IN PURSUIT OF BEAUTY

IN PURSUIT OF BEAUTY

A NOVEL

GARY BAUM

Published in 2025 by Blackstone Publishing
Cover and book design by Kathryn Galloway English

Printed in the United States of America

First edition: 2025
ISBN 979-8-8748-6384-5
Fiction / Psychological

Version 1

Blackstone Publishing
31 Mistletoe Rd.
Ashland, OR 97520

www.BlackstonePublishing.com

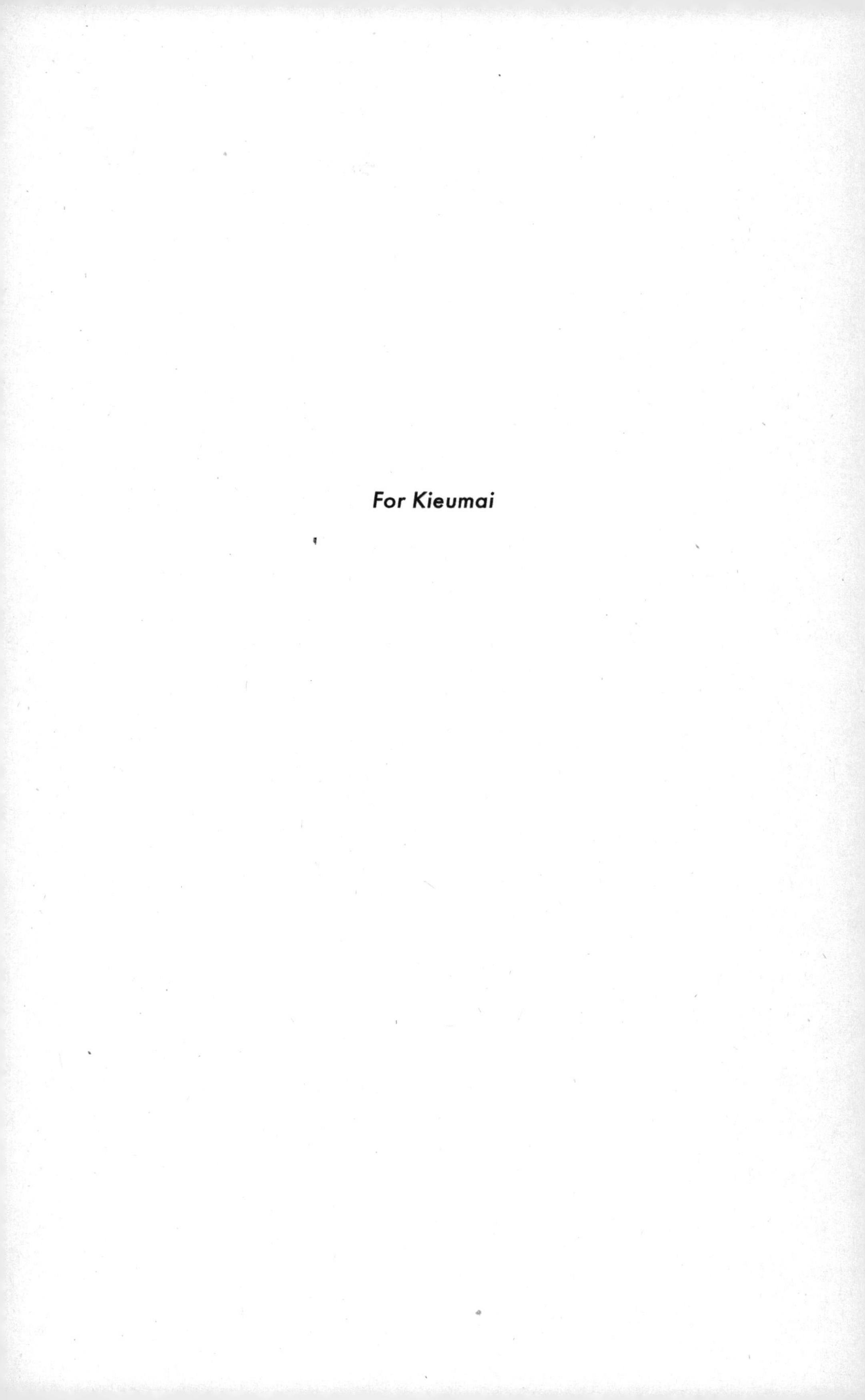

For Kieumai

CAN'T MAKE YOU LOVE ME

Surface matters. It's not merely what's inside that counts. The superficial is full of meaning—and consequence.

My life's work is evidence; my life, the proof. Outer beauty was once my occupation. Banished, I've made it my mission.

What you've heard about me is true. It's just that there's more to it. The headlines had the core of it right: I did commit medical insurance fraud. I did it over a sustained period, in an organized fashion, at an expansive if not enormous volume. I've served my time for it. I've lost the ability to practice my passion because of it. I've come to terms with the fact that "ex-con" will forever be as much a part of the identity of Roya Delshad as "plastic surgeon" because of it.

My crime, in the scheme of things, is victimless. I fleeced corporations to help the struggling. Chump change for those insurers, new lives for my patients. It was illegal. Yet in the unjust society we live in, I don't believe it was, in sum, morally wrong. I had plenty of time to think this over in prison.

The media has labeled me the "Robin Hood of Roxbury Drive." Fair enough. I did take from the rich and give to the poor, and my office was in fact on that street.

I'm also aware of the nickname's double-edged nature, the implied slur. The procedures I provided out of my gilded address to my working-class patients didn't tackle life-threatening concerns. The type that are easy to feel good about no matter your own politics or privilege, the inarguable Doctors Without Borders stuff that helps people breathe again or see again or walk again. I crossed an unspoken line by simply helping people smile. And I don't mean by performing cleft palate repairs on babies.

In my Beverly Hills suite, I provided *elective* services: breast augmentations, nose jobs, facelifts, tummy tucks, lip injections, chin and cheek implants, upper-arm and thigh lifts, vaginoplasties, lipo. The list goes on. I provided those services to women who didn't possess the economic means to do as their more affluent sisters did: improve themselves in their pursuit of happiness.

This isn't a mea culpa. I'm not looking for forgiveness. I wouldn't mind, though, better understanding.

What I did came from an honest place. It was a reasonable response to the inescapably lookist world we live in—and the more equitable one I think we need to envision. If you'll indulge me, I'll make my case.

ONE

You can't begin to turn a "no" to a "yes" until you put in your ask. That's been my operating philosophy as a feature writer. My job has been to get ambivalent or reluctant people to talk, against their better judgment. My primary weapon: carefully crafted correspondence.

I specialize in one of the dark arts of journalism. Reporting in-depth profiles is a confidence racket, a seduction involving some degree of treachery. I happen to have become adept at it.

When you do this kind of thing for a living, you see the news cycle as a cavalcade of potential marks. They mostly fall into a few categories. There are the nobodies who, for whatever reason, have become somebodies. (Not my thing.) There are the nobodies suffering forever as nobodies. (Worthy work; also not my thing.) There are the somebodies who are on a certain slide toward becoming nobodies, perhaps already most of the way there. (A perennial interest.) There are the somebodies at the top of their game. (Dull and often irritating assignments but pay the bills.) And there are the somebodies who've fallen out of favor, experienced some loss, yet are angling to reclaim their forfeited status.

These are my favorite. I've made them a specialty with the editors at various outlets where I ply my trade as a freelancer. These particular somebodies need a voice as they attempt to further their agenda.

In return for that opportunity, I exploit the access they must grant me in pursuit of a meaningful story, or at least an entertaining one. .It's a transactional business, an amoral collaboration. At times, it works out to our mutual benefit.

The successful initial ask bears certain hallmarks. It's concise—extra words are an invitation to hang yourself—and as subtly blandishing as possible, given the implied flattery already inherent in a coverage request. Asks made directly to a mark hinge on the manipulation of egotism, whether latent or apparent: the narcissist's vainglory, the intellect's pretension, the moralist's pride in the rightness of their cause. I've found it doesn't take much to massage away qualms once you first identify the contours of a mark's self-absorption.

The day I made my ask of the incarcerated plastic surgeon Dr. Roya Delshad, I'd just published a profile in *Los Angeles* of a male porn star who'd been accused of on-set sexual harassment by several female costars. I'd turned in my latest revision of a *Vanity Fair* piece about a swashbuckling residential spec-house developer at war with neighbors over unpermitted renovations on a forty-thousand-square-foot mansion in Bel Air. And after months of painstaking wooing, involving quite a few expensed dinners at Craig's, I'd finally convinced the two late-middle-aged daughters of a recently departed Oscar-winning director to go on the record—with leaked substantiating documentation—in *The Hollywood Reporter* about how their septuagenarian stepmother had spent years battering their Alzheimer's-afflicted nonagenarian father and forced him to change the terms of his will to benefit her further at the expense of his biological children. All the while carrying on an affair with the director's much younger home aide.

Roya was a mark from the moment her situation went viral in the papers, on TV and radio, across social media. She'd even become a meme after someone fabricated a quote in which she purportedly aphorized: "Pretty should no longer be a privilege. It should be a right." The problem was, as with many headline-garnering stories, Roya was a mark for everyone else too. And I'm uninterested in the low yield of being part of an active news swarm, angling for small scraps among the vultures.

It's too trivial. Move-the-needle scoops are what move me. My passion is the quest for tricky and on occasion even troublemaking stories, admittedly of a certain glossy sort, that have been, for whatever reason, ignored or neglected.

In Roya's case, I plotted patience, as I often do. Calculated bets on restraint in an otherwise frenzied news environment are my ploy. I knew media interest would be highest in the immediate aftermath of her arrest, during which time her legal team wasn't allowing her to talk to anyone. When she agreed to a plea deal, resulting in a reduced sentence, I planned to continue to wait. I knew that, as with so many curiosities just like her, she'd have news show bookers and beat reporters and feature magazine writers and perhaps even documentary filmmakers lining up to be her suitors. They'd all greet her in a cluster of requests, whether through her attorneys or directly via the warden, each more obvious and ingratiating and overeager than the last, those asks arriving in prison just as she was getting her bearings on her bizarre new reality. I also was confident that the sheer mass and assortment of inquiries would synthesize into a bewildering, repulsive mush.

Which is why I chose to let that all pass. I set a calendar alert for a full five months after she began serving her sentence, when I figured she would've grown accustomed to her new surroundings, no longer bizarre but instead dull, now perhaps a good deal more interested in receiving a letter in the mail from a stranger. Then I struck.

First, I sent a note to her legal team, postmarked the day before the one I sent to her. I could have emailed, but I didn't want to risk that mode of communication's ease of swift, habitual decline, on her behalf and for the record. Better a single letter to the attorneys' office, knowing full well it would need to be passed around, likely resulting in a lack of ultimate ownership of reply—and, fingers crossed, no response at all. The intention was to be able to truthfully inform Roya in my ask that I'd already taken the proactive, aboveboard measure of looping in her lawyers while chancing that, with the case closed and sentence being served, she was no longer their priority. Furthermore, that after stewing in prison for lo these many months, she might be wondering about the benefit by that point of gagging herself when it comes to press requests any longer.

Anyway, the letter:

> Dr. Delshad,
>
> My name is Wesley Easton and I'm a Los Angeles–based freelance magazine writer, whose work regularly appears in a variety of publications, including *Esquire*, *Vogue*, *Wired*, and *Vanity Fair*. I report on fascinating people, some well-known and others far less so. What the pieces all have in common—across subject matter, from politics to entertainment to science—is curiosity, open-mindedness, and an interest in the careful, sensitive sharing of stories that haven't yet been truly heard.
>
> I'd imagine I'm far from the first individual to have approached you about sharing your story, which is of course fascinating and untold. I believe it could be a great benefit to the more than 26 million readers, users, followers, and fans across all media (including print, digital, mobile, and social) of *Elle*, a publication devoted to exploring women's personal power. *Elle* would like to publish a feature profile about you at a generous length, allowing the full complexities of your life, work, and point of view to be rendered.
>
> Now, based on the lack of participation in any media coverage so far (or any in the pipeline that I'm aware of), I'd also imagine that you and your legal counsel—to whom, for your reference, I yesterday sent a related note, attached—won't likely be easily swayed by yet another suitor. That said, I'm not in a rush, and neither is *Elle*. We'd like to develop a relationship

with you and see how it might progress at your speed. To that end, for your perusal, I've attached several recent issues of the magazine, as well as copies of a few of my own stories. My contact information is below. I do hope this is just the start of our conversation.

Best,
Wes

Everything about this was calculating. Let's take the refined exercise in smarm from the top. I was sure to mention that I was locally based, as I surmised most supplicants would be hailing from New York City and you can never underestimate lurking anti–New York City bias elsewhere in the country. Which is why, while I do a lot of work for *New York*, I didn't mention it in favor of the other select publications, which were meticulously curated as a subconscious mixtape of general-interest mass-market prestige. (While an equally echt-Manhattan crowd produces these magazines, even in our digital age their true habitat, the wellspring of their advertiser-supported consumer relationship, remains the supermarket checkout line.) That bit about reporting on fascinating people is, purposefully, an implicit compliment, rather than an explicit one, which would be heavy-handed, and the reminder of the breadth of my extant reporting purview meant to demonstrate a Renaissance interest in human affairs, as opposed to merely a tawdry absorption with life's anomalies.

It's crucial to get out in front of all latent facts and assumptions. Hence acknowledging that I was just one among many courters. After all, the appearance of transparency is a virtue. The language about *Elle*'s circulation across platforms and personal-power babble were shamelessly ripped straight from its online media kit, while the indication that the story would run long was a simple play to ego (and, frankly, a risky one, since an extended word count could also be interpreted as more space for her to look bad).

Then there's the additional recognition and even bowing, practically scraping, to her attorneys' presumed wisdom, coupled with the most important thing—the demonstration of restraint. There's no hurry to do this story. (As long as we get to lock it in!) Let's just begin talking. Here's some reading material. No commitment. You're the judge. The ball is in your court. Finally, the sign-off: I've taken the liberty of advancing from the formal Wesley to the more casual Wes. Nascent intimacy established. Won't you join me?

I should also mention, as long as I'm confessing all this deliberate insincerity, what's glaringly missing from my ask letter: a volunteered personal connection. It's by design. Detailing, as a way of forging some semblance of intimacy, and in the desperately naked manner of a college admissions essay, your own journey to come to terms with some aspect of your physical self. (Even better if it involved a surgical procedure at some point; fewer points if the closest story you can summon, or merely invent, instead involves a loved one.) I figured everyone else had attempted this, or frankly at least all the women who'd contacted Roya. As a guy in this case, particularly coming in on the caboose of these requests, it would've come across as yet another prepackaged sob story of questionable veracity. In that void I elected to rest on my professional qualifications, theorizing that a distanced approach, less unctuous in at least this one anticipated way, would set me apart.

As for the attached stories, I included three for her consideration—enough to give her the feeling of plenty, but not so much as to give her the feeling of homework. The critical thing about clips sent to marks, aside from withholding any conspicuous hatchet jobs, is being aware that these people, if their interest is at all piqued by the possibility of being written about by you, are simultaneously going to attempt to read them analytically (their central concern: how mean or at least snarky were you, on the whole?) while drifting off self-centeredly (what will my own as-yet-unwritten monument read like?). The best gambit to goose the latter is not to provide directly parallel pieces for point of comparison: CEOs don't receive pieces about other CEOs, artists about other artists, et cetera. That way they're less likely to think unhelpful linear thoughts about the procession they're about to join, and their place in it. Rather, I've found the ideal stratagem to stroke the psyches of somebodies (the psyches of somebodies being, again, my chosen calling) is to tacitly cross-pollinate their self-regard—of their creativity, of their bravery, of their status—by supplying a pantheon of examples of individuals involved in unrelated pursuits through which that self-regard might intuitively connect in latent kinship. Hence, the polarizing Beverly Hills plastic surgeon acquired articles about an enfant terrible Danish architect mired in a controversial historic preservation project, from *Smithsonian*; a successful Santa Monica–based restaurateur who reinvented himself as a critically acclaimed conceptual artist only once he reached his seventies, from *Bon Appetit*; and a first-generation Chinese American fashion-merchandising consultant who is now waging a dicey campaign for human-rights reform in the garment industry of her ancestral homeland, from *The Cut*.

Ask letter mailed, the waiting game began. It wasn't a conscious vigil. I don't think much about marks—which is to say emotionally invest in them, their stories and the hunt and ramification of the telling—unless and until I get to "yes.".

Biweekly for two months I sent her follow-up letters. I have automated reminders set on my Google calendar for such messages. The light work of generating gently pestering subsequent correspondence—which is kept brief (just a couple of sentences) and, in this case, was at times accompanied by additional clips to consider along with the latest editions of *Elle* to hit the newsstand—is baked into my morning routine.

I would've kept at my one-way missives for one year. Experience had shown me that was an appropriate cut-off point of diminishing returns. But I didn't need to because after two months she responded in a dark-ink note, nearly illegible in a doctor's chicken scratch.

"Wes," Roya wrote, taking my casual cue. "I'm admittedly charmed by your persistence, and I do appreciate your interest. As you've deduced,

I have serious reservations about speaking with the media. They are by no means yet allayed. That said, if you'd like to visit, we can talk this all over in detail (OFF THE RECORD!) and see if there's some way we might work together which would satisfy us both."

The ask had, as these things go, turned out to be a deceptively easy one. The task she'd set before us, however, would prove far more difficult.

WHAT IT'S LIKE TO BE ME

I grew up in Beverly Hills, but not the Beverly Hills you know. We didn't just live south of Santa Monica Boulevard—and therefore in the flats. We didn't even live south of Wilshire Boulevard. We lived south of *Olympic Boulevard*, meaning that I was a barely-in-the-city-limits, in-it-for-the-public-schools kid, holed up in a duplex a few blocks east of Roxbury Park, our neighbors the electronics-and-shmatte-trade Orthodox Jews who congregated along the Pico-Robertson corridor, not the assimilated entertainment-business Jews of Hillcrest Country Club and Nate 'n Al's.

I belonged, ostensibly and peripherally, to a third local caste, then nascent and now dominant: the diaspora Persian Jews that'd sought refuge after the fall of the shah in 1977. My father, Reza, educated in his hometown of Tehran as well as for a few finishing-school years in London, arrived here in his early twenties. He was one of five siblings, the second of three brothers. They'd expected to spend their lives expanding their family's commercial real estate firm—started by their grandfather and great-uncle—in their home country.

Like so many others, the Delshads lost everything when they left. Yet they soon began doing what they knew best from the moment they first settled into a single sprawling house in Trousdale Estates—then an unfashionable, out-of-the-way neighborhood of modernist tract houses, today one of LA's most sought-after, ultraexpensive enclaves. That is, put simply, and in a way that would no doubt irritate my uncles for its lack of nuance, they researched properties, acquired dumps on the cheap, either chose to hold them for long periods or fixed them up and sold them for more.

My short, broad father—his Middle Eastern nose a capacious prow, his forehead a sloped wall, his swept-back dark curls glistening—met my tall, thin mom, Julie, in 1979. He was overseeing renovations on a small commercial building that was part of the family's burgeoning American portfolio and, once he saw her in her WASPy glory one morning (she of the dimpled chin, the sky-high cheekbones, the petite but shapely bust), began reading his newspapers at a coffee shop a few doors down on lower Beverly Drive where she toiled as a waitress while attempting to become an actress. She had been in LA for six years, circumnavigating the city from her cramped apartment in the Fairfax District to auditions and living with her would-be actress roommates, Marsha, who died of cancer a decade later, and Renee, who now lives in Spokane and is born-again.

In my mom's telling, he reeled her in over weeks of repeated refill requests, generous tips, wry jokes, offhand intimacies, and quotidian chitchat about the news of the day. More than anything, apart from his clear intelligence, he possessed a casual worldliness and foundational confidence, a sense of who he was and surety of where he was headed, that she found alluring—admittedly even more so because, at that time, she lacked her own. When he brought up a story he read about Santa Monica's Villa Aurora, the postwar hub for exiled émigrés, and she took an interest, he noted that Schoenberg's Chamber Symphony No. 1 would be performed by the LA Philharmonic at the Music Center the following Tuesday, and he'd love to take her. "Later he said he laid that trap because I'd made an offhand reference to *Buddenbrooks* a week earlier," she once told me.

The origin story sounded suspiciously highbrow and gauzy. Which may have been why, as an adult, I consulted my father's journal from that period, a dark leather-bound volume of occasional entries that revealed a man on the make, busy cataloging the minutiae of his in-progress professional projects, when not given to bemused new-to-the-country sociocultural asides about, for example, *Magnum, P.I.* As for the successful pass at my mom, his version matched, albeit with some nauseating bits about what he wanted "to do" with her "derriere," etc.

They married the following year. It was a courthouse wedding. It may as well have been an elopement. Her parents, back in Pittsburgh, saw the act as the final California betrayal. They hadn't wanted her out west in the first place, and never stopped urging her to come to her senses and return home. Grandma Alice refused to visit her, and Grandpa Charlie only did once on his own volition. It was two years after her arrival in Los Angeles, on an expedition up the I-5 freeway from Camp Pendleton following a reunion with his old 1st Marine Division tank battalion soldiers, celebrating the quarter-century anniversary of their landing at Incheon.

That my father was a recently arrived immigrant and a Jew would have made the union a nonstarter for the Bryants even if she'd met him while living in Pittsburgh. For the Delshads, that my mother wasn't a Persian Jew wasn't merely a nonstarter. Intermarriage was a New World calamity.

At first, Saba and Savta wouldn't even meet my mom. Instead, it was left to Auntie Gina, my father's baby sister with the baby Cindy Crawford mole, to be an emissary on a reconnaissance mission over tea at the Peninsula Hotel. In the end, my eldest uncle, Nouriel, was the only Delshad at the courthouse, serving as a witness. The gesture was graciously performed, albeit without informing the rest of the Delshads or even his own new wife.

It was also soon leveraged. Nouriel was the one to break the news that it had been decided—all four of the other siblings had agreed, in tandem with Saba and Savta—that my father would henceforth be excommunicated from the family business. He was bequeathed a sum to head off on his own.

My father, crushed and angry, didn't look back. He couldn't. My mom was soon pregnant with me. He charted a new investment course apart from the Delshads' established American standard by partnering in a small-scale, *ground-up* mixed-use development in neighboring West Hollywood. It succeeded. So did several others, the third just as my little sister, Dahlia, was born.

Then came the fifth in 1985, far larger than the rest and just south of Beverly Hills on Robertson Boulevard, which didn't. Worse, he'd gone in on it for the first time without partners, overly aggressively placing his winnings from his previous projects on this one. Construction delays, permitting hassles, a sudden softening in the local commercial real estate market: It all hit him and he lost everything. "Callow shit," he told my mom when he realized he was sunk.

A month later, seeking a reprieve from the gloom and preparing an imminent return to the hospitality industry (my mom had stopped waitressing, at my father's prompting, as soon as she learned she was pregnant), she took Dahlia and me to the zoo for the day. My father had a meeting scheduled with the bank. Instead, he left a letter on her vanity. "I'm so sorry," it read. "I don't expect you to forgive me. Tell the girls their father will always love them, and you." Then he shot himself in the bathtub of a room at the Beverly Terrace motel on Doheny Drive.

When I was older, I asked my mom how she dealt with what happened. She said for the first few years she just didn't. Her raging grief was to the brim yet outwardly contained—except for occasional keeled-over trips to the toilet or into bed, the result of a stress-induced stomach ulcer that, she confided to Marsha and Renee, she'd in one flash of early agony nicknamed "Reza." Moment to moment, my mom focused on the daily, metronomic, practical matters involved in taking care of her young daughters. Of the two sisters, only I was old enough to wonder, every so often, "Where's Daddy?" I remember my mom responding, time after time, until I stopped inquiring, "He went away, and he can't come back, but he loves you very much." She always said it with a smile and a kiss.

As soon as they heard about my father, Grandma and Grandpa flew out and pleaded with my mom to finally return to Pittsburgh. She wouldn't. She saw no future there as a widow with two frizzy-haired, half-Persian daughters who didn't look like anyone she knew back home. Even if the acting career that brought her there was kaput, Los Angeles still offered a climate she prized—not just temperate winters but what had become her favorite thing: those ultraviolet canopies of jacaranda trees blossoming each spring—and an admirable dearth of judgment from which she thought she could best build a new life under trying circumstances. Grandma and Grandpa wouldn't set foot in California again until they saw me give my high school valedictorian speech. (For our part, Mom flew us out to Pittsburgh every Christmas and every other summer for a week. Occasionally Mom's only other sibling, her gay, perpetually ripped big brother, Henry, would rendezvous with us from Manhattan.)

Meanwhile, the Delshads sought to keep her here. My earliest memory, at the age of four, is of Saba, an entirely bald, finely wrinkled patriarch who was defined to me by his conception of dignity and heavily accented English. Saba was on his knees, weeping and apologizing to my mom, who looked on serenely, far past any more tears of her own. He had come alone to our condo in repentance. She told me decades later that he'd said he'd "betrayed" his son.

Saba offered significant financial assistance. My mom agreed to only certain help. In the end, he would cover our debts as well as our existing costs for a year, while she looked for a nine-to-five job. He would pay for babysitting once she started working, until we were old enough to fend for ourselves. And he would pay for college, for Dahlia and me.

At last, Saba welcomed us, the tragic Delshads, into the family fold. For the sake of Dahlia and me, my mom entered an uneasy détente.

That it was born of wariness, guilt, inequity, and original sin was a fact I wouldn't understand until much later.

As I was growing up, the central act of this relationship was monthly Shabbat dinners. We would drive north from our condo on Friday evenings, past Olympic, past Wilshire, past Santa Monica, past Sunset, to attend boisterous, cheek-pinching, hours-long get-togethers at one or another of the Delshad extended-family mansions in the gently rising hills. They all featured retrofitted facades that'd been cheerfully ornamented in an ahistorical mélange of Mediterranean influences—parapets, friezes, columns, cornice moldings, gilded gates, and marble—seemingly inspired in equal parts by Cyrus the Great and *Dynasty*. Neighbors who hated the florid mix-and-match style, which is to say most of the neighbors, came to call them Persian palaces. (These same neighbors, basically all white, meanwhile unconditionally revered their own fake French Regency, Tuscan villa, Greek Revival, Spanish neocolonial, English country manor, and other assorted piles.)

I could tell, when I was older, that my mom likewise thought the Delshads' houses were tacky. But I loved Persian palaces, that indigenous Beverly Hills style, wherever I glimpsed them: They said something bold and resonant to me about the people who proudly built them—that they had sweeping, Technicolor dreams, unapologetically realized. The houses were passionate and expressive beacons. I registered them as authentic in their inauthenticity, which is to say true to themselves.

Persian palaces, as it happens, are now falling out of fashion among the second generation. My cousins are typical: column averse; obsessed with a minimalism ironically perhaps best exemplified by the original, untouched mid-century modern houses of Trousdale Estates. But I believe in a few decades there'll be a movement for Persian Jewish Renaissance Revival architecture. It'll be redeemed.

My mom—a shiksa, nonchalantly nonobservant even in her own practice, Presbyterianism—was always an outsider at those Shabbat dinners, even though they were mostly pageant and banquet, with a mere sprinkling of religious practice. Her participation was that of a passive cultural observer and cordial chaperone. When Dahlia and I were of school age, she took to dropping us off.

The truth is, even if my father hadn't died and the Delshads hadn't cast them out of their orbit for daring to be together in the first place, she would've found the screwy effervescence of those dinners hard to handle. While she was willing to admit that any one Delshad could be "charming," and my father by far most of all, as a group they were loud and assertive in a way that my mom—an introvert from a family that had, through generations, found mutual comfort in its long silences—experienced as exhausting.

Dahlia and I, our father's blood coursing through us, had no such problem. We were energized by the ruckus at the Delshad Shabbats, the endless challah to be eaten, the hide-and-go-seek to be played before dinner, the video games to be played afterward, the aunties and uncles to be hugged and tickled by when we bumped into them throughout. It would take years for us to slowly, fully grasp that we didn't quite belong.

First, aside from a divergence in relative religious observance—my agnostic mom, without my father to intercede, had opted out of sending her children to either Sunday or Hebrew school—came a steadily dawning appreciation for the money gap. Our cousins lived different lives than we did outside of those Shabbat dinners. They remained above Sunset, amid those gently rising hills, behind those bewitchingly gauche facades, flush with all the obvious, readily apparent *stuff* they had: the comparative treasure of toys and trips. (Every so often they'd speak of Paris and Hawaii; we were invited to bunk for a long weekend each May at an annual all-Delshad conclave at some expansive estate or another in Palm Springs.)

Our jealousy only metamorphosed when Dahlia and I grew a bit older and understood that their privilege afforded them mothers who could welcome them home from school with a snack, rather than be stuck working for hours, often until night fell. Most startling, generally, was the discovery of an absence. How, for our cousins, perhaps the key, omnipresent, undeniable governing principle of our family's daily life—

middle-class anxiety over money (how best to responsibly allocate it, save it, stretch it, ensure its continuity; that if we get *this* thing, we can't get *that* thing)—never entered their own orbits.

That our thirteen first cousins were always sweet to us, not ever outwardly snotty (the ones closest to us in age invariably having our backs at school, even if we were never immersed within the protective shield of their pre- and then postpubescent Persian cliques), could be ascribed to simple love, or luck, or good parenting. Or else what I came to believe to be the case: a patina of melancholy that forever surrounded dead uncle Reza's intrinsically injured girls. My mom's drip-drip-drip of who our father was in life was a devoted yet shrewd propaganda campaign. It began with dewy (and in retrospect pretty gag-worthy) bedtime fairy tales, interspersed with Aesop's own, focused on Reza's propensity for cinematic grand gestures. The moment he surprised her with an apartment thickly strewn with crimson rose petals, or the time he took a cold-clocking swing at a guy who'd said something insulting to her as they'd waited for their car outside a favorite restaurant. It wasn't until much later I'd learn the remark had to do with her being on the arm of "an Arab," which my father found doubly offensive since, he was quick to point out, he wasn't one. Over the years this romantically impressionistic sketch was imbued with details meant to anchor him in reality and contrive a semblance of intimacy but that also, now that I think about it, veered toward purging low-level vexations: that he snored (loudly!); that he loved onions, specifically Funyuns (which my mom hated, especially off his own breath!); that he would get the *worst* Top 40 stuck in his head. ("It was always 'Funkytown,' never 'Cruisin'!")

As for what happened to him, the he-went-away-and-can't-come-back dodge somehow bought my silence on the subject, at least until the day little Dahlia was old enough to wonder, after a playdate with a friend, "Why don't I have a dada too?" My mom lost it, to Dahlia's bewilderment. When she recovered, she addressed us both: "You do. He's just in heaven." Ambiguous, evasive, overly conceptual stuff like this kept us in the dark for years, until the autumn of the third grade, when I'd suddenly had enough:

"What happened to Dad?" I demanded one night as she went to turn off the lights while I lay in bed. Caught off guard, but by this time even keeled, she asked why I needed an answer. I told her people were asking me at school.

"Honey, it's a sad story. I'd like to tell it to you when you're a little older." Much debate ensued over the fact that I already was older. Finally, she relented.

"He hurt himself on purpose," my mom said, having tucked herself around me under the covers, big-spoon-little-spoon, a hand firm against my pounding heart.

I asked how. She hesitated. And then, softly: "With a gun."

"Why?"

"I don't know, honey. I still really don't understand, and even when you're much, much older, like me, you may not understand either."

My mom would tell you her primary vocation has been as a mother. But what supported this task was a career spent in various Century City high-rises, first as a secretary—just as the term gave way to "executive assistant"—and then as an office manager at a series of large-scale civil litigation firms as partners continually sought out her proved experience over the decades once they migrated to rival shops. As she once put it to me, they liked her innate reserve, which read in a professional setting as purposeful discretion. They appreciated her detached meticulousness, the product of a youth spent under an ex-marine major's familial command. And they welcomed her hospitality-industry-honed ability to faithfully execute holiday, birthday, going-away, the-ruling-went-our-way and other such company parties—and it was a never-ending stream at these places—far above the usual desultory-obligatory fashion of such affairs. My mom, who to her regret had skipped college to pursue her Hollywood dream, liked to say waitressing was the most crucial educational experience she'd ever had. To wit, a favored refrain: "They're paying you to smile when you don't feel like it. Especially when you're a woman."

About that Hollywood dream: My mom insists she'd been losing interest in her pursuit of acting not just before my father's death or even before their marriage but by the time they'd met. She relished films—across genre, era, style. Not with a cinephile's narrow snobbery but, at her core, with an escapist viewer's vast generosity, the kind forged of a childhood spent fantasizing she could've said a different thing before being sent upstairs to her room, said that thing *better*, or perhaps disappeared into another world altogether, in all those scenes that ended with her father repeatedly striking her mother. (I only learned of this, and their reliably grim happy endings—that Grandma would always forgive Grandpa in the morning—once I'd gone to college.) Yet after years in Los Angeles, which to that point had yielded solely sporadic TV commercial work, futile movie auditions, and a single three-line role on one episode of *WKRP in Cincinnati*, she'd come to realize that she'd never even ascend to being a solidly working actress, which is to say a not-struggling one, much less a star. This despite what she'd assessed to be a reasonable-enough level of inborn talent and accrued skill for the craft. My mom told me she'd met my father just as acting, in her sardonic formulation, "had reached an inflection point of bitterness, apathy, and inertia in my life."

I've often wondered about the opposites-attract quality of my parents' love match. Not just the obvious—the physical, the cultural, the socioeconomic—but others too. By all accounts, he was gregarious and even hard charging where she was restrained. He was comfortable being goofy, while she cringed at appearing even slightly ditzy, the reflex of a lifetime spent self-conscious of being so pretty. He was learned while she was an autodidact on those shared enthusiasms over which they'd first bonded, classical music and European literature. (She'd come to *Buddenbrooks* by way of a highbrow aspiring-screenwriter bartender she'd dated while working another waitressing job when she first moved to town.)

By contrast, my dear stepdad, Fred, a father of two himself whom she met at the law firm while he was still technically married and *saw in secret for years* but we didn't know about it *until my sister went away to college* and they moved in together—long story, another memoir—made far more sense. She and handsome, lantern-jawed Fred are on the same wavelength in all things, from temperament to background to interests to, um, aesthetics. When I see them together now, they look like the smiley, silver-haired, over-sixty-five white model couples in multivitamin advertisements. It's adorable. I just want to affix matching adjustable Velcro visors to their heads and reserve them a tee time and send them on their way. Yet their perfection (all right, seeming perfection) also gives me a bittersweet pang because, while I realize my parents' own union was itself an odd wonder, I do now admittedly find myself asking if Dahlia and I were not a fluke of the universe—or at least of my mom's rightful course within it.

I've already touched on it, but it bears further underscoring: My mom is gorgeous. Really, I'm not just saying this because I'm her admiring daughter. I stand behind my accumulated professional credentials (to the extent they matter anymore) as well as my burnished vocational eye (which nobody can take away from me).

I mentioned the slightly dimpled chin, the sky-high cheekbones, the petite but shapely bust. Let's put aside the fact that, with the most piddling of exercise routines, she's retained—that's present-tense, as in *to this day*, well into her AARP-dom—a Barbie-esque figure, albeit with a more healthily realistic waist-to-hip ratio. I'd just like to focus on her face, also the same as it ever was, slightly upturned nose to bow-shaped lips, win-the-lottery bone structure my patients paid me for, now merely etched with the very finest of wisdom lines.

It's been a focus of my attention since I was a baby; I'd light up when her green eyes connected with mine. But it was only over time that I came to understand the power of her exquisitely symmetrical features. I'd gaze at her often when she wasn't looking. As I aged, a genuine curiosity mounted. I attempted to consider her beauty's full measure: the curve of her chin, the sweep of her milky-skinned cheek. How a slight variation would be less lovely.

Of course, *she* would always downplay her allure, whenever it was pointed out to her. Self-effacing stuff, like by noting her imperceptibly snaggled teeth. My whole life, except for special occasions, my mom's worn essentially no makeup except for a light foundation—the style we these days call a make-under—knowing full well she'd still look great at work. Yes, along with the beyond-demure clothes and the thick-framed glasses (she'd worn contacts in her auditioning days) and the purposefully unglamorous ponytail (I mean, really?), this constituted anti-sexual-harassment armor—a likely futile attempt to reside on the mousy flip side of sexy librarian. But it was also the kind of thing only the most stunning of women can pull off.

I was not born stunning. I was a cute kid: the frizzy hair, the broad grin. Yet I'd inherited my father's physiognomy. Not just his darker coloring but his prominent nose, his beetle brows, the entire broad oval of his visage in feminine form. The rest of my body was Delshad matrilineal—thin lips, wide hips, ridiculous bottom (and bosom when puberty arrived), reasonable if a bit stocky frame. The two things my mom bequeathed to me were her tall height and her green eyes.

The poor hand I'd been dealt was only more obvious as Dahlia came of age. It's amazing. She's basically now my mom, but with luscious olive skin, thick dark curls, Delshad-brand double-D chest, and huge matching rear end. Where I went totally wrong in the blending of DNA code, a misshapen beta model, she went right. It would be hilarious if the cosmic cosmetic joke hadn't been on me. The only patrimony she was also beset by was acne, which she vanquished far more quickly and easily than I with over-the-counter Proactiv (by contrast, I required hardcore Accutane), along with Persian hirsutism, our happy trails more like highways until lasered away.

Our mom treated us the same. The rest of the world didn't. I could get into the accumulation of ugly-daughter slights—triggering microaggressions, in today's vernacular. But I've already worked them out with my therapist.

Dahlia acquired our father's natural sociability as well as his sense of gung-ho certainty, an enviable moxie near devoid of anxiety that I often couldn't fathom. Sometimes I puzzled if it was all in the genetics or if her, as I came to think of it, enchanted buoyancy was the result of coming into a selfhood in the crucial years after our mother's most severe grief had waned, rather than at its peak, like me. I'd add another theory: the blessing of being a knockout. After all, beauty is like money. It doesn't necessarily make you happy, but it allows for a lot.

In Dahlia's case, I watched how, as her looks ripened early, the world bent toward her, the Perfect 10. Not just boys and men turning, eyeing, leering. Girls and women were in awe, often jealous. Her intense carnality and innate charisma combined as an overwhelming force, polarizing, a Rorschach test. In time she suffered the slings and sorrows of her burden, the intense incoming bitchery and assorted dramas that arrive with the territory of being so damned hot transforming her, defenses raised and trauma accrued, into yet another beautiful, fragile Beverly Hills High School bitch.

Not that she ever really was a bitch to me, thankfully. Our squabbles had always been minimal, to our single mom's relief. This was perhaps helped, at least in part, by the fact that the extreme asymmetry of our attractiveness served to blunt a great deal of my envy. She was just so far out of my league, some magnificent alien, an airbrushed figure in a magazine.

It would've been harder to deal with the situation if she were only relatively more good-looking, a composition in the realm of possibility that I'd fallen short of. But because of the wide discrepancy, and because there were others too—I was the quieter one, which I got from my mom, and the one who excelled at academics, which I got from my father—we didn't compete. When she felt wronged, which was often, and Mom (of far more sagacity generally, including of course the slings and sorrows of a life spent so very pretty) wasn't around, she'd confide in me, her faithful female eunuch. I'd offer what advice I could, which wasn't much, her experience at the sensational shiny center of life's adolescent parade having no connection to my spectator's reality behind the barricades.

Now, I don't mean to set myself up as some ogre. I wasn't hideous, only hopelessly plain, and therefore lost to mediocrity in the teenage sexual marketplace, where not to be coveted is not to exist. This despite Dahlia's concerted efforts to put me in my best light. I always had legit outfits, on-trend hair, flattering makeup. Alas, the *She's All That* hustle was never enough to pull me my own Freddie Prinze Jr. prince.

Again, and to keep with the nineties lodestars, my Beverly Hills life was not *90210*—not even dorky Andrea Zuckerman's. There were no Peach Pit hangouts for me, no *Clueless* whimsy. Perhaps I would've been induced to tag along with Dahlia's clique, which did regularly indulge in screen-worthy fast-lane fun—or so I heard, although I was already away in college when it reached its zenith—as a charity case, had she been the cool older sister rather than the cool younger one.

OK, so I'm being dramatic; give me a break, I'm reveling in high school pain as I remember it, a warped lens. I had friends. There were, in fact, guys who were into me: awkward, sweet, studious, geeky guys who were into awkward, sweet, studious, geeky me. Not to mention the previously rejected and on-the-rebound guys who'd decided to try their luck on someone who might be, you know, *grateful*. I was just never interested.

I studied instead, preferring to never be kissed (which I wasn't in high school, as pathetic as it may seem) rather than lower my standards. They were very high: I only wanted to make out with, and in theory fuck, total hotties. As we all do. And for some reason I had the supreme patience to wait the situation out, until I could join their Mount Olympus as an equal. Besides, I had a plan, one that had begun to take hold while still in middle school, when I first recognized the distance between who I was becoming and who I intended to be, what I so desperately wanted and what the world would allow.

I had a crush on this guy named Raj, a handsome Indian kid in several of my eighth-grade honors classes who, yes, was really good at math and science, but also was athletic, and funny in a not-mean way, and floppy haired; he rocked the middle-part bowl cut better than anyone this side of Jonathan Taylor Thomas. Oh, and entirely clear skinned. Nearly no dude that age was entirely pimple-free, and I was a snob about clear skin. (My own severe outbreaks, necessitating that Accutane regimen, wouldn't arrive as a revengeful riposte until the following year).

In eighth grade, dances were immediately after school. Students showed up in cliqued clumps. Raj was with his soccer buddies. I came late, with my best friend at the time, Tina—first-generation Korean; super-duper cute; even quieter than me, at least in part on account of her thick accent; given to a tendency to bite her lip when thinking or nervous. Both socially anxious protoloners, we'd hesitated in coming at all, having to psych each other into the whole thing at our adjoining lockers.

Raj immediately spotted us, coming right over in welcome, looking dapper in his wale cords and vertically striped button-up. We talked about . . . I have no idea, because I was thoroughly fixated on Raj, in all his Raj-ness. Then a pause surfaced in the conversation, just as Toni Braxton really got going on "Un-Break My Heart." Raj, removing hands that'd been scrunched into his pockets, dipped his head down and then up again toward Tina. "Hey, maybe wanna dance?"

She looked at me, terrified, knowing full well of my intense crush and only perhaps mildly sharing it. I granted her a tight-lipped, thin-lipped smile: *It's OK*, it said. *No problem.* Without looking back my way, he led her toward the dance floor, the sweaty-palmed swaying scrum of the wanted. Tina lay her hands on his shoulders in that stiff eighth-grade way, like defibrillators, and Raj cupped the nonexistent curves of her waist. She looked around, seeing others seeing her, a maybe new couple to gossip about, then settled in on his chest, shy and dazed. His long-lashed eyes, though, were only focused on her own.

I'd retreated, a wallflower, watching alone from the distance. I wondered what it felt like to hold him in that moment; more importantly, to be held by him. Tina would soon tell me: clammy. But before she could attempt to dissuade me, while I still stood there in my surging envy, I cupped a hand along my own waist, and imagined.

I wanted Raj. I knew that. Yet what was dawning on me was that I simply craved to be desired, sexually desired, that elemental human thing. What I didn't know then but soon learned was that the longing that followed, this deep insidious yearning, was an emerging gulf, wide and indifferent. It separated me from my destiny. It couldn't hear me scream from one end to the other. It would take me almost two decades to bridge it.

TWO

Drop-dead-gorgeous Roya entered from the far end of the busy visiting room, striding toward the corrections officer in charge. Her tawny skin and well-proportioned features were underscored by makeup of expert application, apparently permitted in this facility. She'd retained a glamorous look behind bars that approached the combative. In these surroundings, there was a conscious sensuousness about it, somehow vaguely political.

What first struck me, though, was Roya's hair. Most of the other inmates either had made the utilitarian decision to cut their hair short, or else wore it up or pulled back. Her own mane—long, curly, frizzy, high volume, a midnight shade—unfurled in a soft, natural bounce down her back and along her chest. It was dramatic in appearance and high maintenance in practice, although given her circumstances she had plenty of time to tend to it. It was also a striking departure from all the pictures I'd seen of her prior to her incarceration, in which she'd cultivated an edgeless, straightened-and-swept look of cryptoconservative professional femininity, with not a tendril out of place.

The officer, checking his clipboard, directed Roya toward me with a nod: the blind date, seated beneath the fluorescent sheen at a laminate wood table for two amid the chattering throng. Her plump lips coiled into a smile. As she walked up, I took in her eyes, sea-green pools. The handshake was firm as we sat. "Welcome to my reality," she said with a half-conspiratorial-half-acknowledging air, warmth spiked with arsenic, her eyebrows arching and shoulders shrugging, an amused ethnographer receiving a fellow colleague at the scene of her fieldwork. I immediately liked her.

The small talk ran short, at her behest. After all, we only had a mandated hour together, until and unless she put me on a special visitors' list, in which case there could be longer sessions in the future.

Roya was all business. She opened a notebook she'd brought, holding a sharpened pencil at the ready. It was classic type A behavior from someone whom I at once pegged as a onetime teacher's pet. Yet here she was, the good-girl-gone-bad in the regulation jumpsuit. "So, let's get to it," she said, at last. "I hope you don't mind if I ask *you* a few questions right now to see if you're the right person to be asking me more than a few questions in the future."

Ah, yes, of course, the dance. It's what follows the ask when dealing with the canny. Or at least those who think they're canny. I was used to it. The inquest into motivation, the interrogation of process, the cross-examination of previous reportorial history—it's all fair game. Another part of the dance is endurance, which is to say patiently sitting through marks' sermonizing regarding how they've been wronged in the past, why they believe you are going to wrong them again, and, broadly, the varied sins of the media. "By all means," I said, leaning back, suffused with congeniality. "Fire away."

"Well, before we even arrive at your interest in me, I'm genuinely curious how you ended up doing work like this in the first place. It's something I've been wondering about with everyone who's contacted me. Is this something you've always wanted for yourself, barging into people's lives, asking intrusive questions—from what I can tell, mostly when they are least interested in it or capable of handling it?"

An interviewing style of such instantaneous, palpable aggressiveness would, in a journalist, betray rank amateurism. Just for efficacy's sake, it's coming in at the wrong angle. You've got to handhold a mark off the cliff.

I calmly provided Roya with a well-worn capsule history of my career. My first love was film; I was obsessed with Lubitsch and Wilder, Stillman and Baumbach. I'd wanted to be a screenwriter. In college I'd worked on the campus paper . . . as a film reviewer. (My hard-line critical mode during this period was undiluted vintage auteur theory.) After graduation, I'd crashed with two friends from college who'd moved out to North Hollywood a year earlier. I spent the first three months on their futon before landing an entry-level night job found off Craigslist at a regional wire news service. I figured I could write during the day.

Several years later, I'd written a ton of things, taken a ton of meetings, sold a few things, made a little bit of money—I mean a *little* bit of money; never enough to live on—and had absolutely nothing made. Nobody had seen my work. What *had* happened in the meantime, though, is that my initially occasional side gig, freelance writing for the alternative *LA Weekly*, had picked up. (I was still working at the wire news service as my primary income stream but had advanced to more humane shift schedules.)

Police sources, developed steadily over time through the wire work, led me to some absorbing crime stories. I figured out how to report and then do feature writing on my own, first submitting to the *Weekly* on spec. Eventually I made my name on what turned out to be a blockbuster piece of real-life noir, about a local serial killer who'd preyed on four prostitutes in low-income minority neighborhoods south of the 10 Freeway over the course of a year. He'd killed himself when police confronted him, but my scoop, which incorporated narrative storytelling with fresh details, first connected the dots to a much larger cluster of cold-case rapes and murders a decade earlier in another part of South LA several miles east. DNA evidence would later confirm his involvement, I explained to Roya, almost as an aside, casually donning my halo. For years now that long-past social-justice reporting accomplishment, wielded adroitly, had been the skeleton key to turning would-be sources.

"You could argue you've never really left the entertainment business," Roya coolly offered upon hearing this. She was pleased with what she meant as an acid observation. I told her I wouldn't argue.

She pushed again, leaning forward. Her corkscrewed hair moved in sharp contrast across her bright jumpsuit. "Don't you feel shitty about invading people's privacy?"

I allowed I did when the prying was against their will, although most of the time I was invited, one person's privacy being another's publicity. I then tendered a warmed-over chestnut about the value to all in better understanding the abstracted and sketchy stories that take root, for whatever intrinsic reason, "in the public square." They become myths, I offered, unmoored from fact. It may be tragic or tough, but it's necessary to at least attempt to anchor them again.

"You make inflicting pain sound high-minded."

All right, time to begin the deflation of her high-and-mighty balloon. "You're assuming it's painful to talk in any circumstance. Sure, there's anxiety, but in my experience, usually afterward the predominant feeling is relief. Roya, not everyone sought out by the media is like you—not everyone has a horde after them to hear their story. Most are just happy someone is listening. They feel alone and voiceless."

Roya sat back. She turned this over while absently brushing a few of the wild Medusa locks away from her face, her pen resting its tip against those plump lips. Then she not-so-absently shifted, pulling her shapeless jumpsuit taut. As she held still against her chair for an evanescent moment, the uniform looked fitted, emphasizing her chest, one I knew to be ample and flawlessly shaped. I realized in a flash that she knew I knew that. The flat unforgiving fluorescent light was awful, irradiating every surface in the visiting room with a surreal alien glow. Yet despite the circumstances—the room, the crowd, the outfit—she was ravishing, pure heat.

The woman I was gazing at, no doubt ready in just a moment to lash my intentions yet again, wasn't born to that body or that face. I was already aware of that much of her story from reading a cached version of her practice's since-shuttered website. She was transparent about how she'd conjured them. She'd diligently worked toward them over a number of years. She'd known pain and shown patience to achieve them. This was an earned beauty. They were her vision and her dream, realized.

"OK," she said, more subdued now, perhaps chastened, at least temporarily. "Tell me about the most painful thing you've ever had to do to pull off one of your stories."

I wanted to quibble with both "had to do" (versus simply "done") and "pull off" (as though it were a scheme I were getting away with), but I let them lie. It was an easy answer. It tears at me to this day.

I was on the verge of bringing down an A-list Malibu residential rehab center and its network of affiliated luxury sober living houses for a *Los Angeles* magazine exposé. My investigation of its questionable care practices focused on the deaths of three $65,000-a-month clients at the properties over a four-year period. Each had been able to repeatedly smuggle their drug of choice (chronologically: cocaine, whiskey, OxyContin) onto the property and ended up overdosing on it. These fatalities, along with dozens of people who would burn cash on lengthy stretches there just to relapse again within days of leaving, were enabled by a de facto system of half-assed detox. I'd found that a demographic of primarily rich and famous addicts were allowed special privileges—such as near-immediate car and cell phone access, even on-site sleepovers with significant others—to the detriment of their recovery.

I'd first been tipped off about what was going on by an anonymous email telling me to put in a state Public Records Act request for complaints made to the (ineffectual) licensing board about the place. From there, I triangulated, convincing the whistleblower, who turned out to be a disillusioned client who'd been close to the whiskey overdose, to connect me with half a dozen dissident current and former rehab staffers who in time would namelessly lead me to the clinching information. But before I could run the piece, which included the rehab owners' rebuttals, I needed to go for comment to the addicts' families—families who hadn't even realized it was the rehab's operational negligence that led to the deaths. (Successful civil lawsuits would come later.)

Two of the calls were painless. In one case, when I told the assistant to a major music-label boss that I was inquiring about his son's passing, I was given the number of the executive's personal attorney. In the other, after I left fruitless messages for the life partner of a decorator-to-the-stars and that decorator's siblings I'd tracked down in other states, the publicist for the guy's most famous client called me back, saying she'd soon be sending along a joint statement on behalf of the life partner and family, from whom the decorator had long been estranged.

The third call was excruciating. I directly reached the mother of the OxyContin overdose, who'd been a part-time office receptionist and would-be housewife. (Her husband left due to her addiction.) She was at home, alone, in an upper-middle-class suburb along the Eastern Seaboard. A second mortgage had been taken out to spring for the best possible care, above the mere insurance-grade stuff that hadn't taken. Her twentysomething daughter's death had occurred only six months earlier. She was still in the depths of her grief. As soon as I mentioned her daughter's name in connection with the rehab, her voice went hollow. Rapidly but softly, my heart a piston, I explained that I was working on a story about what had gone wrong, and that it appeared to be part of a pattern.

She asked how I'd learned about her daughter. I told her that I had sources inside the rehab, as well as that I'd spoken to friends she'd made during her time there who were also battling addiction. I informed her that my findings were corroborated by the facts in her daughter's autopsy report, which I'd obtained from the coroner's office.

The mother was thrown, by the inference of overarching neglect but mostly by the call itself. She was gracious, even amid her agony. "What do you need from me?" she asked, entirely innocent. I said I didn't need anything. But if she or her family wanted to provide any comment or further context or clarification, even off the record or on background, given what I'd shared, I would incorporate it into the story. She declined.

Then there was a pause as it dawned on her. Her words were quiet, stated without rancor, as though to herself in realization: "Do you mean to put her *in* your article? But I don't understand. She's a private person. We're a private family. This is a private issue."

As respectfully as I could, in a quavering tone that should've been far more resolute, wishing I could reach out and take hold of her hand across the continent, I countered that this had become a matter of public interest and the larger community's need to know what was going on trumped the standard consideration for confidentiality. It was a detached analysis of the situation, but it had the benefit of being true. I said—I believed this then and I believe it now—that more people would keep dying if exactly what happened weren't revealed, rendering the specific contours and causal breakdowns of the problem. The exact details mattered. She said nobody back home knew her daughter had been an addict and that once my story ran online it would be her top Google search result forever, what she'd be "remembered by." Then she cried.

"So what'd you do," Roya asked me, softened now. I said I'd run it, of course. And the mother had been right. Her daughter's tragedy as an addict is indeed her top Google search result, likely forever.

"How did it make you feel?"

Journalism's a rude business, even in its finest hours, when it's slaying dragons. "Like I was doing my job."

I let that one sit there, in the fraught pause that followed. I've found it's important how one handles these moments, however awkward or even excruciating. Never be the one to rush in to fill the silence. It's weakness.

Eventually she changed her focus to a rapid-fire series of what at first seemed to be lighter-fare questions regarding my background. These included a bunch of generic stuff like what my parents did for a living (my since-retired father was a finance executive, while my mother took care of us three brothers, of whom I'm the youngest); where we lived (a suburb of Philadelphia called Ardmore); where I went to college (Emerson); where in LA I resided (Venice, just off Abbot Kinney); if I was married (I'd divorced, after a six-month commitment dissolved three years earlier); and if I had kids (nope).

I'd never been on a speed date, but I felt like I was on a banal one. The probing was so broad and up the middle. Her apparent idea of a quirky inquiry, delivered offhand between the others, was about my middle name (Frederick, after a paternal uncle).

Turns out, these questions were precisely and concisely deployed. They were all Roya needed, with some diversionary tactics to spare, in sketching a bare-bones biographic portrait for her narrow purpose, which was to bear down on a key point she felt was important in establishing, as she put it, "the likely asymmetry in our understanding." As she put it to me: "You grew up rich."

There was an instinctual throat clearing and leg twitching. Well, I found myself arguing, not exactly. "Ardmore's an affluent community. We weren't the wealthiest, let me tell you, far from it. We were in the middle, if that. We were *comfortable.*"

"Come on, Ardmore's along the Main Line, *Wesley Frederick Easton.* I'm sure you've read up on me, so you're aware I went to Penn. I know just a little about Philly."

I couldn't help it. She'd caught me off guard, and I was defensive. "I'm not sure what you're aiming at. As far as I understand it, you grew up in Beverly Hills. If you want to talk about rich."

She smiled: I'd stepped in it. "I grew up *uncomfortable* in Beverly Hills, in an apartment at the edge of town. My single mom hung on for the public schools."

Again, I couldn't help it. This time I laughed. "Look, I'm clearly not going to win a who's-more-real contest with you. Not that I would've tried to walk in here and compete with a *convict.*" Her grin had begun to diminish, although she held it fixed. A flush of principle arose as I leaned forward. "And I can tell you that I seriously doubt your realness quotient vis-à-vis just about any *other* inmate in this room. But that's not why I'm here and it wouldn't matter regardless. I'm here about you, not me. My job—my intended job—is solely to be a conduit. It's to be an interpreter."

Roya let that one sit there as all those other inmates and their visitors went about their business feet away, paying our exchange zero mind. Then she said, matter-of-factly: "I don't buy it. Everyone brings their life with them in everything they do. And I believe you know that, which means you're bullshitting me."

Seeking to bring the dialogue's heat down to a simmer, I asked her how my supposed wealthy background precluded me from properly telling her story. She told me it wasn't that I'd grown up affluent that bothered her but my equivocation about it: "You're not transparent about your privilege." She paused, considering the point. "Which is another way of saying you're not being honest about it. Whether you are to yourself I don't know."

Fair enough. I apologized. Would she give me another chance? Another thoughtful pause passed. As a matter of fact, she would. "Let's try again," Roya said, a smirk returning, imbued with a deep well of undeniable self-satisfaction, as though she'd planned this turnabout all along, "on a matter of your privilege of much greater importance to the central issue at hand."

"All right. And that would be?"

"Your hotness."

I absorbed this as a strange amalgamation of trick question and perverse flirtation. My response was to gaze as evenly as possible at her while I attempted to figure out how best to charmingly defuse this ostensible compliment bomb.

Soon she spoke again. "I'm serious. I want you to admit an obvious yet rather uncomfortable fact: You're—objectively speaking—extremely handsome. Stunningly good-looking." Her eyes narrowed in measured professional critique. "Conventionally so: the square defined jawline, high cheekbones, dark brows, long thick lashes, thin eyelids." Thin *eyelids*? Never been praised for those before. This was weird. I just continued staring at her, waiting for the trapdoor to open.

"You want to write about me? You want to be my 'conduit,' or whatever pretentious thing you just said? My story is about the pursuit of beauty.

Specifically: the terrible costs and pains and hopes and dreams of that pursuit. The truth of it, for most people, isn't just uncomfortable. It's irresolvable and it's bound up in all sorts of things—aspiration, longing, regret."

I didn't, and don't, think of myself as stunningly good-looking. If I did, I'd be a total narcissistic asshole, and not the right kind of total narcissistic asshole to be a worthwhile writer, which is to say a neurotic one. The fact is, on a moment-to-moment basis, I don't think of myself physically much at all, and when I do, I get fixated, like any normal fallible human being, on what's wrong with me—slightly yellowed teeth despite multiple dental whitenings, shadow-deep crow's-feet and forehead wrinkles, a mole or three that maybe should get checked out.

And yet, OK, facts are facts. I lost my virginity as a freshman lacrosse player to a varsity football cheerleader. (Granted, she was on the rebound.) I was the highest bid during the senior-year auction for the high school Kiwanis club charity fundraiser. ($245; and yes, I put out.) Hell, I didn't just work at the Abercrombie & Fitch at the King of Prussia Mall during Abercrombie's late-nineties heyday. I was one of the "face guys" working the door, charming mothers and daughters alike, as one of the teen-Adonis six-packed *greeters*. In other words: I was legend.

I'm not going to run up the score by getting into college and beyond. I think the point's been made. I would just like to thank Mr. and Mrs. Easton for the genetics. And it was three of a kind, too—even if the middle one, Kirk, turned out to be a redhead. (To make up for it, he was more than compensated for that indignity elsewhere.)

"So," she said, "what's it going to be? This is make-or-break for me."

I walked the plank. Luckily the visitors' room was so loud that nobody could hear this insane back-and-forth. "OK, I admit it." My voice took on a *Zoolander* register. "I'm really, really, ridiculously good-looking."

Her brow furrowed. She was not amused. "I'm not interested in an ironic admission. I'm not playing a game with you. If you can't even handle this, I've got a well-worn copy of Nancy Etcoff waiting for me back in my cell. Happy to leave right now."

All right, noted, no kidding around. I made a show of sitting straighter in my chair and closing my eyes to refresh before trying again. "Roya, I, Wesley Easton, am a particularly good-looking dude relative to, um, most. It's conferred benefits that I'm aware of and many others that I'm likely not."

Her chin rose in approving consideration of that last line. "Good," she said. "Now let's parse this a little bit further." Every interview or preinterview session is, to one degree or another, an ordeal. This one was proving to be a rather unique gauntlet. "When did you first become more good-looking than most dudes? Was it high school? Middle school? Elementary school?" I told her I honestly had no idea. I hadn't been keeping track. I didn't think most guys would have. "Well, let me tell you this," she responded with surety, "everyone else you were outpacing was keeping track. They were watching you accrue the spoils of your victory."

Roya then wondered what I now did for "bodily upkeep." I explained that I exercised a few times a week, played tennis on Sundays with a buddy, had been proactive about moisturizing since I turned thirty, tried to eat at least fairly healthily, had quit my pack-a-day habit long ago (right after graduating from Emerson), drank only a glass of wine with dinner and never did drugs except for marijuana. To this, she cocked her head and said, unimpressed: "In other words, you have to do nothing."

Next, she asked me if I'd ever considered the possibility of having work done, perhaps sometime in the future. I told her I hadn't, but if anything, I looked forward to growing old gracefully—although, catching myself, I understood it was easier to say this as a man. "It's also easier to say that," she offered, "when you've apparently always operated from a position of sexual advantage. One day it'll begin to slip away." I made a joke about hoping to be happily coupled up for the long term by then. She didn't laugh.

I continued, more seriously, "I think there's something compelling about your view of the world, beauty's driving force in it. I don't necessarily agree with it, at least at the moment and at least as you've articulated it. It sounds like a theory that may be passionately held but overdetermined. Still, I'm happy to talk it through further and, you know, *tussle* until I'm convinced."

Roya hadn't been paying attention to this, I realized as soon as I finished yammering on. Instead, caught up in thought, she wondered aloud, without segue, how and why I'd become a writer. I thought I'd already relayed the story. "No, you didn't," she said, displeased. "Going back to the beginning, long before college and the wire-service job. Artistic types, as far as I understand it, are always somehow at least partially damaged. That's what forges them."

It struck me as bold, if somewhat naive, to come straight out and seek my deepest, innermost truths—such as they were. Again, the angle was off; it was too steep. "I'm not a cheap date," I said, now chuckling. "If you allow me to get to know you, which perhaps consists of understanding your own at least partial damage, maybe then I'll share my own too. We'll see how we do with each other."

Now Roya waited me out as we watched each other in silence. Finally, I bit, to nudge things along. Our time was running short. "So, what's it going to be? Are we on for the *Elle* piece?"

A surprised look came across her. "Oh, no, definitely not. That's out of the question. It's never been *in* question."

"Wait, what?" Irritation prickling toward rage swelled within, registering in a newly clipped cadence. "Then what's this twenty-questions routine been about? Why am I even here?"

Roya smiled in reassurance, her own voice delving toward girlish and accommodating for the first time since we met. "Oh, I'd like us to work together! Just not that way."

I asked, peevishly, what way she had in mind then. "A memoir," she said. "I'm sure there'd be interest from a publisher. You'd be the ghostwriter. We'd work out a fair deal on compensation. Your name would be on the cover too—much smaller, of course. This way I can be more candid because I can approve of what's going to be written, and we can—what's the word you just used?—*tussle* over the revisions together. I'd have a sort of quasi-editor's role, consultative. I know that's not the way it works with journalism, which is why I'm not interested in participating in a profile."

Preserving my calm, I explained that I'm not a ghostwriter. "Not yet," she said, smiling again. "But you're going to be great." Nice trick there, the rhetorical assumption that the project was already happening, with me attached.

"And why are you so sure? For a book-length project, maybe you'd like to work with someone else. There are a ton of great writers out there, many of whom have ghostwritten before. I can pass along some names myself. *Women*, who grew up in an economic stratum more to your liking, and who have had a lifetime of body-image issues—many persisting to this day. Trust me, I've dated *several* of them."

Roya was amused by my sudden willingness to hand things off. "But Wesley Frederick Easton is so *persuasive*," she teased, "and he's already so earnestly 'fascinated' by my story. Why start fresh unless I have to?" I wasn't appreciating this line of enticement, and my stunningly good-looking face must have shown it, because after a pause she ventured another tack.

"OK," she said, wiping the grin off her voice. "My turn to pitch. I liked your article on that Count Dietrich guy." I'd recently written a profile for *Town & Country* on eighty-three-year-old Count Dietrich von Cirksena, a barely closeted German faux nobleman grieving the loss of his Jewish wife, seventies soap star and Bel Air dinner-party doyenne Amelia Moreland.

The couple's story wasn't one of the clippings I'd sent Roya over the course of several rounds of proffered reading material by mail. "How'd you find it?"

"It's restricted and monitored use, but we're allowed on the internet in the library, Wes. Do you think I'm going to limit myself to your curated selections? I've got a *ton* of time on my hands. I've even read a few of your film reviews from the Emerson school paper. Those were tough sledding."

"Thank you for the criticism of the criticism. So, what'd you like about that piece?"

Roya had a ready answer. "They're the ultimate fish in the barrel and you didn't shoot. The empathy quotient was high. I respect that."

I'm susceptible to flattery like any other mark. My ego can be manipulated too. I thanked her and told her I'd take the ghostwriting offer under consideration.

She rose, all business, those sea-green eyes connecting with my own. Then she extended her hand for another firm shake. "Please do."

BODY ACHE

When I was a child, Sunday mornings meant visits to our favorite place, the J. Paul Getty Museum along the Pacific Coast Highway on the way to Malibu. My mom, who'd been visiting since it opened in 1974, was besotted with it, and I soon became so too. Frequently, when Dahlia was bored with or outright irritable at the idea of joining us yet again, she'd be dropped off with a friend. That meant that I'd get Mom to myself, making the experience even more meaningful. After the museum, we'd get our feet wet on the beach across the street, invariably both screeching at the cold shock of the waves, and then order lunch at the counter of the nearby Reel Inn seafood shack, taking our seats at the long picnic tables as sand continued to work its way beneath our matching, now-chipped painted toenails.

She adored the Getty for its strict traditionalism and starchy gentility. Now the PCH property is called the Getty Villa, to distinguish it from its modernist main-campus sibling offshoot, the Getty Center, which debuted in 1997 on a sprawling Brentwood hilltop. It shares those traits with her other LA museum enthusiasm, the cross-town Huntington Library in San Marino, another vanity institution bankrolled by a new-money tycoon with old-school proclivities, which I enjoyed when we visited a few times a year primarily for its endless gardens of every horticultural variety. My mom, who had no use for contemporary art, was interested in one thing on her visits to the Getty's collection of Greek, Roman and Etruscan antiquities: communing with greatness across millennia. It was transportive, dreamy, awe-inspiring; the human civilization equivalent of gazing at the stars—an activity that, as it happened, eluded us in light-polluted LA. Put simply, she hoped to be overcome by a feeling of *Whoa*. In a city with a short history (not that her hometown of Pittsburgh is all that old in the scheme of things), this imported extreme long-term memory was, to her, a balm.

Her infatuation influenced my own enchantment with the Getty too. But the persistent rapture, which has prevailed as intensely as few other things, is due to other factors as well. For one, the physicality of the place itself is sheer romance, a grand sweeping gesture. Not just the elegance and opulence of the formal topiary surrounding the long front reflecting pool, mosaic inlays along the colonnades, illusionistic frescoed loggias, and everything else there that's modeled on ancient Roman gardens. It was J. Paul Getty's notion to replicate—on the other side of the world, thousands of years later, in its initial glory (and not in some tastefully faded, ruinous state)—the Villa dei Papyri, which had been buried by the eruption at Mount Vesuvius and discovered in 1709.

As with Beverly Hills' Persian palaces, art and architecture critics have long scoffed at it, deriding the undertaking as an effort of refined kitsch, thinking the Getty vulgar for treating its sublime holdings as props in a lavish period-correct stage-set production—so LA, so *Hollywood*—rather than with the standard curatorial distance. Such criticism doesn't make sense to me. This isn't reenactment. It's conjuring.

When we visited, my mom and I would often, without verbalizing the decision, part ways. She had certain pieces she liked to call on, like old friends—vessels, urns, plates, jewelry, funerary lions, a favored sarcophagus or two. Proof of her devotion: After the Getty was caught up in its shameful antiquities scandal in the mid-2000s, which she of course avidly followed, my mom used the museum's eventual relinquishment of key artifacts to Italy as a reason to draw up a vacation itinerary to sojourn to their new institutional homes in that country several years later with dutiful stepdad Fred in tow.

By comparison, I found all of that stuff interesting but never compelling. My heart was with the core of the collection—the sculpture, full-body works and busts. Absorbing these pieces imprinted the conscious ideal for human form on me like nothing else since. Not a specific one (I admit I'm beholden to a contemporary ideal) but *seeking* one. If my original sin is some unique composite of lust, greed, and envy in relation to earthly aspiration, then blame the Getty. Blame Polykleitos circa the fourth century BCE and his chiseling acolytes in the classical periods thereafter.

Oftentimes strange or sad things happen when you intensely ponder—which is to say, in some way, love—cultural objects in duration, arguably to overuse. It can outright kill the affection. More often what you first saw or felt so powerfully in whatever it is (personal example: Britney Spears's "Stronger" and its accompanying music video) mutates into something else, or becomes buried beneath other, subsequent responses. This may very well be the case with the Getty sculptures that I visited and revisited countless times in my youth.

Considering them now, what I recall being most moved by was how the marble had softened and contorted with age, the elements misshaping the concerted rigor of the craftsmanship. That makes sense: These pieces were often situated outside, and even when they were inside, they weren't being preserved in special climate-controlled rooms until sometime within the past century. Yet there was something devastating to me about the fact that these carvings, supreme acts against mortality, many depicting the gods but frequently also real people—who'd, of course, turned to dust thousands of years ago—were in the midst of their own slow decomposition. Dust would claim them yet.

It was only once I began practicing plastic surgery that I understood that there was something fortifying, too, about the prospect of such inevitable entropy. Even if the timetable on flesh is much quicker than that on limestone. I did well to remember this whenever I despaired of the temporal nature of my own craftsman's exertions in the operating room. That one day it would all just begin to wrinkle and sag and collapse (often for the second time) on the road toward death; that as soon as the swelling went down, the work would be at its best, like a dish sent out to the table from the kitchen, and not a minute later. It was all for naught. But we're human, so forever doesn't matter.

Decay and loss are what strike me most now when I think of many of those statues. Perhaps because, after a lifetime spent attempting to ascend some physical peak, I realize it's soon, biologically, downhill from here. The full-lengths have forfeited countless appendages. In the case of the heroic Lansdowne Herakles, the Getty's larger-than-life answer to David, all macho-sentimental posturing, carrying his lion skin and club, his member's been severed. It renders the piece, to me, dramatically ironic.

The most common misfortune is missing or otherwise shorn noses. All of those rhapsodized faces, particularly when limited to busts, are brought into sharper relief. It's beyond tragic—ghastly, really. Restorers have decided not to reconstruct them. I guess it's more authentic to leave them deformed. I can't help but be repulsed, put to mind of syphilis and leprosy, wishing I could lend a professional hand. One of the most prominent statues afflicted is Hygieia, the goddess of good health.

Like my mom, I had pieces that maintained a gravitational pull. That a head of Nerva—with his high forehead, hooked nose, close-set eyes, and large Adam's apple—had been reworked from a portrait of his immediate and reviled predecessor, Domitian, seemed somehow disquieting as well as hilarious to me. Then, for more farce, there's the head of Caligula, depicted at the behest of his family as far more attractive than he actually was (according to bitchy descriptions by Roman writers). Not to mention a bust of Commodus, subject to an abrasive sculptural equivalent of a facelift, severe Botox, and microdermabrasion in the eighteenth century—at the direction of some overzealous English earl who possessed it at the time. As a result, it required extensive analysis of its mineral deposits to even verify its ancient origin.

I had a more complex relationship with the female forms than their opposites. That said, I immensely enjoyed objectifying, in all of its entendres, the men, particularly the hubba-hubba ripped marble *Torso of an Athlete*, devoid not only of arms and legs but of a head that could look back and judge me as I judged it. I had a long-standing cool-girl crush on Julia Titi, the daughter of the emperor Titus, on account of her calm-verging-on-insouciant gaze and quasi-duck-face late-teenage pout, but also was jealous over both her dramatic, deeply drilled curls and the way she so clearly *worked them*. Yet the marble sculpture that I would always end up standing in front of in supplication for the longest was Venus. She was rendered beside an accompanying dolphin, in reference to her birth from the sea, her hair partially up and partially down, captured in the process of pulling some sort of antiquated finery-robe over her nether regions while her breasts remained bare.

I could have done, and later did do, far worse than obsess over this representation of Venus, with her meaty arms, rather stolid midsection, and pleasingly if not extremely youthful-feminine facial features. Her jowls, for instance, could have been brought in. Yet this Venus was the first body I utilized as a reference point aside from my mom's. Before I had breasts of my own, I developed a habit of imitating her pose after showering. Nude in my adjoining bedroom, I'd consider my form in front of the mirrored closet doors, hair still wet, my towel pulled partway up in the same manner, right arm holding one of its corners, my face turned to the left in such a way as to elongate my neck most gracefully, everything suspended for a moment.

Then, for a long time, as my hair dried, I'd scrutinize how I missed the mark. That this shouldn't be a competition; that this Venus was one long-gone male artist's (no doubt in manifold ways problematic) ideal; that, in fact, this Venus wouldn't even be considered ideal at all within our current context; that it was irrational for me to think, as a prepubescent, I was missing any postpubescent mark—all of that, and much else, may be obvious and right thinking but was lost on me at the time. I was too consumed with my knobby knees and my belly pooch and, most certainly, the bump along the bridge of my nose.

My mom once walked in on me during one of these sessions. Shutting the door and retreating back into the hallway as I broke the posture and yelped, she immediately registered what'd been going on: who—or rather what—I was imitating and, having interpreted the grimace that'd affixed to my face, how poorly it was going.

After apologies and negotiations, she'd soon worked her way back inside, soothing the awkwardness of the situation with a joking comment about the beauty contest Venus-as-Aphrodite had won against Athena and Hera, wondering whether the judge, Paris, had properly arbitrated it. (Mom had always been an Athenian.) "Honey baby," she said, taking my now-fully-wrapped-in-a-towel self in her arms and squeezing hard as I attempted to wriggle away in embarrassment. "You're most definitely a little goddess. That's for *sure*." She laughed and kissed my still-damp forehead. My eyes remained downcast, unable to connect. "And you're most definitely *beautiful*. But you shouldn't go around comparing yourself to *other* goddesses, mythological or otherwise. It's"—a beat passed, as she sought to calibrate the correct oratorical approach—"not a good look."

I finally did look up at her as my eyes welled. She smiled in reassurance, a mother's heart-to-heart wisdom dispensed. I hugged her back, squeezing just as hard. Tears flowed against her blouse. She thought they were of fresh comprehension and cooed, again and again, "honey baby." They weren't.

I already knew I was no goddess. Not on the outside. And my mom's advice not to compare myself to others: This verged on the nonsensical and offensive when I was growing up in, of all places, Beverly Hills. Plus, even as a preteen it was clear to me it was a lot easier to be high-minded about what envious behavior was "not a good look" when you were dictating it, as my mom was, from the vantage of your own good looks.

While my dorky, private Venus posing eventually subsided when pubescence arrived, the act of considering myself for stretches in the nude in front of those floor-to-ceiling sliding mirrored closet doors never did. It only escalated and curdled. I did, however, transition to contemporary points of comparison, which shared no unified code of specific aesthetic traits aside from a general aura of gorgeous perfection: a few of the most popular girls in school, plenty of women glimpsed around Beverly Hills and beyond, plus preferred movie stars (Winona Ryder, Drew Barrymore), pop stars (Natalie Imbruglia, Gwen Stefani) and supermodels (Claudia Schiffer, Helena Christensen).

My mom knew I kept doing this now with the door locked. She knew it was a losing game for any teenage girl (even the most popular girls in school), and particularly for one with a prominent nose, a broad oval face, thin lips, wide hips, and a stocky frame. Yet all she could do was buoy her daughter with sincerely held pep-talk platitudes. For a while, through tears, I let her.

Now, I don't know if I would've made it through my run-of-the-mill plain-Jane adolescence if I hadn't, by luck, been spared its worst female grotesqueries, its most wildly depressing, to-the-brink psychological journeys. The pathologies that can even turn deadly: the anorexia, the cutting.

However, as I've said, I did suffer a period of severe acne. It was during the length of ninth grade, my freshman year at Beverly Hills High School. And that's the correct verb—*suffer.*

What had been flawlessly clear skin was invaded, at first slowly and then all of a sudden toward the end of fall semester, by outbreak after outbreak of pimples, some constellations small and short-lived, many larger and more long-lasting, colonizing the T-zone of my nose and forehead, then across my cheeks and along my chin. At first my mom thought it was stress—schoolwork, social stuff—and hormones. Soon she realized it was the full force of my father's genes. His complexion had been pocked when she met him, a scarred battlefield. On him, though, it'd been fine. His coloring was darker. He was older. He had such confidence. He was a man.

I'd already begun experimenting with makeup two years earlier.

But whereas the initial forays were curious, a typical girl's research and development with mascara and lipstick, nudging enhancements, I was now concerned with playing frantic defense. In the era before you could search for niche internet video tutorials, I spent hours working with foundations and liquid concealers, hovering close to my freestanding vanity mirror, desperately blending. The toil neutralized the colors. In daylight, though, it was obvious that the texture of previously smooth skin was ravaged. The frenzied yet precise caking didn't matter.

My dermatologist prescribed me a regimen of antibiotics, topical (clindamycin) and oral (doxycycline), along with benzoyl peroxide, first as a gel and then as a cream. I remember applying the peroxide late at night and lying still, face up in bed, less pained than amazed by how it could so viciously sear the topmost layering of my skin. I'd wait out the ten-minute inferno each evening, an immolating monk of acute teenage self-pity, allowing the burn to quell to its embers before I could go to sleep in peace.

I was never outright bullied for my acne. If the condition had materialized when I was still in middle school, I likely would've been insulted for my pizza face to my face. But just a few years later the way people reacted to it was never blatant or crude. Instead, I simply became socially invisible. Already an introvert, shy by nature, I retreated further, the girl who didn't initiate the conversation, even make eye contact. Why would I want to force anyone to look at me? If my few friends (who were sweet and supportive about my situation, and whom I leaned on a bit, but who had their own ninth-grade traumas to deal with—some, frankly, more dire than mine) needed me during spring semester, as things worsened, they could find me during lunch with earphones on in the library. My head was down over my Advanced Placement textbook, as I took notes, grinding away.

While I'd at times been disappointed by my looks and even upset about them, I'd never been repulsed by them until my acne plague, which just kept getting worse. It sounds bizarre now, but there were moments at night when I'd finished washing away the makeup, applying the medication, and popping the whiteheads that I would just marvel at the abject moonscape of my visage in the honest bathroom light. I'd examine pore after pore after pore at close range in the vanity mirror, the healthy ones and the blighted ones, then back away, regarding in wonderment the entirety of this thing, my face, this mask of flesh, which had betrayed me. I was under it, stuck inside, and over it, floating nearby. I found it fascinating and terrifying.

As spring semester came to an end, my dermatologist put me on the far more aggressive isotretinoin, more commonly known as Accutane. The drug's maker, Roche, would take it off the market about a decade later after determining it'd become financially burdensome to continue losing so many jury trials over its major side effect: the apparent inducement of inflammatory bowel disease like Crohn's and ulcerative colitis. I only experienced the minor effects—dry lips and fragile skin, along with muscle aches and headaches. Accutane would eventually conquer my acne, but it would take months to do it, the drug would make it worse before it would make it better, and it would make my exposed skin susceptible to sunburn as the summer of 1996 began.

Luckily, I was in the mood to be a shut-in anyway. And by shut-in, I mean full-on hermit. I would've rented movies, but in those antediluvian days we still had to head out to Blockbuster to browse the rental selections, and the thought of doing the whole makeup routine for the trip was a hurdle I couldn't surmount in my depressive state. The same went with checking books out of the library. Therefore, a heavy TV diet, coupled with whatever self-help volumes my mom had lying around, was more my lazy-recluse speed.

My intake that summer was a mix of how-to-be manifestos (*The 7 Habits of Highly Effective People*, *Your Erroneous Zones*, *You Can Heal Your Life*, *The Magic of Thinking Big*, *Awaken the Giant Within*) and reruns. I aimlessly watched all sorts of stuff, but the two shows that I recall tracking via *TV Guide* listings were *Saved by the Bell* and *Beverly Hills, 90210*. One may have been a brightly lit, lighthearted comedy and the other a softly lit, self-serious drama. But they both were 100 percent pure-grain LA high school fantasias. And like the WB programs I'd follow a few years later when they debuted—*Dawson's Creek*, *Buffy the Vampire Slayer*, *Popular*—their narratives of adolescent angst and aspiration were powerful narcotics that provided, just as they intended, an escape from my own.

For all intents and purposes, by that summer after freshman year I hadn't yet had real high school experiences and I wouldn't later either. Sure, I was there. I went to class, got good grades, participated in my college-résumé-burnishing extracurriculars. But socially I was biding my time, waiting for my future to begin. I didn't date, didn't attend parties. I sat high school out in that sense, partly on purpose and partly because I didn't have a choice. This is easy enough to accomplish when you're an unattractive wallflower. Sad as it may be, those shows—their camera filters, their plot pivots dovetailing with Nielsen sweeps, their cloying and stirring pop soundtracks—synthesized as a glossy carapace in my head, in lieu of actual memories of the period.

My mom at the office, Dahlia at camp, the shades drawn in our living room, I'd splay out on our couch, glass of Crystal Light in hand. The cliquey travails of Zack and Jessie and Brandon and Kelly unfolded in nonsequential order, alighting at the Max and the Peach Pit. It was enjoyable, if somewhat discombobulating, to watch Tiffani Amber Thiessen—God, I wished, at a glandular level, I could've looked like Tiffani Amber Thiessen—switching from kindhearted cheerleader Kelly Kapowski on *Saved by the Bell* to total bitch Valerie Malone on *90210*. Bayside and West Beverly were shining cities on a hill. The real Beverly High was, to me, by contrast both a locus of loneliness and far less glamorous. My main association with its hallways was the lingering ammonia scent of disinfectant from the janitor's mop.

My mom had wanted me to either take classes or work a summer job (as she'd done when she was that age). But my anxiety and depression thwarted those intentions. Instead, understanding I was going through a kind of torment that she'd never had, and wise enough to have stopped condescending to me after I'd repeatedly pointed this out to her, she asked only that during those few months of school break I "give thought" to how I might become a "happier you." The fact that this advised expedition of the soul had come without any appropriation to subsidize psychotherapy had led me to my mom's self-help shelf.

I haven't revisited those books since. Their collective epiphanies are lost on me. All I can say I took away from them is a purpose-driven desire to envision a specific future I wanted for myself and then relentlessly strive for it. Perhaps my focus would've been more internal than external had I in fact seen a shrink. But as the summer passed and the Accutane took effect, I longed for a different life, a far prettier one, and began to formulate a plan to get there. It was utilitarian. It would take time. That was OK. I wasn't in a rush.

I materialized from my sequestered cocoon in the fall of sophomore year. The acne scars were lasered away by Thanksgiving. I was healed.

My mom was relieved. Dahlia, perhaps sensing the arc of an impending genetic scourge, was too. My tiny, tight circle of girlfriends remarked on the impressive improvement. This only served to remind me how much remarking must have gone on the previous year when the condition was worsening and then at its depths.

As soon as the affliction lifted, I began to obsess, as never before, about my nose: its size and especially its bump. I wanted to do something about it. I'd brought it up in the past, before the plague, and my mom had waved me away, genuinely thinking the concern silly. She really did, in her motherly way, believe me beautiful. "There's nothing wrong with your nose," she'd say, laughing, squeezing my nostrils between the knuckles of her pointer and middle fingers and lightly pulling. "Except your attitude about it!"

Now it was different. My fixation was anchored in the abyss I'd begun to climb out of. My mom knew that. She would tell me again and again, as I'd whine again and again, that my nose was fine, that it "fits," that it's "yours." Finally, she even told me it possessed "strength—strong character." I snickered. "What kind of strength?" I challenged her. "The strength to knock someone out? To require a turn signal to keep clear?" I *had* been bullied about my nose in middle school to my face. The taunts stuck with me.

She considered me carefully. Then she responded: "The strength of your father." By this time, nearing sixteen, I was less interested in paying obeisance to established pieties within our condo regarding my haloed father. The fact that he'd left us, left my mom to care for us, when the going got tough, no matter the mental burden, didn't connote strength to me.

A moment passed. "I don't want his strength," I quietly said. "I want yours."

She cried and I cried and then she kissed my nose, again and again, the way she always did when I was younger, right before she put me to sleep. Wiping away her tears, she looked at me and said, "I would kiss his nose at night too. I still miss doing that."

Wiping away tears of my own, I looked back at her, holding firm, snot in my own snout, and said, "Well, I would kiss your nose at night too, before you turned out the light. I want your nose, not his. Dahlia has it. Why can't I?"

I didn't win the argument that night, but I won it in time. Sociologically, right on time: Sweet-sixteen nose job gifts were then and are now something of a phenomenon in Beverly Hills and other Jewish LA enclaves of the unfortunate schnoz. The places where, no matter how dubious the claim of a deviated septum might be, its medical seriousness is invoked to position *this* teenage rhinoplasty as, unlike all of the others, not *purely* a vanity affair. In practical terms, I paid off my student loans at least several months quicker by servicing this particular niche.

Once convinced, my mom found my specialist, Dr. Pankaj Viswanathan, through the recommendation of a fiftysomething female partner at her law firm with whom she'd become quite close over the years. She hadn't been aware that this woman had ever had her nose done, which was apparently proof positive of the surgeon's skill. Another implicit endorsement, perhaps far better: Even with a called-in favor, I couldn't land a consultation date for sooner than four months out.

I was impressed with everything about Dr. Viswanathan. His office on Camden Drive didn't look like a typical physician's suite. It was a feat of interior design, more like a high-end spa, full of bleached wood floors, frosted glass partitions, and diffuse light. The staff members were all attractive, albeit in an understated, tasteful way that didn't announce them as billboards (whether in reality or merely in theory) for their boss. Then there was the doctor himself, a good-looking, well-built man in his late forties—extrapolating from the dates on the diplomas on his wall; otherwise, who could tell in this business?—with stubble that shifted from mostly pepper along the jawline to primarily salt across the chin. He reminded me a bit of Raj, all grown up. (Raj attended Harvard-Westlake after finishing middle school, disappearing into the private school vortex, never to be seen again, except for one random run-in at the Beverly Center's food court junior year: still a cutie.)

Dr. Viswanathan also struck an admirable balance in his presentation between knowledge, perspective, and wisdom. Aside from displaying a mastery of his chosen specialty itself—its bones, its muscles, its tissue, its folds and flaps and curves, however they manifest themselves in each patient—he knew how to think about it. He never spoke of "improving," only "adjusting." He talked about "symmetries" and "proportions" and "context." When my mom and I brought up our idea, the replication of her nose in the manner that Dahlia had already been blessed, he observed how the proboscis must be considered within the full scope of the rest of the face. When I broke down, wondering, somewhat innocently and somewhat provocatively, "Are you saying I'm not pretty enough for my mom's nose?" he didn't take the bait. He said, "What I'm saying is you should be seeking—if it's what you want to be seeking—*your* best nose, not your mom's or your sister's."

At his desk a short while later, with the clickety-click of his mouse, Dr. Viswanathan reshaped a profile portrait of my unsmiling face, deleting the bump, shrinking the size, pulling up and rounding the tip. He placed a before-and-after diptych side by side on the screen. "This can be you," he said.

It would be, in time. Surgery was scheduled for the Tuesday after I finished my sophomore year. There was a moment that morning when I was left alone after Dr. Viswanathan marked up my nose with a felt-tip pen. I looked in a mirror one last time. He'd warned me during my consultation that some people, even if they are happy with the result, later miss the face they dreamed of changing. It harbored memories of their life before, their real genetic roll of the dice. Yet they can't admit this fact to themselves or others because once the procedure's done, it's done.

I ran a finger down the bump and flared my nostrils. I thought of the diptych, a full-color printout of which I'd kept and revisited with devotion at home since the consultation. The past didn't compel me. I could only think of my future.

I can't now remember the pain of recovery. For ten days I was back on the living room couch of the condo, Crystal Light in hand, rocking a plastic splint secured with tape across my cheeks and periorbital bruising around both eyes, the shiners a result of the nasal bone having been broken. Ingesting my smoothies and watching TV, I counted down the hours until the bandages would be unwrapped. Christmas morning never held that level of allure.

I asked that my mom remain in the waiting room on reveal day. Before the unwrapping, Dr. Viswanathan cautioned that the bruising wouldn't disappear for another couple of weeks, and the swelling wouldn't dissipate for several months, yielding the true final result in as much as a year's time. Still, despite the dramatic swelling and bruising, when the tape came off and the handheld mirror was brought up, it was obvious to me that I'd been transformed. I actually gasped and began to cry. Dr. Viswanathan, knowing what he'd done, just another day at the office, put a hand on my shoulder and looked into my eyes. "Remember this," he said. "This isn't your new nose or your different nose or your better nose. It's your nose. It's been there all along."

Before my experience with Dr. Viswanathan, I didn't understand cosmetic surgery. To the extent I'd thought of it at all, I considered it to be a superficial endeavor of medicine—a permanent cosmetology, a next-level dermatology. It's not. It's foundational and fundamental, melding the psychological and the physiological, this transfiguration of the body. It's a practice rooted in our evolving understanding of who we are.

I was thrilled with the result of my nose job. My mom told me, politically, "I loved how you looked before. I love you just the same now." But Dahlia—who at one point curled up next to me on the couch during my recuperation, saying, with not a hint of condescension in her voice, "I'm sorry you have to go through all of this just to get what I got straight out"—later confided that my mom had told her she'd privately written Dr. Viswanathan a note extolling his handiwork.

My small circle of friends said nice things when they realized it was OK to say anything at all. Most people at school didn't notice. This was both because, again, I was socially invisible and because I'd opted for a new haircut just before class started in the fall to divert focus from the nose job.

I did gain some confidence, that grail so often alluded to in my profession. But it was only a limited, circumscribed confidence regarding my looks. I was elated with my nose, to be sure, but now I was focused on everything else. I'd found a skeleton key and wouldn't stop until I unlocked each door. The confidence I'd attained wasn't the one advertised—self-confidence. My confidence was in physical beauty itself: that what I'd started could be finished, that through cosmetic surgery I had the power to reshape my fate. It would be accomplished on my terms, under my direction, through my control.

I shared this view with my mom back at the Getty Villa, while we strolled through the main colonnade one fine Sunday as I took a rare several-hour break from cramming for the SATs. She in turn marshaled the same pieties I'd heard all my life. About how it's what's inside that counts, how a fixation on vanity itself isn't attractive, how being pretty—however I might define it at the end of the rainbow—isn't necessarily, or even likely, going to make me happy. I nodded at all of this, knowing it to be both true and moot. Then I said, with quiet conviction, as the seated Hermes observed us from his perch on a rock nearby, "You can still be a good person and want to experience a life of being physically desired by those you physically desire."

She told me she took my point, and that she'd "always support" my "journey toward fulfillment, whatever that may be." Yet she said her own direct assistance had come to an end, for both philosophical and practical reasons. She couldn't afford to fund more work. (Dr. Viswanathan's bill was nearly $7,000.) I thanked her again for her generosity—I'd thanked her countless times already—and privately resolved that this wouldn't stop me. I would pay my own way in the coming years. There was still so much left to do. In the next decade and a half, while I racked up steep student loan debts from medical school, I'd outpace the rhinoplasty fee tenfold on other procedures, piling on significant credit card debt in the process. Those debts would only begin to be substantively paid down beyond their monthly minimums when I started billing some of those same procedures myself as a private practice physician.

My story is nearly, if not wholly, universal. It's natural to want. It's human to strive. It's American to dream beyond born circumstance. I believe there to be a modern noble grace in seeking your own ideal rather than settling for the one imposed on you.

To reinvent yourself, to perfect yourself, to navigate your heart and emerge triumphant from the chrysalis of your past self: It's what my life is about. It's what my practice was about. It's what led me to do what I did. So that I could support as many other people as possible on that precarious journey toward fulfillment, whatever it turned out to be—particularly for me.

THREE

I'd decided to ghostwrite Roya's memoir by the time I'd returned to LA from meeting with her. I figured it was a way into doing books. The proposal would likely get picked up; the question was for how much.

For the past several years, I'd been scheming for a way to transition into the book space. The business of journalism, especially as a freelancer, had turned precarious in the extreme. The rational move was to get out. I just needed a viable escape plan, seeing as how my preferred route—cashing in as a scriptwriter during the streaming boom—had already been a bust.

Several times, when one of my biggest stories was published, some New York agent would get in touch, asking if I'd be interested in fleshing out a version of it. I invariably either was tired of the subject or didn't think it could sustain the fleshing. There was also the issue of access. Often after my pieces were published, the central relationships that had conjured them were shot or altered. There was no going back.

Meanwhile, here, with Roya, was a golden opportunity, if I played it right. Her story was marketable, and I was, as yet, still itching to tell it. Still, it didn't serve me in the long run—in our creative collaboration, in my business negotiation—to be an easy yes. I'd wait her out.

To wit: I received a four-page letter from Roya in her near-illegible chicken scratch, dated the day after our meeting, which was meant to seal our deal. There were some additional pro forma flatteries. But mainly it was a confessional, outlining, in frank terms, moving themes of race, class, and gender through the prism of the body, specifically her body's evolution most of all.

It was all there . . . if you could find it in the thickets of deep-purple prose, grammatical trouble spots, mixed metaphors, and underdeveloped notions. To protect the guilty, I've chosen not to reproduce any of it here. I couldn't tell if this was just the way she wrote, when she wrote earnestly and at length, or if the purpose of the letter was, in the lame discharge of its task, a brilliant cynical gambit to attract my help. Regardless, it worked. I felt called even further to action, rescuing my damsel from further distressing any more dangling participles.

The book deal itself was only one factor. My interest was broader—and baser. From the moment I left Roya, I wanted to see her again. I wanted to get closer.

The women I'm attracted to are usually inscrutable, enigmatic. They often share a languid vibe, a chilly poise. Maybe I'm a bit chilly too and it meshes. Roya, the native California girl, was none of these things. She struck me as direct, vivid, alert. And the surface pleasure of her sheer gorgeousness was amplified and underscored by knowing how hard she'd worked to secure it, as well as how much pride mixed with certitude she took in the result of her efforts.

In short order I told her I'd write the memoir, her criminal attorneys brought in a civil colleague to negotiate her deal, and I was hooked up on my end with a lawyer through a writer friend to push for my own interests. I ended up with no royalties and a smaller onetime payday than I would've preferred. But I did get a "with Wes Easton" byline on the cover (in minimum two-thirds smaller type than Dr. Roya Delshad's), and more importantly, I fought off signing a permanent nondisclosure agreement, instead only promising not to write about the experience, if I ever did, until the paperback edition had been out for eighteen months.

"What about my own memoir one day?" I'd joked but not joked to my attorney, who was rather eager to fold when we received aggressive initial pushback to our refusal. "About you writing someone else's book?" he said. "I'm not your literary agent, but it doesn't sound so exciting. Maybe it's a chapter you could skip."

As soon as I'd decided I would take on this assignment, the question became how to do it. Having never written a memoir before, I needed a model. I'd read plenty of the classics in school, from junior-year AP English (*A Moveable Feast*) to college courses at Emerson (*Speak, Memory*). Postgraduation, I'd become something of a connoisseur of the form, from the Holocaust stuff (Primo Levi, Elie Wiesel) and the affirming stuff (Cheryl Strayed, Elizabeth Gilbert) to the funny stuff (Steve Martin, David Sedaris) and the celebrity stuff (Bob Dylan, Patti Smith) to the political stuff (Barbara Ehrenreich, Ayaan Hirsi Ali) and the all-purpose read-it-through-your-fingers stuff (Joan Didion, Jeannette Walls).

Once I digested Roya's note, however, I knew my—our—ideal lodestar. That would be Jose Canseco's number one. *New York Times* bestseller from 2005, *Juiced: Wild Times, Rampant 'Roids, Smash Hits, and How Baseball Got Big.* A classic if unintentional example of Joseph Campbell's hero's journey, it was one of the few books my nonreader brother Kirk, a varsity high school pitcher turned sports-radio call-in show devotee, had ever insisted I purchase.

Written in a straight-talking, disarming, chatty style, it's the quintessential tell-all by someone who sees himself as a truth teller and a rebel, even a prophet, and whom the public has deemed a pariah for unconventional, path-breaking choices. Despite being, by all accounts, a major-league douchebag—the humblebrag kissing-and-telling about turning down a desperate Madonna, the entire chapter about his extensive car collection (title: "My First Lamborghini"), the clinically detached misogynistic section that delineates "slump busters" from "road beef"—Canseco, who at one point provides his side of the story regarding his *domestic violence record*, somehow comes across as charming. It's incredible, and not merely a superb feat of strategic storytelling, because like Roya he's got a Big Idea that he's bent on selling, which he interweaves with his captivating personal history, scandal, and sociopolitical agenda. For both, it's about attaining physical perfection.

While Roya believed in a radical democratization of beauty, Canseco held the provocative position that steroids, which he illegally introduced to the game (he called himself their godfather; others referred to him as Typhoid Mary) would soon be accepted not just among players, executives, and fans involved in all professional sports but by the public at large. Furthermore, that if those steroids were utilized correctly—along with human growth hormone—to reset natural lifespans, they'd not just build better bodies but forestall aging and even death. This utopic futurism, which Canseco placed in the context of concurrent advancements in stem cell research and other developments in biomedicine and biotechnology, was the endpoint of his story. It was built on total transparency about what he did (pioneering the taking of steroids and then surreptitiously teaching his fellow players how to do it) but made no apologies.

Rereading *Juiced*, I found it remarkable how much Canseco's narrative dovetailed with Roya's own. Both of their stories centered on the focused, methodical remaking of their own bodies, universal truths emanating from those journeys. Each had spent time in prison. (Canseco served a much shorter sentence of just a few months, supposedly for failing a drug test while on probation; he claims someone purposefully switched out his urine sample.) His credo could be hers: "Despite what we're all used to thinking, genetics is not destiny. It's a starting point, that's all." It's a shared, seductive, quintessentially American view of the world, in which your fate is your own. "All I'm saying," he adds, "is that the lives we lead are the product of the choices we make."

I mailed her a copy of the book, saying as much, eager for her take. Roya's response was swift, although she didn't engage on these issues, apparently thinking them obvious. Instead, she was engrossed by Canseco's wounded grievance as a Latino and therefore an outsider in the league: how he conceived of his bad-boy status, that it was a racially tinged media construction, especially relative to his Oakland A's steroid-abusing counterpart, the super-doofus white dude Mark McGwire. "Whatever you think of the rest of his story," she wrote me, "this strikes me as emotionally true." Then she went on a tear about how the gendered nature of elective plastic surgery in the public consciousness—how it's still thought of primarily as a female concern—has held "truly aggressive, forward-thinking, public-policy-level discussions about its merits back."

In the following weeks, as I prepared for our first properly scheduled session together (at which time I'd begin extracting material from her for the book proposal), I Priority Mailed her a few other memoirs to, as I put it, get her "brain buzzing," including Mary Karr's exquisite trilogy. Again, I was looking to spark some sort of useful dialogue ahead of our collaboration. But instead of responding to the memoirs, she did her own further reading online, in the form of Karr's republished interview about memoir writing with *The Paris Review*, electing to quote the following two unrelated random bits to me in a reply letter. She omitted the original context of the questions in the process, which skewed their meaning. (The meaning had become Roya's, so no matter.)

> Being looked at in this culture invents you as a woman long before you're getting laid.

> People have different ideas of what natural is. Since the Romantics, we've all been big fans of the natural, as though natural equals good. Shitting in your pants is natural, wanting to boink the pizza-delivery kid is natural. Stabbing people who get in front of you at the cafeteria line—that's probably a

> natural impulse. Where do you draw the line between what's good natural and what's bad natural?

"Wise chick," Roya scrawled underneath, in a note that arrived three days before I was set to see her again. "For the sake of this project, let's not romanticize the natural. It's a mere baseline, after all. Humans are advanced social creatures. In any field of their endeavor, ARTIFICIAL is the departure. That's our achievement!"

BRAVE NEW GIRL

I now reflect on the eight years I spent back east for college and medical school, which roughly coincided with the Bush administration, as my personal ice age. An Angeleno by birth, West Coast by temperament, I was drawn by the romance of real seasons, the history and tradition of old America. Once I got there, my mild eczema became exacerbated by the weather. My latent seasonal affective disorder, yet undiagnosed, flared.

Still, it was college. I was able to tailor my studies to focus (mostly) on what I was interested in, which was biology and art history. I fell in with a (mostly) satisfying clique of friends. We went to (mostly) fun parties, where we discussed both smart and stupid things in equal measure. Life was good.

The best part of my time at Penn, though, wasn't my classes or my friends or the parties. It was my first-ever serious boyfriend, Kevin. Well, not "Kevin"—he's married now, and either he or his wife, whom I catch more than stray glimpses of via the Facebook pictures he posts of her and his two adorable little kids, would quite possibly kill me if I used his real name.

We met during our freshman year. A loose swarm of friends from our dorm, Speakman, was carousing through Philly with fake IDs that evening, peeling off into smaller and smaller groups as the night wore on, and we ended up pretentiously talking about pretension at some cheery Irish pub. Kevin was an English lit major with a minor in philosophy, full of all sorts of ideas passionately if quixotically held. "There's nothing more innate to being human than inauthenticity," he said, taking a valiant contrarian stand in defense of affectation as I fell hard for him over my third Guinness. "Life is pretense."

I'm not going to natter on about our strolls together along the snow-hushed quads, our foodie explorations of the city, our memorable trips in the summers down south, then cross-country, then backpacking around Europe. It was all so *nice*. He was great. First love in all its glory. What a bore in the retelling.

Brass tacks: What's relevant here is that he took my virginity, and I took his. Penn had been Kevin's Ivy safety. He'd gotten into Harvard, Yale, Princeton. But at least one and in some cases several of his classmates from his competitive private high school in Charlotte were going to each of those, and he decided he wanted—needed—a clean break from his past.

At Speakman, he was the full package: intelligent and sensitive in all of the evolved ways, while devout about his gym ritual to maintain that six-pack. Yet at his tiny, elite, casually cruel prep school, where he'd first matriculated in the sixth grade, he'd never escaped the two things he arrived with—a soon-conquered stutter and a far-more-slowly-vanquished tubby torso. "I was always shy there," he confided early on. "I'd want to curl up inside myself."

Kevin told me he'd had little luck with the girls there. Partly it was that he'd been a late bloomer, only shedding the last of his baby fat in his senior year. Partly it was his bashfulness. He'd become, according to him, "a veteran of the friend zone."

I found Kevin's faint North Carolinian drawl sexy and told him so. He said he sounded like a "total uppity city slicker" where he came from. The apparently new-to-the-scene six-pack and the pale-blue eyes and the dark floppy hair did it. As for me, he liked my body, whose surgical transformation was still nascent—beyond my high school–era nose job, I'd gifted myself a pair of Dahlia-esque plump lips, charged to my credit card, via an augmentation procedure during Christmas break of freshman year. (I received Juvéderm Ultra Plus hyaluronic acid fillers, although I subsequently favored Restylane Silk in my own practice.) I didn't have to question his attraction; an erection is an honest barometer. He would comment most on the softness of the skin along the nape of my neck where it met my hair. Not only had I not previously known this was one of my ostensible virtues, but I also appreciated the attentiveness with which he'd discovered it.

We teased each other when we fooled around together. I'd hunt and peck on his six-pack as though his abs were giant computer keys, or else I'd drum on them while we were listening to music like you'd do on your steering wheel while car dancing. Meanwhile, he was a fan of the playfully light titty twister and the wet willy in the belly button, particularly while he had me distracted by making out.

More than anything, he made me feel comfortable with my body not through compliments or even consideration but through a discomfort with his own body handled with a funny ease. I would, for instance, apologize for my inexorable thunder thighs. Not only would he respond by intently smooching them on his way up *there*, but when he got done, after making sure I was done, he would make a show of solemnly apologizing for his unevenly sized testicles, levitating himself in a pull-up to exhibit them—then, with a laugh, say, "Will you kiss it and make it better too?"

I remember him leaving my room for class the morning after we finally had sex. I looked out the window at the spring-green quad and cried. It had been what I'd expected it to be: embarrassed, quick, a bit painful, one-sided. Both times. (Things would improve in the following days.)

But these were joyful tears. I'd spent so much of my life hungering to be hungered for. And here it was, mutual infatuation expressed as rapture.

This is no great revelation, or even a small one. The act had granted our relationship a dimensionality we hadn't previously known, a complexity we couldn't have otherwise understood. I cried for what I felt I'd missed so far in my life, for how untouched I'd been, for what by circumstance I'd been denied. I couldn't wait to be with Kevin again, to do it better.

We would, with avidity and precocious curiosity, straight through to graduation, when he joined the Peace Corps and headed off to a village in Mali for two years. Understandably, things took their natural course.

I headed off to my own self-imposed isolation. Med school at Johns Hopkins was, for me, a journey into darkness. Whatever my struggles in life, they'd never been academic. Until Hopkins, where the searing ambient ambition was unlike any I'd ever witnessed before—everyone else had been high school valedictorian too, everyone else had earned their undergrad degree magna cum laude as well—and I often drowned against the grading curve.

I had friends there, my class a mix of incredible people intent on doing amazing things. But it was relentlessly, brutally competitive, full of gunners, and the bleak, often nihilistic camaraderie we established in that Baltimore crucible was akin to wartime trenches. I spent staggering arcs of hours in the library studying, fueled by titrated doses of Red Bull, peanut butter, and celery sticks.

Free time during med school—and, later, residency—was in such short supply that in many ways I became socially and emotionally stunted, or at least flattened. The process is a funnel for monomania edged by despair. In retrospect I remember less the specific intake of material, particularly the extra-unholy deep-immersion jags I endured in the lead-up to my boards exams, than the rip in the space-time continuum that emerged for several years between any semblance of a real life and me.

I found that romance at Hopkins was distorted too. There were, somehow, several actual couples that discovered each other there. But the scene was otherwise pure hookups, mine included: desultory, furtive, ambivalent, ennui ridden. People hardly had the energy to gossip about it. Think of a mumblecore *Grey's Anatomy* without the pop soundtrack, as directed by Ingmar Bergman.

It wasn't all hell. I found gross anatomy to be a moving, even transcendent experience. You have a different relationship with bodies, dead or alive, after cadaveric dissection. They are both more intimate and more abstract to you, more humanized and more dehumanized.

You never forget the atmospherics of the lab. There's the omnipresent, pungent, pickled scent of formaldehyde and bleach. There are the rows of stainless-steel tables. There are the red plastic buckets awaiting waste disposal.

And then there are the cadavers, which first appear wrapped in layers of plastic and cloth. We were asked not to name them. Students used to, but now it's considered disrespectful. I shared my female cadaver, who'd died at seventy-four, with five fellow students. We were supposed to refer to her by the table number. Still, in my mind she was Jane. Not just preserved tissue and muscle and organs but the site of a life that was lived, memories accumulated, pleasure and pain registered.

It was exactly what I shouldn't have done. But I couldn't help but personify her as I took her apart, just as some of my classmates did with their cadavers, all of those signifying wedding band depressions and piercings and gold teeth and pacemakers and lamentable tattoos dead-end portals into lost consciousness. Who had Jane been? What had she wanted? What didn't she get? What were her regrets?

She was white, although her leathery skin, blood replaced by embalming fluid, now shone a wan yellow gray. Her height and build were average, as were her looks. (Yes, you can get a sense of that, from bone structure and perverse imaginative extrapolation, even considering serious limitations like a lack of makeup and, of course, death.) Her short, straight hair was silver. She had a large recent scar across her abdomen, from a hernia operation, as well as a far more faded one from a cesarian. Jane's most striking trait, however, was her nails, both fingers and toes a matching spunky cherry red, still glossy and remarkably chip-free. I still wonder whether this was her doing or that of someone at the mortuary.

Donating your body to science is a generous act, a noble one. I intend to do it. I made the decision in anatomy lab, focused on Jane as I made my first-ever incision, a thoracic-abdominal Y cut, the scalpel's blade descending. The cadaver of my own body, this gift in service to biology, will be something else, a relic of and marker for advancements in today's modernity. The students who work on it will likewise know nothing of either my emotions or my exploits. They will, however, come to possess a granular understanding of its improvements, its customizations. (The summer after gross anatomy, I added to my burgeoning credit card debt load with a session of lipoplasty to address what my diligent gym routine had proved unable to do: conquer my thickset physique, especially my back, abdomen, and thighs.) I'd be willing to bet that, if I die in old age, they won't by then find such tailoring of the flesh and bones remarkable.

I do know this about Jane: She suffered. Many of the cadavers in the lab, these dear strangers, endured the indignities of infirmity. The giveaways are right there, the stents deep in the abdomen, the staples across the sternum. For Jane it was cancer. She'd already had a hysterectomy. Yet that reaper got her in the end.

Gross anatomy is a sightseeing trip. You pack your instruments—your flexible probe and your curved hemostatic forceps and your cartilage knife and your fine-point iris scissors and your bent teasing needle and all the rest—to dissect and transect, excavate and chisel, skin and strip. In the end you're hacking away with a saw. And everything's fascinating, not merely the obvious powerhouse highlights (the heart, the brain, the genitalia). The multifaceted, layered weaving of musculature along the back is a wonder unto itself. How, say, the iliocostalis and the longissimus and the spinalis run parallel and buttress one another as the serratus posterior inferior crosses above them like a stacked interstate highway exchange. To say nothing of all the nerves and capillaries and veins that inhabit the same neighborhood.

I'm a woman of science. I believe our body is our cells. Our thoughts are our neurotransmitters. However that came about: *Bravo, what an achievement.* In many cases self-healing, in some cases self-cleansing, unlike most other species (often) self-aware—I mean, really, it's the ultimate system. Bow down. Yet not until I scrutinized firsthand, for gross anatomy's duration, the intricacies of this unique machine we call home did I truly appreciate it.

When the lab is over, the bodies are cremated. There's a little ceremony, during which students discuss what the experience has meant to them. Family members of the donors are invited to attend. A surprising number of them do.

It was beautiful. It was stirring. It was also an absolute mind fuck. I kept searching the crowd for Jane's survivors, a widower, siblings, whichever child resulted from that cesarian. If they were there, I couldn't determine it. In my mind, they held her as she passed. I had held her as I passed through her.

I could never explain how beguiling the journey was to my mom or my sister, my friends from back home or Penn. They'd blanch or snicker or go bug-eyed: "Definitely *gross*!" That this adventure, this pilgrimage of knowledge, was a privilege—a consecrated desecration in quest of virtuous understanding—never really conveyed, no matter how hard I tried. I guess the ick factor, that grotesque divide, is just too large.

Aside from med school's relentless studying and the cutthroat classes, there was what we'd been waiting for: rotations with different specialties, real-deal time spent on the wards. Others entered Hopkins with an idea of what kind of doctor they'd want to be, but often they'd change their minds once they spent weeks working with that specialty or became entranced by up-close contact with another one. Most people had no idea what they wanted to do, and the practical aspects—hours, salary, lifestyle stuff generally—frequently determined their eventual direction. I never wavered on plastics, but found the rotations, from ortho to cardio to neuro to psych, varying degrees of compelling.

Every patient is, of course, unique. But a doctor, even a mere med student, recognizes in each hospital admit which of three final realities their patients will face. There is recovery, there is death, and there is the limbo of the chronic condition.

The ideal of recovery, or some sense of it, is why most physicians pursue this profession. We find you damaged—your husband dislocates your jaw in a rage; your tibia busts through your skin when you trip down the stairs—and we heal you with our hard-won expertise. No matter what went wrong, or why, we get to be the boomerang in the universe that makes things more right.

Patients arrive at the ER traumatized, and I don't mean "traumatized" in the contemporary code for "distraught," although they are often distraught too. I mean bleeding, bruised, broken. (Public service announcement: Please don't ride a motorcycle, and if you won't listen to someone who's seen more motorcyclists than she can count—those who survived long enough to make it to the hospital—ejected from their steeds and rearranged upon impact like Picasso figures . . . then, for Chrissake, at least wear a helmet.) Often they've lost consciousness. They won't find out how bad things were until the worst has passed.

You can see the voyage in the postop ward, even through the painkiller haze. How close these patients came to their end, bodies verging on shutting down. They may not physically be the same again (to say nothing of emotionally), but at least they're still here. You can see how, as a result, the organizing principle for their lives has shifted. There was a before and this is their after. They've been transformed.

Then there are those who arrive complaining about something, perhaps suddenly in acute pain, or else realizing something they've been contending with for a while is getting worse, or just not getting better. What was a rough patch they thought would pass has become their existence.

It turns out that cough that just won't go away is the result of all of those years working in the coal mine. You've got pneumoconiosis. You'll be on a respirator for the rest of your days.

You developed this butterfly-shaped rash across your face, along with strange joint and muscle pains and this vague feeling of fatigue. Sorry, it's not fever. It's lupus. Welcome to a future of habitual discomfort, steroids, and vampiric avoidance of the sun.

You thought you'd been suffering from a really bad, really prolonged case of food poisoning. Maybe gastroenteritis. Turns out you've got Crohn's disease. Let's fill you in on the ins and outs of your new appendage, the colostomy bag.

These people enter the hospital assuming they'll be healed. That's what doctors do. Instead, they're managed. We can alleviate their agony, not cure it. They sign in under the delusion they're temporarily sick and come out the other side permanently infirm.

"Does this mean I'm not running at state next month?" one sweet high school jock inquired of his hollow-eyed parents after he'd been informed that he had hypertrophic cardiomyopathy. (He'd collapsed during a practice run.)

"It means," my attending explained, "we're lucky we're able to have you here right now asking that question."

Some of the most profound moments I had during med school involved death—or, rather, the dying. I still vividly remember the angry old widower I met one afternoon early on in my rotations, a stage IV cancer patient who'd arrived after passing out in the hallway of his condominium building. He refused palliative care or discussions of a hospice transfer. "I'm *done*," he rasped, a hard look on his chemo-withered face. "Send me back *home*!" We couldn't let him go without stabilizing him, and it became apparent that he had no relatives or close friends nearby to come be with him.

There was nothing left to do—except, my attending observed, make sure he didn't die alone. I chose to stay with him long after it was time for me to go home that evening. I remained by his side straight through to the next morning. "I don't need a doctor babysitting me," he said, not looking my way.

"I'm not a doctor," I quietly responded. "I'm just a person who wants to be here with you."

He'd weakened far further as daylight broke. He was awake, but barely. I asked him questions. He didn't reply. So I leaned over, placing my hand over his, and kept it there, holding still and maybe dozing. A while later, his hand turned, ever so lightly squeezing mine, in a strange rhythmic, repeated pulsation. Alert, I clasped my other hand over it. His eyes were closed. Then his grip gave way and he flatlined.

By the end of med school, I'd had more than my fill of this. I'd had enough by the end of residency. I admire those who pursue this honorable labor every day. My experience with it was meaningful and so depressing I could hardly bear it.

Med school is an exercise in self-sorting. It sorted me into confirming and affirming that I'm a recovery physician of a particular kind. One who is most compelled, for better or perhaps for worse, by those patients who've *elected* to recover from their damage, real or perceived.

Plastics is not curing cancer. It's not making a stopped heart start again. Yet it's life-changing, cathartic work that allows people to feel born anew. It constitutes a (foolish, yes, but still understandable) rebuke of annihilation, a utopian and very human resistance to decay—a fierce, proactive declaration of vitality.

FOUR

Interviews are fragile exercises. The stakes and personalities fluctuate, which means the tactics oscillate. But the process—interaction to extract information—in practice remains constant, forever strange and unstable: humans attempting understanding.

Before my second visit with Roya in prison, I generated a lengthy list of questions, much as I would've done if we'd gone through with the *Elle* profile. It covered everything, from her legal case and conviction to her life leading up to it to her existence now, serving out her sentence. There was stuff I already knew from ambient media attention to her situation and stuff I already knew from her four-page explanatory letter. But I wanted to take it all from the top, fresh.

I wanted to know all sorts of things, on all emotional and practical levels: the full Barbara Walters. What had Roya learned from the experience? Would she do it all over again, seeing as how she at least still presents as holier-than-thou about it? Did she ever really think she'd get away with her scheme, or given that it seemed to have been established as her new way of doing business, was she just waiting to get caught to make some sort of political act out of insurance fraud? If righting perceived socioeconomic injustices within the medical sector was so important to her, why not quit her fancy Beverly Hills practice and open a nonprofit clinic, raising funds along the way? What did her own history as a plastic surgery patient mean to her, and how might it have played a role in doing what she did? When did she realize the jig was up, that she'd been caught, and how did that feel? How was she handling incarceration? What specifically did she miss about her lack of freedom? What did she intend to do for work when she got out of prison, seeing as how she'd lost her medical license? And on and on and on.

We'd get to all of it, but only a sliver at this first session, during which we'd agreed in advance to begin by narrowly focusing on her early years. Her attorneys had spoken with the warden, who after some back-and-forth—including an extricated promise, signed by all parties, for this official to review any manuscript material about the prison in advance of publication—allowed Roya and me to utilize one of a series of adjacent small rooms at the prison reserved for legal counsel to confer with their clients. The upside, at least compared to the massive general visitors' room in which I'd first met her, was that we were granted privacy and quiet, and as long as I applied for and received prior approval, I could sit with her for many hours at a time, throughout the day, rather than the short spans available to regular guests. The downside was that the beige-painted room, devoid of windows except a small vertical one embedded in the door to the hallway, could not have been more grim or claustrophobic. Also, any more austere: Its only ornamentation consisted of a pair of fluorescent lights affixed to the ceiling, a massive, bolted metal table, and several armless chairs.

These legal-counsel rooms were at once specific places, brutal in their bare aesthetics, and placeless abstractions, chambers so visually banal that, after a brief immersion in each successive interview session, they melted away, like a stark black minimalist stage set for a Beckett play. Roya was all that remained.

She strode into the counsel room that first day with a knowing smile and an entertained hello, her notebook in hand. The guard soon stationed himself in a seat just outside and shut the heavy door behind her with a firm click. We were alone.

"So where do we start," she began, all business as ever, before I could attempt chitchat. I had to reacclimatize myself to Roya, the tension between her detonative energy and her inert surroundings, her unflattering jumpsuit and her stirring looks. The contrasts were their own enticement, pheromonal. They worked on me and she knew it.

"Uh, well, at the beginning, generally. But before we do, we should get some housekeeping out of the way." I placed my iPhone face up on the table between us, tapped the Recorder app, and noted that we'd be on the record at all times—unless one of us pressed the red pause button.

"Now, keep in mind, I'm not your therapist. We're going to be talking, a lot, about you. But fair warning: Don't confuse my sustained interest with empathy. Everything you say may be used against you in the court of my first draft—"

"—which I'll be giving you notes on!"

"Just remember my role, and don't hold it against me as we move through this process. It's going to be a tricky one if it's going to be a rewarding one."

"Interrogation, collaboration—I'm feeling it," she said good-naturedly, unconcerned by my offered caution. "All right, really, hit me. Let's get this going."

I made a show of pressing record and started with something broad, all encompassing. How, why, and when had Roya decided she wanted to be a plastic surgeon? Once she was in medical school or before?

"Oh, long before. Since I first went to a plastic surgeon myself, in high school, for my nose. I was taken with his power to transform."

Taken with his power to transform? That sounded pat. She held forth with passion and verve at considerable length about her rhinoplasty specialist, Dr. Pankaj Viswanathan: his intelligence, his presence, his creativity, his technical skill, his "wisdom about the profession." It was all a bit much.

"You know what I think?" I said when she'd finished, my brows inching up in fun and voice calibrated toward teasing in case I was about to have seriously misjudged things. "I think Dr. Viswanathan was more to you than the dude who fixed your nose and inspired you to fix other noses."

There was a pause, not a long one, during which Roya—slouching in her chair, feet crossed on the edge of the table—looked at me evenly and thought, *Fuck it.* "OK," she said with a laugh, "so maybe he gave me a nose job during high school and a rim job during residency, when he was between wives."

Oh-kay is right. I tried not to react, because Roya delighted in these sorts of rhetorical stunts. "Was there a relationship in between?"

She said she'd sent him a handwritten letter thanking him for his work months after her final postop appointment, which took note of her newfound interest in plastic surgery. He supportively wrote her back via email, and in turn a pen pal intimacy developed over the course of a year as he detailed his upbringing in India, schooling in Britain, and finally training in America, while filling her in on the challenges of life in practice. She, in turn, opened up about her own experience growing up half-Persian and fatherless in Beverly Hills.

The correspondence ended when Roya, crushing hard on Dr. Viswanathan, escalated things by sending him two unsolicited photos of her mid-masturbation: a suggestive close-up shot of her face, eyes closed, lower lip bitten in orgasmic agony; the other an explicit nude, two fingers curled deep inside. "I'm sorry but you've gotten the wrong idea, and unfortunately our conversation now needs to end," Dr. Viswanathan wrote her, Roya recalled. "You are a lovely girl, but still a girl. I've already destroyed the images. Roya, you've put yourself in danger by sending those pictures, and me too."

It was a narrow escape for both of them. More than a decade passed without contact, most of it spent in her case back east for college and medical school, before she ended up returning to Los Angeles for residency at County/USC, where, during a cocktail party at the head of the plastic surgery department's home, they ran into each other again. "His first words to me," she said, caught in the bittersweet reverie of their star-crossed romance, "were, 'You're still lovely, even more so, and definitely no longer a girl.'"

"So you said you caught him between wives."

"Well, he was definitely already *on his way* to being between wives."

My brows rose again, this time inching in scandal. "And you helped nudge that along, I take it."

Roya's eyes narrowed but didn't appear irritated, only puzzled. "Are you here to judge me?"

Chastened, I added, "Of course not, I'm just clarifying." It turned out the affair, during which she was also cheating on a guy she was seeing ("I guess he would've considered us serious at that time"), had lasted eight months. She went on to bestow a disquisition regarding Dr. Viswanathan's already long-dead arranged first marriage and how she "essentially catalyzed" his ability to find new happiness. Saint. Roya the mistress, apparently. It was fascinating how she'd fashioned a self-serving narrative of utility out of her contribution to infidelity. I couldn't help it. I asked if those rim jobs were the key to helping the good doctor self-actualize.

She finally blushed. Not for the rim jobs—for the sanctimony. Still, she played it off. "Well," Roya joked, "they may have been. I guess we'll never know, with such a small sample size and all. Maybe they were placebos." She had me chuckling, yet I already knew that this Roya, both her actions and her attitude about those actions, would never be found in the book. This Roya was incompatible with the enterprise at hand.

We moved on. But it soon emerged, as we talked, that there would need to be a substantive distance between her truth and the published truth. This person—this *woman*—could only be so complicated and still hope to ever acquire more than a small quantity of the goodwill she was looking for. We were facing an uphill battle in making her likable for what was, simply put, an insurance scheme hatched to pay for beauty treatments. This tell-all was to be a public relations project and a redemption mission engineered via the carapace of a carefully deployed human-interest story.

Yet I didn't tell her for some time that a good portion of what she was telling me was useless. After all, Roya and I were still in the early stages of developing our rapport, and I wanted her to feel comfortable telling me anything. Plus, you never knew where these conversational trails might lead, in terms of actionable stuff. (And there are worse troubles than subjects providing juicy, problematic material, such as being unable to wring juicy material out of subjects at all.)

So when I asked about her relationship with her younger sister, Dahlia—crucially, it was pointed out to me at the outset: born attractive, not self-made—and one of Roya's first stories was creepy and arguably predatory, I just rolled with it, exuding detached nonjudgmental inquisitiveness. She explained that during high school she was a frequent denizen of internet chat rooms (mainly on AOL), where she'd talk to guys (mainly older). Roya posed as herself, a bright, curious, creative, and provocatively expressive geek . . . in her sister's hot body. A wet dream for dudes on the internet, like someone the two nerds would've created in *Weird Science.*

This early catfishing was easier to pull off in the late nineties, long before the triangulating advent of social networks and the proof of digital video. Group chats would lead to private messages. Guys would ask to see imagery. She had a routine, sharing suggestive low-resolution tableaux—a vibrator on her nightstand, panties bunched on her floor. Then there was a series of pictures she'd pilfered from Dahlia. These close-ups, which were meant for a boyfriend, showed her sister lying prone among her bedsheets: hair tousled, expression clearly aroused. There were a few other shots to mix things up, full-lengths. One in particular was taken at the pool of a friend's home. Dahlia was still dripping wet, sandal dangling from a raised foot, an impish smirk, areolas displayed at pert teenage attention through the semisheer bikini fabric against the unyielding Californian sun.

Roya relayed this with limited emotional affect. She didn't seem burdened by the memory she was uncoiling. I wondered how it felt at the time to appropriate her little sister's identity like that. She thought for a moment. Then Roya said, casually, "I didn't see it that way. It was more like borrowing clothes from her closet." Did she feel somehow maybe entitled to the imagery? Again, she paused, before allowing, "Maybe that's why I didn't ask." I declined to press the point that she perhaps didn't ask her under-eighteen sister for permission to send semiexplicit personal pictures to anonymous men on the internet—under the guise of being Roya's own, no less—because the answer would've been *No way, you psycho.*

Unsurprisingly, these men seriously perved on this jury-rigged combination of Roya's confident online personality and Dahlia's real-world physique. She was quick to sext by private message but never talked on the phone, much less met anyone in person. Roya revealed she blissed out after they'd ogle the shots and effuse. "More than one guy—several of them—wrote, and I quote, 'I want to fuck your face,'" she said to me, wistful, head shaking, still amazed. "It's just so *primal.*" Roya considered this, dropping an octave toward melancholy. "I'd never known it. To be achingly, stupidly coveted. I didn't know if I ever really would."

Even if factual, was this how Roya truly felt at the time? Or was she now refiguring a memory of her past into overripe fiction? I didn't press. Instead, I inquired as to whether Dahlia ever found out what had happened. She did.

"It was just a few years ago," Roya explained. "By that point we'd both lived much more life. She was cool about it, actually." I prodded a bit about how this had transpired. But Roya was done, turning her attention to her mother, Julie.

From the telling, Roya had been loved as a child. Her hardworking, widowed mother was all unfaltering sacrifice and endeavored understanding. The worm in the apple here too, though, was anchored in a matter of, as Roya would term it, "hotness." She went on at some length about her mother's classic WASP beauty before drawing me in—unprompted, I should add—to another psychosexual vortex of projected craving.

Roya told me that at a young age she came to understand how men leered at and flirted with her mother, despite Julie's mostly failed attempts to minimize the interest by dressing and primping in as demure and plain a manner as possible. Her mother ignored the looks and the comments, or else outright glared or even, occasionally, when things were really over the top, told these guys off. Julie—who was constantly complaining about casual sexism, and inculcating Roya and Dahlia to beware of it in their own lives and futures in a sermonizing way—trailed these encounters with her daughters by informing them of her irritation, disgust, or both. (Things grew only more combustible when Julie caught a ripening Dahlia on the receiving end of the same type of looks.)

"Invisible" Roya—that's what she kept calling her former self, "invisible"—told me she wasn't repelled but rather obsessively intrigued. Her imagination "ran wild" from pubescence onward. She couldn't stop thinking about her mother screwing and being screwed by these dudes. Roya concocted scenarios (let's just say they involved aggressive unwanted advances), ticking off the more memorable in bizarre and rather disturbing detail, which I'm electing to omit here. The fact that Julie never dated during Roya's childhood, didn't even talk of the prospect of it, hadn't turned her mother into a neutered entity in her mind but rather a tabula rasa of sexual intrigue.

There must have been an unexamined reason for why she was consumed with those thoughts then and even now was so compelled to share them with me, still an unfamiliar figure if no longer a stranger. It's a reason I'm unequipped to even begin to unpack. Regardless, Roya wasn't just unashamed of her fixation. She evinced a remarkable enthusiasm for it. Conceiving this erotic adventurism was gratifying to her.

I didn't ask her about these things then, not ready to plumb such depths so early. What I did inquire about, couldn't help but probe, was why she'd placed herself at such a remove from her own desire. These were her fantasies: Why not shape them as she wished, turn those male gazes toward her?

"It strikes me as a failure of imagination, of directed pleasure," I told her, gently.

She weighed this, responding with a firmer tone: "I suppose what should strike you is that even in my illusions I wasn't deluded enough to think my body could be the subject of longing." Roya kept hitting this same talking point. Perhaps my face showed it because she tried again. "You have to try to understand, to make the psychological leap here because you've clearly never processed this idea," she said, her eyes imploring mine. "It wasn't so much some wish to inhabit my mom's body, or even a rejection of my own, but a baseline conception of myself at the time that, physically, *I didn't even exist.*"

OK then. That was enough. It was time for snacks and smaller talk. I'd purchased sodas, chips, fruit yogurts, and unspeakable sandwiches at the vending machines in the visitors' lounge. "This is draining," she said, Cool Ranch Doritos between her fingers. It was for me, yet I got the sense she found it stimulating. Roya had been through therapy. This was different. She had a captive audience—yes, paid to be there, but inquisitive. It was a platform, an exorcism. No doubt about it: She was enjoying herself.

Less enjoyable for her, or at least less satisfying, was my pointillist questioning that followed. For a while I meandered—chronologically, topically, thematically—through various subjects in the interrogative mood. Ones I'd planned to go back to in future sessions in much further detail. It was discursive on purpose. I wanted to get a broad idea of which areas, aside from the obvious ones, would be easy to extract, information-wise, and which would be tough. Sometimes people have strong clear memories, or they effortlessly limn (or gild) the gaps.

As it turned out, except for the intricate varieties and vagaries of the pain that powered her, of which she was a loquacious expert, Roya didn't possess much of a robust recall. It was a misfortune coupled by a left-brained literalist's rigid conception of fact. If she couldn't recollect every detail, it was as though all were lost. I explained that the goal here was capturing even degraded history. There was no expectation of perfect access to her past. It would be my job to reconstruct it.

Yet at query after query she'd shrug, considering her life mislaid by time. "Even before I got to this place, where the routine is unending and blurring," Roya said at one point, frustrated, "I couldn't tell you what I did the previous week, let alone about some *specific incident* five or fifteen or twenty-five years ago!"

She also was quick to critique the sheer idea of reminiscence, its fallibility. Not only how memories are unconsciously biased when not purposeful lies, but that the process of remembering and retelling memories only further misshapes and distresses them, clouding what remains. "It's a dirty dataset," she said. Spoken like a scientist.

In lieu of telling her to get over herself, I parried that this wasn't the point of utilizing the ore of her memories. "They don't need to be precisely true," I said. "They need to be vividly true—emotionally true to you *now*."

Roya murmured her assent and was still thinking this over when I followed with a proposition that sounded as though it were a logical response to her fog but had been my plan all along. I suggested I interview those around her: friends, relatives, colleagues, employees, mentors, lovers, etc. A chorus of voices that—whether or not we ended up quoting them in her account (probably not, I thought at the time)—would provide helpful context and perspective.

"Like, *This Is Your Life*?" she said, brows jumping in skepticism.

"Like, this-is-reporting."

Roya pursed her gigantic lips. "It's my story, not theirs."

I explained that in order to best tell her tale, I needed to not be limited by her cognition of it. Consciously or unconsciously, by her own admission she was an unreliable narrator, and it was my duty to not just be a stenographer of her thoughts but challenge them, applying pressure by talking to other people as a neutral interpreter. That would be the only way to shape an effective chronicle. "Also," I said, "why else bring on a reporter to work with you on this project, if not to allow him to report?"

Roya gave in. Under the condition that she retain the final say over whom I would reach out to for the interviews, which she'd help facilitate. Roya also attempted to stipulate line-item veto power over areas of discussion in advance of these chats—a move I quashed, in the highest dudgeon of self-froth, as an unconscionable trampling of my integrity and autonomy. "You want absolute control," I told her, "that's understandable, but I'll walk. This process is about trust."

"Fine, fine," Roya said in an over-it tone, simultaneously dismissing my exasperation and finalizing the terms of the agreement while scooping the remnants out of her fruit yogurt cup. She pointed her loaded plastic spoon at me for effect, already on to something else. "All right, trust. I've been wide open with you. You told me when we first met that you'd tell me some secrets too. Your 'partial damage,' you called it. Let's hear it."

As always, here was Roya, coming in like a sledgehammer. It was both off-putting and weirdly endearing. As though people just divulge their innermost mysteries unprompted. "I told you 'Maybe I'll share my own,' *in time*. This whole thing isn't a game of you-show-me-yours-I'll-show-you-mine."

Roya had the spoon upside down in her mouth, considering this. There's no other way to describe what she was up to than that she was fellating that utensil, and she was doing it on purpose, plainly lasciviously, either to fuck with me or because she wanted to fuck me or both. Her zealous lewdness was remarkable. A turn-on while also being a turnoff. Comical and a red flag. At this rodeo, of course, I was the designated bull.

"How about you just answer a few more things for me, then?" she said.

Here we go again. "OK."

"Or maybe only one thing, for now." The spoon dropped into the yogurt cup. She leaned forward. "What do you think of me—physically?"

Roya knew my answer. "You're beautiful."

"Be more specific. And I'm not fishing for superlatives. *How* so?"

"Listen"—my cheeks and ears burning, her noticing and smiling because of it—"it's inappropriate to discuss this. You're putting me in an awkward position. This project requires a special dynamic, a unique intimacy . . ." She looked amused while I grappled. "Think of me like a brother. Or a priest confessor."

Now she outright laughed. "I'm Jewish, if I'm anything, Wes. And didn't I confide in you about what my shrink termed my 'interior erotics of the family,' as though she were going to present her findings at the next annual meeting of the American Psychological Association? Just think if I had an immediate relative to project my baggage on who's actually got a *dick*!"

At least she was self-aware. "That's not my point . . ."

"Well, *my* point, which I'll remind you that I've already made, is that you can't fully understand me—where I'm coming from, why I was so driven to help people as I did—without being candid and rigorous about desire."

"And this manifests itself, conveniently enough, in me paying you very explicit and revealing compliments about your own body—obviating professional boundaries in the process?"

"Aha. Why would they be 'revealing'? Maybe because they're a direct route to those 'vivid' truths, those 'emotional' truths you were going on about a little while ago."

This felt like it was about to go off the rails. But I was tired of debating, and besides, I had my "specific." I'd had it since I'd met her. "Your hair," I said. "The way you're wearing it, it externalizes your personality. It's bold, it's . . . sensual." It was as voluminous and uncontainable, obsidian and feral, as in our initial meeting. She was quiet, tugging a thick strand across her upper lip, a fleeting mustache, twisting it around a finger, then letting it go to coil back into that crazy nimbus.

"Good answer," she said. "Ever since I was put away, I wanted it unleashed." As I'd surmised. She uncrossed her legs, cupping a palm over her crotch. Her voice turned husky, lewd: "It's unleashed down here too."

Roya closed her notebook, signaling an end to our session. "I know you've wanted to fuck me since you first laid eyes on me," she said, her tone morphing toward appreciative and matter-of-fact. "It's even hotter for you given the circumstances: that I'm incarcerated and we're working on this professional project together." She tucked her pencil into the notebook as she rose. "Wes, let there be no doubt when you're driving back to LA in a few minutes, and I've got my fingers jammed deep up my cunt in my cell: I want to fuck you too." She grinned, this self-conceived babe behind bars in full command. "What I want is to fuck your face."

GIRL IN THE MIRROR

I was lucky enough to match at my first choice for residency, the USC Keck School of Medicine's plastic and reconstructive surgery department, back home in Los Angeles. The next month, April, I had returned to the city to scout apartments in advance of my move in July. I ended up in an apartment building in South Pasadena. It was a quiet and quaint neighborhood, a quick drive from the medical center. I'd previously only known it as a kid from those occasional weekend visits to the nearby Huntington Library a few minutes farther east in San Marino. I'd sometimes stopped in town at the Fair Oaks Pharmacy & Soda Fountain with my mom, who during my LA absence had left our place at the anxious edge of Beverly Hills, joining Fred at his Manhattan Beach ocean-view condo in mutual early-retirement glory.

What I remember from that weeklong spring apartment-hunting trip was the jacaranda trees in full bloom. Growing up in Southern California, I hadn't appreciated them. During walks to school on gray May and June gloomy days, I took them for granted, my head down, focused on the gelatinous mess of dark, wet petals littering the sidewalk, their sticky liquid coating the soles of my shoes, a nuisance. Yet the time away had altered my perspective. Now all I could see was the breathtaking canopies of purple-blue trumpet flowers, aware with a pang that they flowered more intensely during droughts, hoping to reproduce in the face of their potential demise. And no, this is not an unsubtle allusion to baby fever; I was not then, nor am I now, interested—on either an unconscious or a conscious level—in being a mother. (Although I certainly wouldn't mind being the fun aunt.) It was all just so vibrant, so beautiful, so biological. Those blossoming jacarandas, exquisite against the sky, literally in full flower, somehow reminded me just how far I'd come since I left town.

My few friends from high school who were still in LA were domesticated. I didn't have much time to reconnect with them anyway, given the obscene hours of residency. I began at Keck after national duty-hour restriction reform had been enacted, meaning our forebears saw my generation as having an easy ride. But we still worked up to twenty-four-hour shifts at the hospital, eighty hours a week. I thought I'd become intimately acquainted with the term *fatigue* in medical school. Then I entered residency. Cognitive impairment? Limited mobility? Symptomatic? Check, check, check.

My day-to-day during residency was monastic. I ran errands, went to the gym, hiked the San Gabriel foothills, made a habit of the Rose Bowl Flea Market. But I had tunnel vision about the Keck program, busy putting in the proverbial ten thousand hours to master my craft. Still, I'd only conceived of myself as focused, not blinkered, until I went on a dinner date—an infrequent luxury—during my second year. The guy, a friend of a friend, a civil litigation attorney at a big firm in downtown LA, asked me about my passions, my hobbies. I struggled to summon them. Somewhere along the line I'd forfeited the dynamism of a well-rounded existence in pursuit of this dream. Every thought went back to my residency.

One way to convey the fullness of this commitment, or obsession: Near the end of the Keck craniofacial fellowship that followed my residency, I finally reached the horizon of my physical transformation. I'd undergone several more procedures. Among them were corrections of my zygomatic arches to produce higher cheekbones, a genioplasty to augment my chin, and breast augmentation. (My left had been larger and a bit droopier than my right, plus I'd wanted my areolas to be reduced.) This work had, at long last, brought me in line with Dahlia's own natural looks. Yet even while I'd begun attracting, some might say enduring, the same concentrated male-gaze interest—and, frankly, female-gaze interest—that my sister and at one time my mom knew so well, I wasn't of the mind to enjoy it. The wink, the flirt, the compliment: They were registered with something akin to a researcher's curious detachment, not the engaged appetite and ache of a true player in life's game.

My evolving appearance over those years drew what I took to be polarized interest from others in my tiny clique of residents, fellows, and attendings. I can honestly say it never affected me. I knew these had all been successful procedures performed by topflight Beverly Hills physicians and knew these colleagues couldn't help but admire excellent work when they saw it.

Still, I incurred a degree of disapproval from some quarters, the abstemious reconstructionists who I could tell were embarrassed by what they interpreted as my fangirl enthusiasm for partaking in the obvious pleasures of the craft, unencumbered by some falsely conceived remove. It was considered gauche. They never said anything to me, but I could feel their eyebrows raised, the notion that I'd gotten high on our own supply. For whatever reason, the only socially acceptable plastic surgery for your average plastic surgeon—and by "your average plastic surgeon" I mean an aging male plastic surgeon—is blepharoplasty: eyelid procedures, particularly to create smoother anatomic shifts between the cheeks and the lower eyelids.

My vulgarity knew few limits, although I was deft enough to at least know to keep my deep, abiding love of *Extreme Makeover* and my favorite, *The Swan*, under wraps. I had no interest in dark, heady and/or satirical fictional engagements with the subject of plastic surgery, whether on TV (*Nip/Tuck*) or in film (*Brazil*), no matter their quality. I was a sentimentalist in search of unalloyed melodrama, and I found it on these reality shows of conversion.

I'd watched both during their original respective ABC and Fox runs in the early to mid-2000s, revisiting my favorite episodes online years later. They were talismans, admittedly hugely problematic ones on several levels. The most consequential: Many of these women appeared, even from the brief edited biographical clips in which they explained their situations, to be seriously insecure, troubled in a way that would lead psychologists to recommend taking a slow journey toward surgery rather than speeding along a ton of concurrent procedures to meet the separate and unforgiving needs of a show's production cycle. Also ludicrous, in that stretching-it TV way, was how the "before" interview segments featured these working-class women telling their beyond-grim sob stories under the hot lights without foundation, much less mascara, and in the frumpiest possible attire. The "after" looks were benefited as much by the programs' respective clothing stylists, hairstylists, and makeup artists as by the teams of physicians.

Yet despite all of this, I was hooked on these series. Particularly *The Swan*, with its ingenious double reveal. First the audience sees the woman, the ugly duckling turned swan in her borrowed gown and jewels. Then the camera pans in to capture her jittery fingers. She stands before heavy draped curtains, which pull away as the audience watches her observing herself in a mirror for the first time since she embarked on her metamorphosis. It's primal, perfect entertainment: truly cathartic art.

"Civilization began with the invention of the mirror," the head of my program once told me, paraphrasing Shimon Peres. The swans grin wide when they see what's been wrought. Sometimes they do a little dance. They lose it in teary exhilaration and self-rediscovery, palming their faces, caressing their bodies. "I look like a stranger," one says—thrilled, not confused, at least in that initial moment.

The host leans in, assuring, buoyant: "A *gorgeous* stranger, right?"

No matter how many times I watched, I'd cry. This was, of course, my story. These were the stories—of lives unbound, of new courses charted—that I so desperately wanted to help others tell.

I did confide in the brilliant head of my program, Dr. Sandra Collins, about my *Swan* fandom, because I knew she'd understand, at least on the fundamental level. World-renowned for her specialty, facial reconstruction—at once a creative innovator and a technical master—she was the best and most important mentor I've ever had. While a reconstructionist of the highest order, she was anything but abstemious, expansive in her conception of the field's purpose. Plus, just a really, really cool chick.

Lean Dr. Collins, fair of skin and strawberry blond of shoulder-length hair, Boston Brahmin of extraction and the zenith of distinction, has it both ways. In recent years she's made a fortune as the pioneer of the nonsurgical Collins Lift, which involves Botox, fillers, intense pulsed light, laser treatments, and specially designed barbed threads inserted into the subcutaneous tissue of the face via a long needle. Meanwhile, she's sainted for her regular grant-funded adventures rendering aid in developing countries.

She appears on television as a medical expert, weighing in on daytime talk shows as well as the evening news. She's quoted in newspaper and magazine articles. Hollywood producers seek her counsel on their scripts. Within the profession, she regularly publishes and traverses the conference circuit. All the while running the program, seeing high-profile patients in her part-time private practice and still balancing a personal life with her costume-designer wife, Wendy, and their two adopted young children. She was and is my professional lady crush.

She liked to quote Stendhal to her protégés, marking a credo: "Beauty is only a promise of happiness." Dr. Collins chose reconstruction during her own stint in medical school, when she helped treat two dozen children for severe burns after a school bus caught fire. "You don't draw a line between medical and aesthetical indications of suffering," she once said. "To be happy with yourself is not at all a superficial desire. The procedures we do aren't just for patients' bodies. They are for their souls."

Dr. Collins called the field "psychiatry with a knife" and intoned, "We perform a surgery of emotions." This isn't to say that she was all touchy-feely—she was stern about reminding us that this was a craft whose accomplishment could be measured in millimeters—but she had a sagacious perspective about our specialty that suited itself to education. "We're not doing *orthopedics* here," she once told us with an intersurgical snobbery that made us snicker. "You need to not just empathize with your patients but figure out how your patients perceive themselves. This work is solving people's deep, often abstract interior mysteries and expressing them externally, for everyone to see."

She actually talks like that. Dr. Collins doesn't blanch at the grand verbal gesture, in a one-on-one conversation or at the podium in a conference hall or in a cable news studio, stringing together sentences that call to be soundtracked with swelling orchestral music. Yet somehow it never comes across as self-important, only life-affirming. I've tried to take notes.

Dr. Collins's grant-funded program at Keck, an internationally recognized humanitarian effort to mend the physical injuries suffered by impoverished battered women and girls, grew out of her early involvement with Operation Smile. She knows founding couple Dr. Bill Magee and registered nurse wife Kathy, working alongside them everywhere from the Philippines and Vietnam to Madagascar and Haiti in the 1990s, personally handling hundreds of cleft palate and cleft lip corrections.

Like Operation Smile, Dr. Collins's project, Renew, partners with local government officials, NGOs (the Peace Corps, UNICEF, etc.) and medical professionals while soliciting funds for surgical equipment and supplies from manufacturers, foundations, and donors. It's primarily backed and facilitated through Keck, and it's considered both an honor and a rite of passage to be selected to join her on one of her regular trips.

I made three of them, to Bolivia, Nicaragua, and Ethiopia. I bring it up not to brag of the unspoiled do-gooding on my résumé. I do it to be transparent that, even then, I knew I wasn't an authentic do-gooder, the selfless kind.

I'll be honest. Like most people, sad stuff just brings me down. I'd rather not look, prefer not to dwell. While Operation Smile dealt in improving upon dastardly fate, those kids—mostly young children—

never knew a different life. They'd been born into their stigma. The arrow could only point up from their current circumstances.

Whereas Renew's patients had each been diminished from their previous lives, however tough those lives may already have been, by additional misfortune. These physical attacks were nearly always purposeful, whether premeditated or from flying off the handle. They were at times not just brutal but sadistic, most frequently taking the form of domestic violence. With vanishingly few exceptions these women and girls were abused at the hands of men: their husbands, fathers, brothers, cousins, uncles, boyfriends, neighbors, teachers, village elders, bosses, coworkers, soldiers, complete strangers.

Not just facing this pain but digging into its core to treat it, day after day, was ennobling, yes, but also debilitating, even crushing. I wept with my patients but far more often sobbed in private, finding the misery unbearable. There was always another case. Everything was appalling. It was a black hole of torment. Many of my colleagues were lights, finding grace or some sense of the sublime in being a bulwark against the unending darkness. I was simply sucked in.

One of those lights was Marcus (as with Kevin, not his real name), also at Keck in residency but in the anesthesiology program. He joined me on all three of those Renew trips. We hooked up early on during the first in Bolivia and ended up dating, turning serious over the course of the several years that followed.

Marcus had grown up in leafy Baldwin Hills, the so-called (by him, firstly) Black Beverly Hills, a bastion of advantage adjacent to LA's struggling African American inner-city communities. He was the never-conflicted son of an anesthesiologist, proud to follow his father into medicine. He was also gorgeous, straight-up strapping, with a strong jawline and liquid eyes, and he got teased by everybody we knew about it, especially because this was the pop-culture height of Shonda Rhimes's TV doctor melodramas.

"Dr. Taye Diggs," they'd call him, referring to Sam Bennett, the internist Diggs played on *Private Practice*, and some people would even make comments about how I bore maybe-sorta-kinda a passing resemblance to his then-wife Idina Menzel. While *I* certainly didn't mind those comparisons to a universally agreed-upon sex god or to a universally agreed-upon adorable celebrity couple (for the first time in my life, I'd become the communally observed, rather than the observer!), they made him uncomfortable, even upset, because Marcus was no loose Dr. Feelgood, no social animal. He was an introvert both by nature and for nurtured reasons I'm not going to share here.

But on those trips, he flowed out of himself. He heeded Dr. Collins's call that this work of ours constituted "victories over despair," connecting with patients at the clinic in gentle, casual, liquid-eyed conversation on just the right empathic level. They loved him. Then again, of course, he *did* look an awful lot like Taye Diggs.

Yet I found no transcendence, only constant and instinctive recoil at the in-your-face immediacy of by turns infuriating and nauseating injustice upon injustice. That this almost entirely rural patient population, beyond the afflictions we were treating, was immersed in a climate of strict misogyny, intense religion, and absurd superstition in heartbreakingly poor villages, without access to meaningful education or any real hope of economic advancement beyond employment as subsistence farmers and other menial labor (carrying water, chopping wood). That, for fuck's sake, many of them had waited months or even years in some cases to save up the *bus fare* to travel the four or six or eight or ten hours to be treated by us at our clinics in the nations' capitals or major provincial cities. My livid, bleeding, liberal, first-world heart hemorrhaged out. I returned home from these trips each time with a bout of depression that wouldn't lift for months.

I knew it was too much for me—the totality of the context—in Bolivia. I went again to Nicaragua and then Ethiopia because Marcus came away from our first trip inspired and even more committed. Besides, I didn't want to disappoint Dr. Collins. Marcus knew of my feelings but was quick to point out that, in real terms, my Renew-related distress got nobody anywhere, including myself. "There's good work to be done," he said one evening, that strong jawline fixed tight. "The neurosis—excuse me, the emotional pain—behind you getting it done doesn't matter. As long as it happens." He was right.

I'd like to say I carry the memories of the people I helped on those journeys with me, that they remain crystalline, that they forged my aspiration to practice the other, lesser, cockeyed altruism that followed. But the truth is that large swaths of those experiences are now lost to me, closed off by a thick rind of (political? privileged? idiotic? worthless?) fury about societies ultimately far beyond either my comprehension or my ability to change them. I could heal the wounds I found; I had no power to stop the wounding.

There's a Jewish concept that I've always loved: *tikkun olam*, the repair of the world. Dr. Collins's organization is a prime example. So it should've been enough for me to go where we went, to do what we did. Instead, it felt like our acts of humanity only put us—well, me, at least—ever closer to, or rather face-to-face with, life's starkest shittiness. I wasn't cut out to handle it. (Praise be the infectious disease field specialists whose whole discipline is enveloping themselves in such shittiness.)

Still, there are some memories that break through, or to be more precise that continue to haunt me. Like treating the lovely Zuleyka in Nicaragua. The circumstances of her care were so lurid and horrific that they are almost beyond belief. Just know that they weren't rare. A year before I met her, when she was fourteen, she'd been caught masturbating by her inebriated stepfather, who'd walked into her bedroom late at night as a pop ballad played on the stereo. After she'd completed her orgasm, he made himself known, pinned her down under the sheets with his knees, unzipped his fly, and ejaculated on her face while warning her not to say a word. Afterward, he remarked that she hadn't been smiling like she had while pleasuring herself. So he took a utility knife from his belt and, with a pair of decisive flicks in either direction, carved a jagged Heath-Ledger-as-the-Joker grin past the edges of her lips in arcs up across her cheeks. Then he bashed her nose in with the wide bony base of one hand.

We restored Zuleyka's nose and erased the coiling, raised scars that had marred her otherwise smooth cheeks. A psychiatrist on our team counseled her, although I couldn't imagine what meager good even a concentrated series of sessions over just a few weeks would do. I would've needed a lifetime of therapy.

The psychiatrist told me Zuleyka hadn't masturbated since the attack, and likely wouldn't again for a long time to come, at best. It shouldn't have been a surprise to me, but I was gutted. I remember responding by taking a short walk outside the hospital in Managua, along a cobblestone path, grabbing ahold of a low fence post, and dry heaving in the sticky midday heat.

We were removing external shame and social hardship. We were providing no internal agency or opportunity. Long-lashed Zuleyka, who despite possessing no classroom instruction past the second grade, responded to my presence (via a translator; she spoke the indigenous Miskito language) with what was clear to me was an extremely bright perception, would now—due to our handiwork—be suitable for imminent marriage to some guy in some village far enough away from her own that her "dishonorable" past wouldn't ruin her practical future. It would only plague her mind.

That night, over dinner of nacatamales, I told Dr. Collins of Zuleyka, of her tragedy in all its facets. She listened—listened in a way that told me she'd thought a great deal about such tragedies too, arriving at equanimity about them long ago—and then said, "You can't save the world. You can only put your dent in it."

Maybe so, yet it wasn't enough. I didn't know how, but I understood even then, inchoately, that I wanted—somehow, some way, eventually—to harness and wield bodily female beauty as a tool for female empowerment. And all such empowerment is, of course, political.

There is a direct line on this still-patriarchal planet between how a woman looks and what she gets out of life. Men, we are told, are visual creatures. It's genetic. And it's our battlefield. To subvert it, or shift it, I believe women require absolute control of the presentation of their physical selves. (Among, yes, many other things.)

It can't be ignored or wished away, regardless of the dismal truth of it. I would argue it's not so dismal; we are all naturally drawn to outward human splendor. This reality may not be where we'd like to be fighting for our equality, or where we necessarily should be, but it's where we are. Let beauty be a promise of happiness.

FIVE

"Roya-shomon," she called it, riffing on Kurosawa in a letter postmarked the day after I left our interview session, the one in which she bid me adieu by telling me she wanted to fuck my face. Roya provided me with what she titled the Delshad Dossier, a neatly penned list of names of the people who she claimed knew her best, or at least the ones with whom she was willing to let me speak, accompanied by phone numbers and email addresses when she had them on hand and, in the cases she didn't, blue-ink arrows pointing to those on the list who might possess them. This was the fruit of my request to report around what I presumed to be her unreliable narration.

Out of personal whim and professional habit, I also ran an unsanctioned background check on Roya to see if anything interesting popped up. There was nothing notable in the quick-turnaround data portfolio—no bizarre address listing or tantalizing concealed-weapon permit or curious financial lien. Still to be reviewed, though, was her litigation history, which would arrive on a delay. In my experience, that readout is often a map to El Dorado.

At the top of Roya's list were her mother, Julie, and sister, Dahlia. Soon I had arranged back-to-back meetings for the following Saturday. Julie lived with her second husband, Fred, in a Manhattan Beach condo featuring unobstructed views of the Pacific and the Pier. Not to mention the Channel Islands far beyond, although it wasn't clear enough to see them on the cloudy morning I visited.

Fred, a retired attorney—I soon learned that their place and a house up the coast in the hills of Santa Ynez were the spoils of a career spent as a partner at a Century City firm specializing in patent law—didn't hang around the condo once I arrived. He puttered only long enough as I settled in with Julie for us to size each other up before he went out to run some errands and hit the gym. The brittle-sweet Julie and genteel-sociable Fred struck me as the sort of easygoing, clubbable couple my parents and their friends would've welcomed into their circle back home.

"Julie spent yesterday getting ready for you, pulling out the scrapbooks," he said, blue eyed, silver haired, lantern jawed, broad shouldered. Fred, a decade or so older than her, had the commanding if vulnerable look of a fading matinee idol, casual in his workout clothes. He held my eyes square, his presence warm, strongly masculine, assuming a shared trust that had better not be broken: "Now don't let her cry." Before he slung his paddle tennis racket over his shoulder and headed out the door, kissing Julie goodbye, a peck on the cheek, he offered his own unsolicited rumination on his disgraced stepdaughter. "Women are complicated," he said. "Roya more than most."

Julie had laid out the scrapbooks on their coffee table, along with tea and cookies. The living room, open to the terrace, was filled with all-white furniture, a decorative choice that always made me feel like it was tempting the fate of spilled beverages, as well as what looked to my untrained eye like some quite expensive oil paintings, especially given the full framing-and-spotlight hoopla, and a pair of ancient worn-and-chipped marble sculpture heads on adjacent pedestals, one of a grim-faced bearded man and another of an ecstatic woman. There were also several flowering trees. "I don't like cut blooms," she told me without prompting, explaining the absence of flowers, as though I needed to know. "Why wouldn't you want flowers that are living rather than dying?"

Roya had told me her mother was beautiful. This was true. While

Roya had cultivated a lusty pinup's quality, Julie was a different kind of sexy: restrained, fit, classically elegant bone structure, a conventionally attractive white American face. She's the woman approached by a modeling scout who ends up booking catalog work with high-end department stores—the woman whose form other women idealize and aspire to inhabit.

Julie met me that day in a turtleneck sweater and fitted jeans. She wore an understated coating of makeup. The recessed lighting in the room was diffuse on a dimmer switch, acting as a soft-focus lens mixed with the foggy marine layer slowly rolling inland off the sea through the opened sliding glass doors. Yet despite those advantages, I could still see that the years had begun to diminish Julie, her skin papery, her hair thinner than in the family pictures arranged on the buffet in the entryway.

Our conversation started with the expected small talk: about who I was, and how I'd gotten involved in this project, and what this "listening tour" (my way of positioning this interview series) was all about anyway. We expended a nonnegligible amount of time discussing the care of Fred's several young grandkids, who have complicated sleeping, eating and excreting needs when they stay, as two of them recently did, overnight at the Nichols'. *Much* more complicated than she recalled of her own children. I registered this errant step-grandma irritation as the price of admission.

"Roya tells me I should be free to be very open with you," Julie said. "Apparently you've earned her trust."

"I hope so, and hopefully I can earn yours too."

"So, what can I tell you about my darling daughter?"

I told her that I was most interested in speaking with her about Roya's formative years. But first I was curious about how she was handling the idea of her darling daughter, formerly a dazzling doctor with a Beverly Hills practice, now being incarcerated, bereft of her medical license, and facing a future shackled to a criminal record. (Of course, I put this to her far more gently.)

"Xanax helps," she said, lightly laughing. "Seriously, though, once I moved past that this happened, and how it happened, and why it happened—it took a long time, and many talks with her and Fred and my therapist—I became OK with it. She's an adult. I raised a woman who makes decisions out in the world. Sometimes not the best ones."

Julie turned, for what would be the first of many occasions, toward the sea. "I was very concerned, once she was sentenced, that she could be in physical danger in prison," she said. "That's what worried me, as a mother, most. That, and just the psychological toll. You go in one person and come out another." Her breathing was steady, precise. "So I was relieved to learn that she's sort of a folk hero in there for what she did. Those other ladies apparently see her as the media christened her: this Robin Hood of plastic surgery, taking from the rich insurance companies and giving to her underprivileged sisters." A beat passed. "At least that's what Roya tells me when I visit." I told her that, for what it's worth, she had told me the same thing. Julie exhaled.

As for Roya's future, "she'll still be pursuing her calling, advocating for women, I'm confident of that. The question is how she's going to support herself while doing it. I've never had an ex-con in the family, but I understand it can be quite a challenge to successfully reenter the job market. She tells me she's thinking social activism, nonprofits." Julie gave me a knowing look laced with trepidation. "It's not my world. I can only be supportive."

I took this nod toward practicality and self-sufficiency as a way to transition all the way back to her single motherhood. I asked how she did it, taking care of her daughters on her own in the aftermath of her husband's suicide.

Again, Julie looked to the sea. "There's no how, there's just do," she said. "Moment to moment, hour to hour, day to day, one foot in front of the other. I went into mama-bear mode." Tears formed but did not overflow. "In its very hard way it was strangely easy because it was all so clarifying. I took to a blinkered mindset. I didn't even try to pursue my own joy for a long, long time. I just plowed a field, subsistence emotional living." A thought came to her and she chuckled, brightening through the gray. "'Subsistence emotional living,' that really did just come out of my mouth. That field: It was easy to plow because it's where I'm from. It's home."

We started talking about Roya's childhood. The scrapbooks were put to use, a curated assemblage of school papers and projects and pictures, interspersed with family photos and other Delshad effects. "My straight-A girl," Julie said proudly, fingering the yellowing academic mementos. "Dahlia struggled, generally C's. B's were her A's."

In the family photos, both formally posed and goofily candid, Julie and her first husband, Reza—Roya and Dahlia's mustachioed father, a big-boned dude much shorter than she—looked inescapably happy. He had a shit-eating grin in each shot, arm around her, oozing sexual appetite and satisfaction, the Jewish immigrant who'd snagged the shiksa goddess. His moppet girls, Dahlia still a baby, squirmed like puppies around him. Julie appeared relaxed, fulfilled, even blissed out. A young family life like that must have been full of its own microstresses and anxieties, but it didn't infiltrate the frames.

After his death there was a gap of several years. "I just didn't really take any pictures," she says. "I wasn't up to it. I wish I did now, for their sake." The trio resurfaced again in snapshots on adventures to the beach, Dodgers games, the manicurist, the mall, the park, a Chinese restaurant close to their condo beloved by the girls as much for the drama of its rotating center trays as for its dumplings. "They could never get enough of spinning that lazy Susan," Julie explained, caught in reverie.

Roya herself was frizzy haired and moonfaced, gawky like all kids are, her nose a bit prominent, but certainly no troll. Yet in each shot it couldn't be denied she was at a remove from her mother, who even when playing down her looks—apparently just about always—was stunning, and meanwhile Dahlia as a child possessed the vivid features of an animated Disney princess. The unfairness was constantly and immediately present. You could see how a girl would develop more than a garden-variety complex.

The reality was there in the most basic emotional exchange embedded in the photos, in Roya's expression. As the years passed, her smiles in those pictures—with a spatula making cake, in a reindeer-strewn Christmas sweater at Julie's parents' house—always seemed at best tentative, hollowed out. They were the smiles of a person, I came to realize as Julie flipped through the scrapbooks up past Roya's high school graduation (she was one of three valedictorians in her class), who didn't believe her smiling face was worth enjoying. She didn't believe, to be more exact, her face was worth smiling back at.

I floated the idea of Roya's youthful sadness to Julie. This begat a tender lecture on the tough, hidden, generalized trauma of girlhood—the "permanent condition, no matter what," she called it—that even the most well-meaning, right-thinking, fully evolved boys and men "such as yourself" just would never profoundly understand. It led at last to her own girls' traumas, and her own trauma in dealing with it. "Dahlia was your prototypical difficult child, spirited and rebellious and not great at school, boy crazy and chased by boys," she said. "I worried about her in those ways, but not that things wouldn't eventually work themselves out."

Roya was different. "She was always so smart and creative and perceptive and determined," Julie said. "She could also be stubborn and isolating, and her sense of humor—about herself, about the world around her—was not a salve. It was embittering." She went on, "When Roya got low, she didn't grow heated like Dahlia. She was distant, inward, impossible to reach."

I inquired about clinical depression, self-harm, even suicide attempts. Julie told me Roya had seen a therapist but was diagnosed merely with being a malaise-stricken teenage girl within the normal bounds of the circumstance. She never hurt herself or spoke of considering it. Still, "I worried about it all the time, and no number of tight hugs and urgent kisses from me, or eye rolls and frustrated denials from her, alleviated my concern." It wasn't until, at college, Roya met her first boyfriend, and Julie was subsequently introduced to both this North Carolinian fellow named Kurt ("so sweet; I could tell they adored each other") and, perhaps even more importantly, her clique of new friends, that Julie's "heart took a rest." Roya, she explained—scrapbook resting on Julie's crossed legs, open palm against chest, lost in thought—"never had a group" before. She let that hang there and then added: "It was that inwardness, that isolation."

Finally, Julie snapped out of it, gazing at me with more attention. "I see you're not married," she said. "Do you have kids?" I explained I did not. "If you ever do, you'll understand this: Whoever they turn out to be, you'll hope—above all else, even above their happiness, which can ultimately be a silly and shallow thing to wish for yourself or anyone else—that they aren't going to be lonely. At least not for too long. At least not in the end. I worried about that with Roya. At times I still do."

Our discussion wended its way along until we got to Roya's slow-burn physical transformation over the course of a decade and a half. Julie explained that grappling with it had, in turn, altered her. Initially she'd been steadfast against it, attempting to fight and reason with her despairing daughter. Yet in time she came around, Roya's corporeal chrysalis triggering an emotional one of her own.

"At first I couldn't understand it, couldn't even conceive of any legitimacy—I was blinded by my love for her," she said, her tears now running over, a tissue delicately dabbing. "But eventually it penetrated. To have a daughter who feels that her body has betrayed her, feels constrained by it, it's crushing." Julie took a moment and then continued. "One day I just realized that somehow Roya had—in her agony, on her own accord—clearly envisioned a better future, a specific one, *this* one that she was reaching for. And she was doing all of this, going *through* all of this, to grasp it! Why should I do anything but support her?"

Julie went on, making a (well-meaning, poorly considered) connection between her daughter's struggles in reconciling fleshly identity and the far, far more severe ones of those in the transgender community. I didn't bother to parry that this was an amalgam of foolish and offensive, but I did jot a mental note to find the right time to tell Roya about it so her mother didn't go around repeating it.

I gingerly brought up the topic of Roya's current appearance: what she thought of it, how she felt about it. "She looked beautiful before, she looks beautiful now," Julie insisted, a sentiment whose lack of illumination was compensated by its genuineness. "At least she still looks like her sister, even arguably—objectively—more so." I asked if Dahlia had ever expressed unease about Roya's evident copycat impulse. Julie pled the Fifth. "I hear you're meeting her later today," she said. "That's a question for Dahlia."

Julie then offered, unprompted, that Roya "never went through a goth phase where she cut off her hair or turned it blue or wore all black or anything like that." Her daughter didn't self-frump like she did either. "She never uglified herself," Julie said. "All she ever wanted was to look conventionally pretty, intensely so. Maybe it's unimaginative, maybe it's retrograde, but it's understandable. I get it now."

Her getting it now, she went on, didn't just have to do with comprehending her daughter's pain. It had to do with, for the first time, experiencing diminished attention herself—exacerbated, she pointed out, by living in Manhattan Beach, a locus of fitness and youth, even by LA standards. "Increasingly I find myself self-segregating in age ghettos, perhaps to retreat, so it's less in my face," she said. "Aquatics exercise classes at the gym, river cruises for vacations." Julie added, with a laugh, "Sometimes I see these girls in their bikinis around here and I regret not wearing them more often when I was still at a bikini-appropriate juncture in my life."

She was candid about feeling old in material terms—joking about menopause—and confessed to utilizing Botox and fillers as she attempted to "preserve" herself in an understated way, a respectable way: a rich woman's self-care way. "All of the upkeep injections and suctioning and nipping and hormones," she said. "Nearly every woman I know gets them, but few of them talk about it."

To better combat creeping wrinkles, Julie claimed to be reconsidering her long aversion to a facelift and explained that Roya referred her to a Beverly Hills colleague for Cellfina cellulite treatment before the legal mess began. “It’s strange, I beat myself up so much over this stuff, and I don’t know why,” she said. “Fred has no equivalent anxiety about using Propecia or, you know, Viagra. He just sees all of it through a utilitarian lens, very much like Roya—as tools.”

We talked some more about her career and Roya’s career, about the various waves of feminism she and then her daughters had surfed and sparred with. But the conversation came back to the mind and mindset of incandescent, troubled Roya, her “darling girl.” She told a story of a lazy weekend afternoon when her kids were still kids. Julie had fallen asleep on the living room sofa with a novel splayed out across her chest. When she awakened, she saw Roya, then twelve years old, gazing at her from two feet away.

“What are you doing?” she groggily asked of her daughter, a little creeped out.

Roya cocked her head, examining her mother’s features with clinical detachment. “Trying to see myself in you.” Sleep still veiled Julie’s consciousness. She didn’t fully function in the moment. “You’re very pretty, Mommy.”

“So are you, honey, and I without a doubt see myself in you.”

Her daughter forced a conciliatory smile. “I love you,” she said. “I’m sure I’ll see it eventually.”

Later that afternoon I was knocking on Dahlia’s door. She lived in a courtyard-facing unit of an atmospheric Spanish-Mediterranean apartment complex just inside the gerrymandered border of West Hollywood, in the shadow of the Pacific Design Center. Dahlia was, as promised, a Perfect 10. I’d been prepared for it—the curves and coloring mixed with her sister’s and mother’s piercing emerald eyes—both by Roya’s descriptions and by the up-to-date pictures on Julie’s entryway buffet. What nevertheless destabilized me was the force of her natural magnetism.

“So here at last is the Delshad whisperer,” she said, the tone of her voice (huskier than her sister’s, by either the virtue of genetics or the vice of carcinogens) striking a note somewhere between coquetry and camp, opening her door just enough to let me in while positioning a long leg to make sure her eager bichon frise wouldn't scurry out. She was dressed in an all-black ensemble of leggings, boots, and what read to me as a luxuriously expensive hoodie whose cowling appeared more ornamental than functional. Her contoured makeup and long dark hair, impossibly shiny and cascading in soft swirls (not coiled curls like Roya's), undermined the casual effect.

"My mom tells me you're a very nice boy."

"Well," I said, "I do well with moms."

She smirked. "Oh, *do* you?"

I blushed, absorbing the combination of her toying talk, her strong floral perfume, and the dog's paws frenetically seeking a way up my trousers. "Well, I mean, conversat—"

"It's OK, everyone has their thing!" Dahlia was already relishing teasing me. "I've been with plenty of age-inappropriate men in my day." A mischievous beat, a conspiratorially arched brow. "No judgment."

Full tilt from hello: what a piece of work. And here I thought Roya was a lot. My thoughts went back to Julie. How did she handle raising these two? Forget the practical aspect. Just the emotional impact. It must've been so wearying. That was a *ton* of explosive personality under one roof.

Dahlia's one-bedroom had been settled weeks earlier and was still only minimally furnished and partially unpacked, a sanctuary whose chief feature was a Jenga-like stacking of moving boxes. She explained to me, by way of context, in a manner seeking neither sympathy nor further discussion, that she'd broken up with a boyfriend and moved out of his condo in Brentwood on what I took to be rather short notice. It was unclear whether the decision was hers, his, or by mutual decree.

Dahlia acquired this apartment largely because it was walking distance from her job as a manager at a spinning studio, one favored by an entertainment-industry clientele, which according to her involved a lot of "drama," most having to do with instructors carrying on relationships with each other and their clients. I asked if she'd dated at work, and she said, wearily, that she'd "sworn off it," before segueing into a mini rant about how, postbreakup, she'd been ganged up on by "both my best friends *and* my mother, intervention-style" to reactivate dating apps and sites she'd previously renounced. "At this point, since I do want kids, and should probably get that going fairly pronto, I think I'm ready to agree to those gross millionaire-matchmaker services," she said, her eyes flicking down at her chest and beyond from a perch on her sofa as I sat across from her in her provisional living room.

I noted she'd said *agree to*, not *sign up for*. She'd long been scouted out, heavily recruited. "Right now, my goods are at their peak value." A pause, for either comic or tragic effect: "Who am I kidding? They've already started dropping." I didn't know her well enough yet to determine if her vocal inflection—resigned and amused in equal measure—was in fact a signal of fundamental misery or absurdity or both.

We talked for a little while longer before Dahlia announced that her dog needed a walk, she needed a coffee, and any substantive dialogue would need to occur in a space not quite so devoid of other voices. I understood. I've found that many interviewees feel much more comfortable sharing intimacies amid the anonymity of a crowd, lulled by the background din in a public place, rather than alone in the revealing privacy of their own home or office suite.

Dahlia flirted with me along the way to the coffee spot. I couldn't tell if her interest was sincere, but I hedged against it. I played it poker faced even though I found her attractive, excruciatingly so. My gut said she was sniffing me out for some moral or ethical deficiency to report back to her family.

Aside from the obvious allure—the wallop of the physical—Dahlia, like her sister, had a nutty charm, and unlike her sister, she was far less fraught, at least on the surface, with warping pain. Dahlia may not have been as book smart as Roya, but it was clear from just a short time talking to her that she had a similar inborn intellect, or conversational quickness. It was the kind of thing sparks can ignite on, at least for me.

Even as I was thinking about this, I caught myself. Dahlia and Roya had to know that anyone who was aware of both of them was making just such calculating assessments. I couldn't conceive of how the sisters' relationship (which, if like most siblings' relationships, was to some degree competitive) endured that external dynamism.

Dahlia was easy about allowing me to extract her backstory over our coffees at a nearby café, and in letting me keep the process expeditious—aware she was the bridesmaid of this tale, useful for context and contrast. She told me an archetypal, unremarkable Westside-of-LA story, fast-forwarded to begin in early adulthood. It was one of aimless ambition leveraging obvious physical and social assets to land a succession of pretty-person gigs (bartender, waitress, VIP-nightclub hostess, salesgirl, model, bit-part actress) while on what she termed, with retroactive self-mockery, a "nine-year academic plan." She made her way through first Santa Monica College and then, after transferring, Cal State Northridge in the Valley, where she completed an undergraduate degree in marketing. This voyage was buttressed by her mother, a North Star "always holding out hope I wouldn't permanently fuck things up," as well as a large circle of party-oriented female friends of varying merit who appealed by turns to her better and lesser angels. (I got a very cokie vibe off Dahlia—not the I'm-on-it-right-now vibe, but the I'm-always-down-for-a-bump one.) Also buttressing: a succession of men of dubious merit who caused her predictable grief.

Roya, I noted, was not part of this constellation. When I brought this up, Dahlia, as if waiting for the prompt, explained that her relationship with her sister consisted of four parts. She remembered her sister while they were growing up as being "sweet, smart, introverted, and withdrawn," observing that she both "felt bad for her and looked up to her," seeing Roya as "a tragic figure," although she "wouldn't have put it in those terms at the time. I think I might have said 'pitiful.'"

Second was the eight-year stretch when her sister was back east for college and medical school. They hardly saw each other except for Roya's brief visits home, or Skype calls. Check-in texting took place from time to time, often to triangulate the whereabouts and moods of their mother. But mostly they weren't in touch. "The distance and the duration was just a . . . drought," Dahlia said, between sips from her cappuccino. "We were busy, living our lives, you know?"

Then came Roya's return to California for residency and fellowship, which segued to her years of surgical practice in Beverly Hills. "It was totally different—*she* was totally different," Dahlia said, lips puckering, brows rising, as though I already knew what she was talking about, which I didn't. Dahlia proceeded to depict Roya as aggressively competitive, in both her professional and her personal lives.

By Dahlia's account, she invited her sister to start hanging out with her LA clique once Roya settled back in town because Roya didn't really know anybody who was the same age, single, and still going out—her few high school friends had since domesticated into social oblivion or moved away. Things were cool for a little while, a bit of a golden age since Dahlia was in a relationship. But it soon became apparent that Roya's assertiveness, in her new guise as a fellow hottie, manifested itself in noncopacetic behavior, variously defined, involving fellow girls' suitors—potential, current, ex—that transgressed delineated norms.

"Everyone was fair game," Dahlia said, exasperation calloused by time. "I'd talk to her about it, she wouldn't get it, I'd talk to her about it again. She had this mixture of naivete, like a foreign exchange student, mixed with just not giving a shit, or wanting to push boundaries, or wanting to make up for lost time."

I told Dahlia that Roya had intimated to me that her residency and fellowship were monk-like years of restriction. She made a face. "It was that, sure—in between slutting it up with one-night stands and booty calls and hookups with random dudes she found on the internet." There was contempt for the misrepresentation while at the same time zero disapproval for the actions. After all, as she was quick to clarify in the next breath: "Not that I cared. That was my life around that time too." She laughed—a big, throaty, unbidden laugh, followed by a moment of tickled self-reflection. "That's pretty much me *again* these past few weeks." Her emerald eyes sparkled at the impish thought.

Dahlia did finally have enough of Roya after a while, when she was single again and her sister started making passes at guys she felt she'd already claimed at parties or in clubs. "It was just so . . . *high school*," Dahlia said, eyes rolling at the reminiscence. "Or like one of those old movies—*Grease*, *American Graffiti*—with the hot rod racing. She'd pull up and need to rev her engine, just because she finally had one. It was lame. Since high school I'd spent years looking to hang out with girls *not* like that."

I asked if Dahlia ever revved back. "Sometimes," she offered, "if it was egregious." And in those cases, who won? Dahlia looked at me like I was a nitwit. "The natural, of course." I took a beat to puzzle over whether she meant natural as in physical or social or both, and it dawned on me that she had flirted with me purely because Roya had already done the same. In that moment she sang to herself while employing the slightest of shoulder shimmies, eyes closed in the diverted moment, channeling Tammi Terrell's Motown melody: "Ain't noth-ing like the real thang, bay-bee; ain't noth-ing like the *real* thang, oh no."

Wow: There was a deep well of bitchery to tap into. But I knew that this gossip, while edifying, wasn't going to get me anywhere productive book-wise, since it would never end up in it, and could even backfire, as Dahlia would just be agitated for the rest of our time together, her nongermane responses colored by needlessly surfaced spite. So instead, I inquired whether she'd ever worked out all of this with Roya, seeing as how it still came across to me like a fresh wound. "Oh, it's just fun to talk about," Dahlia said, waving me away with her smile. "We're all good now." She saw I was skeptical, so she went on: "What loving sister doesn't like to talk a little shit, though? Besides, you wouldn't believe anything else I told you if I didn't first give you some *goods*, right?" She had a point.

We briefly touched on the fourth part of her relationship with Roya, which was the most recent one, beginning with her sister's downfall and its run-up to the then-present in the slammer. She kept in less frequent contact than their mother did, making far fewer prison visits and phone calls. Yet I got the sense that their intimacy was more frank.

Dahlia appeared to possess a more granular understanding of Roya's true life behind bars, the reality of its grim doldrums and frustrations. "I thought she read a lot in medical school and residency," she said, stroking her dog, who had been on barking patrol against passerby before settling into her lap for a nap. "The monotony is what really gets her."

Aside from acknowledging the stress it put on their mother, Dahlia shrugged off Roya's professional implosion and subsequent incarceration. She was long past the shock of finding out her nerdy sister had turned radical bandit, engaging in a brazen and extensive if idealistic medical insurance fraud scheme, which Dahlia termed a "victimless crime." Cocking her head in contemplation, she ventured, "I never—not in a million years—would've thought she'd spend a night in jail before I did." Dahlia added, "Now, though, it seems somehow preordained." There was no further elaboration.

I was curious what Dahlia thought about Roya's incremental transformation, and in particular its unmistakable arc toward her. She contended the whole thing had a certain "frog-in-boiling-water quality" to it, due to its timeline. People didn't notice its totality unless they looked at old pictures, or a mutual acquaintance or relative who hadn't seen her in a long time pointed it out. As for the copycatting, she was sanguine: "It's clearly a compliment. I know she went through a lot to get what I had handed to me. What else could I possibly be but gracious about it?"

Fair enough. But how far did her magnanimity extend? I brought up, with a bit of dexterous half apology, Roya's confession to me that, when they were teens, she'd taken Dahlia's semiexplicit pictures and circulated them online as her own. Turned out Roya told her about it after her return to California. Dahlia explained she'd been "massively" upset yet forgiven her sister in short order. After all, while the closeness of the betrayal stung, by then it was just another one of the many times people had laid claim to her body "without my say-so. I'd learned to process it."

I thought that was fucked up, if ambiguous. Not to worry, she was just getting started, a portal opened without need of much prompting to the details of her damaged abyss. She told me she was glad she wasn't a teenager now because, Dahlia explained matter-of-factly, brooking no doubt, "there'd be even more of me on the internet"—in compromising positions against her will—than there already was, what with advances in camera phone technology and the prevalence of social media platforms.

She said she'd shared a topless selfie with her college boyfriend. He lost his phone at the campus gym. The picture ended up circulating first around CSUN, then beyond. Several years later, "not learning," she was talked into a sex tape with "another winner," who, once dumped, uploaded a scene to a revenge-porn site in which "I wore the tackiest eye shadow and giggled like a *numbskull* after he came on my face and part of it went up my nose." The jilted ex then sent the link from a made-up email address with her name on it to everyone she knew whose contact information he could find. It took two months and several cease-and-desist letters sent by a lawyer friend of Fred's (by then her stepfather) to get it taken down. "Every so often we have to send out another letter," she said, blasé about the perpetuity of her psychological terror. "It's downloaded to all of these creeps' computers, and it keeps popping up again."

Dahlia went on to describe a (disturbing to me, banal to her) history of sexual assaults and incidents of harassment throughout her life that had, at least so far, "luckily" fallen short of rape. Then again, as she coolly observed without outward bitterness: Unlike her, I "walked freely at night," beatific in my moment-by-moment male ignorance to the constant and immediate bodily threat of being a woman—pepper spray not at the ready, car keys not in hand, self-defense class never taken. All of it was relayed in much the way one might chronicle a lifetime of minor medical traumas. It sucked at the time, but that's how it goes; you carry on. Which, I suppose, was her brutal point.

While she noted there were plenty of episodes she'd just let go, that were memory blanks, she rattled off an extensive series of still-limpid indignities. There was the one at a high school house party when she was pinned against a wall by a drunk dude who pressed himself against her. ("I can still remember his razor burn and his Binaca-and-beer breath.") There was the one when she went to a new doctor about persistent soreness in her throat and he gave her a "gropey-as-fuck" chest exam while his female nurse was out of the room. And on it went, stories of forcible kissing, penile exposure, public masturbation, unsolicited dick pics, unnecessary hugs, grazings in close quarters against her breasts, "so many random hard-ons against my ass at clubs I always now dance with someone I know behind me." None of this included the lewd and even just bland catcalls, or the condescending "smile, beautiful!" admonitions, which were her daily white noise.

Dahlia asked me which such stories her mother had shared. I said the line of inquiry hadn't come up. She contended Julie wouldn't have been anywhere near as forthcoming as she'd been, but that her mother's experience had been similar, adjusting for the unique disgraces of her era, and in some cases worse. It was a tie that bound them. Their plight was the hidden side of being exceptionally beautiful, Julie told Dahlia when she was blossoming into her full gorgeousness and first understanding its distinct burdens. Her mother had educated her about what was to come: the uninvited acts, the inciting insults, the requirement to be constantly on guard. Most women dealt with this to some degree. But those "like us," Julie informed her one evening, arms wrapped around her, "carry the heaviest weight."

It went unsaid that Roya never received this lecture as a child, had no need for it. Yet Dahlia's sibling, remade as a glamazon, had nevertheless since joined the charmed, cursed sisterhood. She'd ached for its pleasures. She'd also since discovered its woes.

"Roya always complained about being invisible—I'm sure she went on and on about it to you—and I guess as a result she's resistant to complaining about being *visible*," Dahlia said, tilting her empty cappuccino cup at angles, considering the grit at the bottom. "She doesn't like to talk about this stuff. It causes her whole post-third-wave-feminis t-beauty-power-ecstasy-whatever thing to short-circuit. But the dirtiest, darkest secret of all—and if she's ever truly honest with you, she'll own up to it—is that she takes this perverse pride in finally being worthy of the mistreatment. It's a triumph."

WORK BITCH

The journey to become a professional doctor was interminable. Then—at long last, as I came to grips with the idea of my impending mid-thirties, updating my routine with, among other remedies, a pricey new eye cream to combat incipient crow's-feet—one day I'd reached my destination. My USC mentor Dr. Collins helped me land the junior-most spot at the seven-doctor private practice Bedford Cosmetic Associates in Beverly Hills, which around town was known as Dr. Norman Landler's group. His specialty since the late 1980s, utilizing pioneering techniques at the time, is perfectly enhanced yet natural-seeming breasts. You may not know his name, but you know his work since a long list of A-list celebrities have benefited from it. Sorry, no names spilled here; my nondisclosure agreement and sense of discretion are still intact.

I maintain a tremendous debt to Norm, an unwaveringly generous man in every way, who provided a finishing school for me in the art of being a plastic surgeon—it's much more than just a science—at the sprawling empire of an office he'd built over decades on Bedford Drive. This discipline, an elective medicine, is governed by an inimitable set of conditions, impulses, standards, and incentives that are both evident and not. Norm took the time to guide me through them, unlocking the hidden doors of how to become the kind of physician in an incredibly competitive field (not just plastic surgery but *Beverly Hills plastic surgery*) who might succeed. That my achievement was so short-lived is a failure entirely my own.

Norm, a transplant from Maryland, got a kick out of the fact that I grew up in the neighborhood. "The local kid made good," as he liked to put it. I have to say, there's odd kismet in how this Beverly Hills teenage misfit, who scrammed across the country the first chance she got and then stayed there for years, returned to seek adult fortune and establish a professional reputation in her hometown. Then again, her hometown happened to be the world capital of what she wanted to do. Likewise, there's a chicken-and-the-egg quality to the whole thing. That I had a life-changing rhinoplasty experience (it sounds like a joke, but how else to describe it?) in my native Beverly Hills—one of the few places where plastic surgery enjoys full, noncondescending societal respect—rather than in some community that looks more askance at the field likely was a nonnegligible factor in determining my future career path.

Norm's surgical skills are stellar, truly top notch. Don't take my word; ask any of his direct competitors in the Golden Triangle—he's super well-regarded. Yet that's not what made him, and more importantly kept him, the undisputed number one. boob guy in Los Angeles. It's his way of engaging people.

Discretionary procedures can be a sordid business since your patients are also your clients. If the tension that exists between those two overlapping identities isn't apparent to you as a physician, and doesn't make you even a little queasy, I've got a Hippocratic oath to reread to you. Anyway, what's best for those people is, on an inherent level, ethically debatable. Your (let's assume valid) professional opinion may advise a course of action. Yet decision-making is always at risk of being influenced by your financial bottom line. Even if you could somehow preclude, on the subconscious level, your practice's profit motive related to the treatment process, the financial bottom line still exists in the minds of those potentially being operated on.

The disposition of monetary sums *always* factors in. Let's call this what it is, regardless of whether it should be: a luxury service. And the outlays are significant, often burdensome, to many who are weighing these decisions. It's mostly the middle classes, not the rich, who keep our schedules full.

When Norm talks to patients, the problematic nature of all of this is baked in. Yet he finds a way to defuse it by being so candid, contextualizing the options, the pros and the cons, explaining his decision-making process in layman's terms, ensuring they fully understand the details by walking them through what, when, where, why, and how. His warmth—jokey but not too jokey, hands-on but not too hands-on, if you know what I mean—helps a lot too. No matter your reputation, and the inspiring before/after photos you can share to close the deal, ringing up a customer in this line of work is a leap of faith, since it's a creative, interpretive, intangible specialty whose outcomes are based on personal satisfaction rather than recurrence or some other, more concrete metric. "Fruitful sessions," Norm would remind me, alert to and properly repulsed by the specter of grift, "are about helping patients actualize their futures, arming them with facts and stripping them of delusions—while *not taking advantage.*"

Norm, through specific advice or just observed example, taught me everything I learned about how to run a practice. (And, again, I feel the need to underscore, nothing untoward about how to crater one.) All of the things they don't teach you in class, the awareness of small differences that manifest success—an awareness bordering on narcissism that to outsiders may read as snobbery or vanity or, most likely, imperceptibility. There's the practical: making wise staffing decisions, honing work-life balance, playing surgicenter investor politics with fellow physicians. There's the tonal: how to aesthetically connote status vis-à-vis such stealth weapons as employee uniforms and wallpaper selections.

More than all else, Norm modeled the joy of being a private-practice physician. I still smile when I think of him in his peak-nineties neckties and curtained gray hair and monogrammed white coat sweeping down the hallway, whistling Chicago's greatest hits ("25 or 6 to 4," "If

You Leave Me Now"), which I was unfamiliar with until he earwormed them into my heart—I told him if I ever get married, I may end up playing "You're the Inspiration" as my first dance song. While there's plenty of stresses (mainly, the rare patient disappointed with the result), frustrations (insurance claims), and irritations (paperwork!) in running a private practice, there's also the gratifying, productive hum and ballet of it all, when colleagues are working in concert to provide patients with what he called "the happy kind of surgery." I'd worried when departing USC that I might be a bit bored if I was no longer amid the bustle of the hospital. Yet I found office-and-surgicenter life to be the right rhythm for me.

I found Beverly Hills itself to be the right rhythm for me too. I'd left with teen angst, my nebulous sense of myself as an outsider magnified by its outsize, oppressive glamour. Now, save for a few capitalist-critique reservations, I'm onboard.

While it's a globally famous municipality, it's also Mayberry, and that sense of woven community was something I overlooked when I was spoiled by never knowing anywhere else. To be clear, it's a particular breed of Mayberry, one where hardening wads of gum on the mica-glittering sidewalks are removed at the break of dawn with steam cleaners, heaven forbid tourists catch sight of the lingering shame. Yet in its unquiet way it's sincere in its blatant wish to impress you with an ordered, manicured, palm-tree-lined, city-design-commission-mandated world. This is a town where the fire hydrants are spray-painted a *très chic* matte silver, reframing them into more visually appealing Duchampian Readymades.

Earning just north of $300,000 per year straight out, aggressively paying down my student loan and credit card debts, I took an apartment walking distance from the Bedford office, grabbing an espresso at the Brighton Coffee Shop on the way in each morning. It was fitting that I'd cross Rodeo Drive at Dayton Way to get there, always taking a moment to gaze at Robert Graham's self-explanatorily titled aluminum block sculpture *Torso* towering fourteen feet tall on its bronze base in the flowered street median. The flawless, powerful female form gleamed in sunshine and in shadow, forever-pert nipples saluting the hills to the north, fit posterior mooning the Beverly Wilshire hotel from *Pretty Woman* at the T intersection down the block. I was confident that Graham's ancient precursors, the ones whose works I'd come of age with at the Getty Villa, would approve of his piece. I approved of its placement too, an apt mannequin-beacon of the central business district's pair of world-renowned pillars: retail and surgery.

If not geographically, then circumstantially, my apartment was far from the inconspicuous Beverly Hills building I'd grown up in. My mom, who helped me decorate, remarked: "You're not living off Pico anymore." This one had a doorman and reception desk, "valet" cleaning and laundering services, plus one of those envy-inducing rooftop pools with a long row of upholstered lounge chairs and a soundtrack of moody, piped-in music that made you feel like you were forever staying at a hip boutique hotel. I'd made it. My pride before the fall.

Hindsight being what it is, it's funny how well things were going for a minute there. The career, the apartment, my relationships: not only with my mom and my sister, but also finally having the time to reconnect with old friends. I even had this steady, mature, well-rounded, at-the-right-pace, just plain *nice* thing going with a somewhat older (not *icky*-older) investment adviser whom I'd met at the gym. Aside from an acute newfound obsession with death and its harbinger, deterioration—as instigated by the periodic detection of stray gray hairs and defended against by a mixture of exfoliating agents, moisturizers, and serums—life was *good.*

I'll admit my mania about decay was likely spurred by the friendship I developed with the cosmetic dermatologist Dr. Penelope Greene. Penny was my colleague at Bedford, who'd joined the practice several years earlier. She's a vivacious brunette; the youngest of four Washington, D.C.–bred daughters (all others being attorneys); a fellow connoisseur of Britney Spears; a lover of all things shiny. We got on.

When we weren't, say, busy marveling at how one of our other young Bedford colleagues had so swiftly cornered the Beverly Hills ultraniche market on umbilicoplasty—belly button reshaping; part of the larger "mommy makeover" hustle—we liked to (annoyingly, in retrospect) riff over chopped salads at our desks on the utopian ideals of our respective trades and how we hoped to eventually promulgate them to the masses. The harebrained scheme I eventually ginned up would leave me broke, banished, shamed, and ruined. Her plan . . . well, there's a reason why I've since taken to calling her Money Penny, and while she responds by telling me to fuck off, it's with affection.

Penny's forte is the emergent arena between facial and facelift, specifically quick-turnaround procedures. She wields fillers—adroitly and minimally, since too many looks freaky—by injecting them right above the bone so that there are no bruises. For reference, when I was at Bedford, I employed direct cheekbone, chin, and jawline Radiesse filler injections to create definition as part of the practice's "facial sculpting" menu—it's the real-deal version of what makeup artists claim to do with contouring; when you think someone looks Photoshopped on TV, this is what's done. Penny also tightens skin and produces additional collagen with what we call "lunchtime lasers."

A lot of this stuff is cutting-edge: She's one of the few dermatologists in the country who're currently allowed to do a recently FDA-approved, minimally invasive yet technically delicate "string facelift," so called because the skin is raised with strands composed of glycolic and lactic acids that later dissolve. Penny's all about complicated work, having developed a following among stars for a regimen to contend with merciless high-definition TV screens, which makeup and lighting are no match for anymore. She calls it the Sequence: a very light microdermabrasion, trailed by a toning laser administering five thousand pulses of low-energy light, and then a flower acid peel and, finally, a layering of vitamin C serum. It costs several thousand dollars for her to do it for you each time. She's currently in the process of developing a branded DIY kit version with a multinational cosmetics firm that costs under one hundred dollars (!) and can be utilized half a dozen times over the course of a year. Plus, a nontrivial percentage of proceeds will go to a charity dedicated to advancing the cause of women in STEM research careers.

In short, Penny will be rich beyond imagination and likely hanging out with Oprah around the time I'm finally wrapping my probation's two-thousand-hour community service requirement. Now, kids, let this be a lesson: *That's* how you plot to make the world a marginally better place, by working not just *with* but *within* the system—instead of, inanely, as I did, against it.

Looking back, the first of my inane decisions was departing Bedford far too early. I'd intended to be there for many years, maybe indefinitely if I was made partner one day. I hadn't thought it all out. But a little over two years into practicing, my auntie Gina gave me a referral by recommending that one of her Beverly Hills Persian girlfriends bring in her seventeen-year-old daughter for a rhinoplasty consultation. Honestly, I wish I could've had the body and face of this adolescent when I was her age. (I would've settled for just one of the two!) But her nose was more of a honker than mine ever was. I was kind of shocked it hadn't been addressed already.

So I did my thing, and there was—surprise—a massive improvement. The girl was delighted with the result. The family thought I walked on water. They told everyone they knew. Referrals rolled in.

All told, a happy, archetypal story of familial connections and competent skill yielding business dividends. Except this one surgical success led to a drumbeat that didn't let up until I found myself warily hanging the shingle of my own solo practice a number of months later. My father's successful brothers, Nouriel and David, were among those who heard of my handiwork and later saw the results firsthand at, respectively, a bat mitzvah and a wedding. Based on evidence and buzz, they told me I needed to open my own "shop"—and they felt so strongly about this, they were volunteering to back me under terms far more favorable to me than any bank loan.

I demurred, explaining I didn't think I could yet muster enough patients on my own. "You've got the community—*your* community—behind you," David assured me, during a sit-down at Gina's place, a few doors away from Saba and Savta's old house in Trousdale Estates. I noted that there were, as it happened, several well-established Persian Jewish plastic surgeons in the area; I couldn't count on tribal loyalty. Nouriel shook his head, smiling, confident, ready to welcome the progeny of the excommunicated Reza back into the family business fold.

While I was flattered by what seemed to be interest straightforwardly derived from my professional ability and their perceived monetary benefit, rather than any detectable residual guilt over their tragic nieces, a leap into my own practice seemed premature, risky, even reckless. Why not wait a few more years, or even plenty more years, gaining skill and contacts and making more of a name for myself first?

Then again, why? I had an impeccable medical pedigree, had been top of my class and a star during residency and fellowship, and would be transitioning from one of the most prestigious cosmetic surgery groups in Beverly Hills. Would a *dude* in my situation ultimately limit himself with such reservations?

When I didn't immediately consent, they flipped my mom. Afterward, by phone, she explained that my uncles had made an "inarguable" point that was "worth keeping in mind" as I thought through my decision: "If your father was still alive, he'd have already underwritten you with the same offer. That's just what Delshads do once their kids have proved their worth in the world."

There was nothing else to argue. This was happening. I found myself soon signing for tenth-floor office space in a building on neighboring Roxbury Drive. Penny told me I had chutzpah, that she was proud of me for making a move so quickly. I was worried what Norm would say. He'd be justified in feeling affronted after such an abbreviated tenure; if the situation were reversed, I likely would've been. Yet he was bighearted about it, a profile in the act of being a mensch, sending me off with a lavish staff lunch and sweet toast at Mr. Chow, as well as offering me pointers on keeping subcontractors in line during the suite's build-out. I didn't tell him I had a pair of uncles with decades of experience in construction doing that for me.

During those last few weeks at Bedford, I was consumed with the specifics of winding down my responsibilities there while making frenzied plans to set up the new business. Yet amid all of that something awful happened, an aberration that continues to haunt me, a reminder of the stakes involved, not just financial but fundamental. It may be elective, it may be cosmetic, but what I perform is still surgery, and surgery is always serious.

One morning I'd finished with a consult, and returning to the reception area to drop off files, I found staffers and my next appointment looking out the open windows (typically sheathed by blinds, despite the tinted glass). Their mouths were agape, heads shaking, murmuring concern. I asked what was going on. One of the front desk girls nodded across the street, a few buildings farther over on Bedford Drive. At once I saw a woman, elevated a few floors above us on the roof: entirely naked, legs dangling over the precipice, blond hair. "Oh my God," I said. "How long has she been up there?"

Without looking away, one of the staffers explained that it'd been at least an hour and a half, but she'd only heard about it about ten minutes earlier from a technician who worked in the urologist's suite next door. We watched the woman, body glinting against the sun. She swung her legs forward and back, as though she were seated at the edge of a pool, playfully kicking water, rather than at least 150 feet in the air, atop a medical tower whose facade of dark-brown glass dated it to the eighties.

We weren't close enough to make out her face too well, except to note that it appeared slightly smudged, discolored. "Wonder what happened," said my next patient, a woman in her early forties whose nose I'd worked on the previous month. Her voice was frightened. I summoned a comforting nonresponse.

Then the second of the staffers, still glued to the view, mumbled, "She's probably jumping because she saw the bill."

Half an hour later, after having finished with the checkup, I returned to the waiting area and found an even larger crowd assembled, the Bedford staff and doctors now idle without patients to care for since access to our building had apparently been cordoned off at least a block away. The woman was standing on her tiptoes, turned directly toward us, her crotch shaved bare. She likely couldn't see us behind our tinted glass. From our perch, the street was partially visible, a mess of police cars, fire department vehicles, and at least one ambulance standing by farther away. Bystander pedestrians, looking up, loitered around a perimeter defined by caution tape. Above them, office workers in adjacent buildings were pressed against their windows too.

I was absorbing the woman, inscribing her body in my memory, its movement disconcertingly loose and unselfconscious, when, without special warning, she took two steps forward and tumbled to the street. If there was a thud, I didn't hear it. Some people in my office gasped. Someone said, "Holy shit!" Emergency personnel had set out one of those bounce mattresses on the sidewalk. Intentionally or accidentally, she'd missed it by several yards. At that height, with that velocity, I wonder if it would have made much of a difference.

We found out later that she'd been a fifty-four-year-old Silicon Valley tech executive and a patient of Dr. Shane Murray, reputed to be discreet regarding his high-profile client list and exacting in his daily practice. He'd performed a facelift on her the prior afternoon (he's known for charging some of the highest rates in town—up to $150,000), and she'd stayed in aftercare in an adjacent part of his office surgicenter overnight. We heard a monetary settlement of unknown quantity was subsequently reached.

Among the rest of us, there was a distinct there-but-for-the-grace-of-God feeling. It could've happened to anyone, we thought. Speculative theories circulated: that she'd taken her bandages off too soon, or that she didn't like what she saw, or that she'd had a bad reaction to her medication, or that she'd suffered an unrelated psychotic break. The LA County Coroner listed the cause of death as "postoperative delirium." The family released a statement attesting that her "fall appears to be linked to a postoperative neurobehavioral disturbance" in which the woman "we knew and loved for her calm, positive disposition never regained consciousness."

Like every plastic surgery patient, she no doubt had her reasons—complicated, subtle, and profound reasons—to undergo such a procedure in the first place, whatever they might have been. Only she was aware of the true shape and merit of the risk she took. I'm confident of this: Like every plastic surgery patient, she was brave.

SIX

I continued to make my way through the Delshad Dossier—haphazardly, with mixed results—over the next couple of months, between regular jailhouse chat sessions and the Roya-assigned cramming of pertinent books. Their titles uniformly conveyed their gist. Some of them I shirked. Most I skimmed.

Key examples included *Looks: Why They Matter More Than You Ever Imagined*, *Beauty Pays: Why Attractive People Are More Successful*, *The Beauty Bias: The Injustice of Appearance in Life and Law*, *The Beauty Myth: How Images of Beauty Are Used Against Women*, *In Your Face: The New Science of Human Attraction*, and the one by Nancy Etcoff she was referring to in our initial meeting, *Survival of the Prettiest: The Science of Beauty*. She'd acquainted herself with a certain portion of this material before her arrest. But she ingested the rest of it in her newfound free time. Roya had ex post facto burnished her in-the-moment problematic judgment with rationalizing bona fides, laying the intellectual groundwork for future social-advocacy efforts to boot. I largely disregarded the reading list because, for one thing, I thought it was propagandistic. For another, as I explained to Roya, she could synthesize and filter to me the parts she felt relevant to her thinking.

I had a pair of tugging questions that'd arisen early in my time with Roya, which I hoped this reporting process might resolve. One of them was why her abiding obsession with physical attraction—a subject nuanced to the point of murk—was, in her words and deeds, ultimately so stunted in conventional notions of external beauty. I confess that I never got beyond the easiest answer, either with her or with those who knew her: that the values of her native Beverly Hills shaped her.

The other, which I truffle hunted here and there even though I wasn't sure what if anything I'd do if I found what I was looking for, was whether Roya's relationship with her mother was as unwavering in its supportiveness as it had been portrayed to me by each of them. Julie seemed too understanding, too note-perfect. My bullshit detector pinged. Every woman I'd ever known well had shared more with me about friction in their own relationships with their mothers, at present or in the past or both—and almost all of those women were less fraught figures than Roya. It struck me, the gumshoe journalist and failed screenwriter, as somehow both grail and MacGuffin, a hidden riddle nobody wanted me to solve. Which may be why it hovered.

Roya had urged me to reach out to her oldest, closest Beverly Hills childhood friend, Tina Choi. They'd met in elementary school when she was still Tina Chang. Now living in ritzy Hancock Park, she took care of her three young children, with the substantial assistance of a nanny, while doing intermittent from-home work managing parts of her family's sprawling real estate investment portfolio, which her father and husband co-ran. Tina's dad, I'd been informed, had doubled down on now-humming Koreatown after the 1992 post–Rodney King civil unrest decimated much of the neighborhood.

Roya told me that Tina had a heavy accent when they were growing up, so heavy she barely spoke to anyone but her intimates. When I met her in the middle of the day in the middle of the week at her neo-Georgian-style house—she was kitted out in designer athleisure wear, her hair in a bun, the casual epitome of a certain class of LA mom—only the faintest trace of that accent remained.

Tina was not just untroubled but glad to talk about Roya, with whom she seemed to be perpetually tickled. "Sometimes you seek your opposite in a partner," she said atop a stool at the island in her airy kitchen. "She was that in a friend. I was shy, anxious, follow-the-rules, definitely *not* a risk-taker. She was brash. She'd make me laugh. She'd buck me up. She'd eventually go on crazy adventures to help poor people in foreign countries, and now she's ended up in prison for helping poor people here."

I asked her about sad Roya, shut-in Roya, pitiable Roya: all the Royas that Roya and her mother and sister had made me think were essentially who she was as a kid. Tina shrugged: "We are all sad, pitiable shut-ins at times. Maybe I didn't see that side of her as much, or don't remember it as much. With me she sparkled. But that's how best friends can be."

For her part, and fascinating to me, Tina didn't see much noteworthy difference at all between the Roya she knew as a child and the Roya she'd visited a few months earlier in prison. Circumstances may have changed. Yet "she's still the same person: ambitious, committed, never satisfied, on healthy terms with the absurd."

Pressed for more about this relationship with the absurd, Tina brought up a formative Roya crush named Raj Khurana. "Oh my God, she was so *obsessed*," Tina giggled at the memory. "And a large part of the attraction, aside from the fact that he was charming for an eighth-grade boy, was that he had clear skin—no zits. This was really important to her. Anyway, she never lands the guy, he ends up going to some other high school, and the next year she's, like, *overtaken* by acne." This sounded to me like grim teenage karma, but the absurd? "Roya doesn't go in for fate," Tina informed me, no longer giggling. She'd been there, nursing her pal through the dark time of Accutane. "She goes in for meaninglessness."

Later I looked up Raj, out of curiosity. He's a big deal, who after a career working his way up at places like Powerade and Coca-Cola is now running his own marketing firm that aligns major consumer brands with top entertainment- and sports-world celebrity endorsers in exchange for equity. In one advertising trade journal, the Manhattan-based Raj—who pops up fit, confident, and broad chested in many an online Hamptons party-circuit photo—described a new low-fat, low-calorie, GMO-free potato chip line he'd recently started working with as a "truly disruptive force."

Roya had provided me with the contact information of her closest friend from Penn, Alice McKenzie, now a financial analyst back home in Dallas. Alice had been in letter-writing contact with Roya while she was behind bars. Informed I'd regularly been visiting her in prison, she probed me hard for further details about "how things are *really* going." I ended up providing her with far more valuable intel than she did me.

As for those coed years, she had thin reflections ("Roya excelled at drunk Britney Spears karaoke—she really got into 'Crazy'—and, umm, flip cup"), soon throwing a lateral to Roya's college boyfriend, by the name of Kurt Myles, the same guy Roya's mother had mentioned to me earlier. Alice deduced, through some Facebook clicks while on the phone with me, that he was living in Charlotte, North Carolina. "They were in one of those couple cocoons the whole time at Penn," she explained. "You've got to talk to him."

Unfortunately, Kurt, an English teacher at a private high school, didn't want to talk to me. Roya assumed all would be copacetic since they'd remained in sporadic, platonic phone, email, and Facebook contact over the years ("none whatsoever in person"), with Kurt offering continued support in a few cherished handwritten letters since the arrest. But it turns out his wife, long simmering in disapproval about the rapport, had had enough. "She thinks I'm going to willy-nilly snatch her husband away one day," Roya told me with irritation when I mentioned the impasse. So did the wife, whom she described as "unreasonably jealous," have even an iota of legitimate concern? "Not at all. I mean, I *could*, but I'd never."

Kurt either ducked a litany of questions I'd sent him (once I'd given up on any verbal communication) or offered boilerplate gracious, useless ex-boyfriend patter about what a wonderful "lady" Roya was and continues to be. Except for one point, which was that she was innocent. Not of her crimes. Just, generally, *an innocent*. "You might disagree with her," he wrote me. "I certainly did and do. Still, you have to give her this: Whatever it is she's saying or thinking or feeling at any given time, she trusts it. It's a confidence that may lead her astray. But she has that going for her, even if she can be its victim. She believes in herself."

From what I could tell, Roya's boyfriend during her residency years at USC, Terrance Franklin, never met or compared notes with Kurt. Yet he'd come to a similar conclusion about her core sincerity. While understandably wary, Terrance—now an anesthesiologist working at a hospital in South LA—consented to a brief phone interview. He was most comfortable speaking about their work with Renew, a nonprofit providing plastic surgery procedures performed by American doctors to, mostly, female victims of physical abuse in developing countries. She hadn't yet talked to me much about these trips, so he filled me in, contending they were crucial to her social-justice formation. "She fronts like she's the poor girl from the rich town," he said. "And while that may *technically* be true, on *narrow* terms, she's still one of the luckiest people on Earth. Roya realized this in those places—it really came through—and I think her conscience sort of bled out, as an occupational hazard, when she tried to go back to what she thought was 'real life,' doing plastic surgery in her rich town."

Terrance's counterpoint was Roya's USC residency classmate turned roommate Drew Lennox. The ear, nose, and throat specialist Skyped me, shirtless and ripped, from the terrace of his condo in an enviable Miami high-rise. The waters of South Beach were visible behind his bleached-blond, close-cropped head. Even more so than Dahlia, he made the most of the unhindered freedom to speak that Roya had granted him. ("Girl wants the truth on blast," he said, literally rubbing his hands in joy, "then girl can have the truth on blast.") Drew was someone who already liked "to fucking dish," as he put it, and absolution in advance was near-heavenly.

Roya had positioned the duo's relationship to me as that of cloistral study buddies (when not at the hospital on their respective arduous rotations), cramming for long hours at the library or on the couch or at their dining room table among piles of textbooks and other paperwork. Drew confirmed this, explaining that "we were nesting in mutual misery." Yet he also corroborated and furthered Dahlia's characterization of the period, aside from an extended stretch with Terrance, as peppered with nights of Dionysian release, in which they'd go clubbing, mostly to gay ones ("the fag hag in full effect"), and on their two-in-the-morning drives back to South Pasadena from West Hollywood, "she'd be texting booty calls." Drew laughed. "It was always this challenge—not unspoken; we joked about the competition—because then I'd need to fuck someone too, if only to drown her out." He was doubled over, his whitened teeth gleaming. "She was just so *loud*."

Drew recovered and turned contemplative. "I would tease her, telling her that she screwed dudes like an eighteen-year-old guy fresh off the turnip truck and out in the big city—in other words, like me when I first left Ohio for college in Chicago," he said. "But I stopped when it hit me that her 'transformation,' as she called it, was her own liberation. She'd escaped her reality. She'd Houdini'd it. I respected that, and I still do."

Roya and I would later discuss including a more candid depiction of this era in the book. She appreciated Drew's assessment and was keen to flex her feminist credentials, clarifying she wasn't at all embarrassed about her "number." For the record, I never asked for her to share it.

Nevertheless, she agreed that this wasn't what we were selling. While accurate and even revealing, the stark facts of her posttransformation sex life, the catalytic roots of its phosphorescent bloom, would serve only as a distraction impeding her purpose. Her narrative needed to be kept PG-13 for maximum possible impact. "Another memoir, another time," she kidded.

There was, I took it, some cloaked politicking among the elder rungs of the extended Delshad clan about who would, and should, speak with me. Roya was squeamish about including any of "that generation," as she called them, on her initial dossier, despite my request. (One favorite cousin around her age, by contrast, was listed.) I eventually got her to capitulate—arguing that neither she nor her mother had proved able to flesh out her father's coming-to-Tehrangeles journey as well as one of his siblings likely could—and I contacted the eldest brother, Nouriel. Roya well knew there were mixed Delshad-wide feelings about her since her rich uncles, Nouriel and David, so proud of their niece the doctor, had lost the money they'd invested in underwriting her practice when she professionally imploded. Finally, I received word: Her aunt Gina, baby sister of her father, would receive me at her home.

"So fucking *old-school*, I love it!" Roya said when I passed along the news. "Auntie was the one sent as an envoy to at the very least give my mom the once-over because my saba and savta were utterly opposed to the idea of my father ending up with 'some random white chick.' I'm just surprised this isn't going down at the Peninsula Hotel too. At least there'll be tea—for sure, there'll be tea. History rhymes!"

Gina Boloorian welcomed me into her home in Trousdale Estates four miles due north of Rodeo Drive and two blocks away from Roya's grandparents' former address. She was completing a renovation on her property, attempting to restore "the original luster" to the gaudily over-the-top, pretty much universally derided architectural style known as the Persian palace, which the previous occupants had let languish. Initially the house, like that of Roya's grandparents and for that matter every other one in the neighborhood, was in fact a mid-century modern marvel. The tract's current vogue derives from *their* refurbishment.

I'd no sooner let slip to Roya at our next prison visit a smidgen of disdain about this, figuring I was in safe company, than she nearly bit my head off with a vehement defense of Persian palaces as "heartfelt" masterpieces of pure artificiality—genuine fakes—that had "just as much validity" as the oh-so-tasteful mid-century piles with which they intermingled. "It's beauty that isn't afraid to flaunt itself," she said, a decided edge to her voice, "and there should be *nothing wrong* with that."

In her early fifties, Gina came across as composed, with a formality just shy of starchy, and pretty in a put-together if discordant way, her makeup contemporary while her hairdo and clothing were arrested in a Persian ideal of Beverly Hills power doyenne three decades removed. Seated in her living room, which looked out on a pool being skimmed for leaves at late morning by a maintenance man, she, like Julie, offered tea and sweets for our chat, although her own presentation was far more elaborate and elevated (fine china and a porcelain pot were involved), served not on her own but by a uniformed Latina housekeeper.

She'd read my work, beyond those standard first pages of Google hits, and quizzed me about articles in a polite if bloodless manner that suggested less an actual interest in them than an interest in letting me know she had done her homework about them—and, by inference, me. Gina was helpful and even amiable about certain things, particularly when I sought her help in building out a portrait of Roya's father. "Reza was by far the most American of any of us, from the moment we flew here," she said. "He was enamored of the popular culture. His big personality just *meshed* with America's big personality."

She was more guarded if still insightful on other subjects. Reza's suicide and now Roya's very public disrepute had greatly impacted the Delshads. They were central defining facts of their collective narratives, held tight near the surface. Gina was candid about this, if somewhat elliptically so. "My mother has had dementia for a number of years now, so she only saw Roya rising, not the plunge," she said. "When it happened, I told my kids, who had all remained close to her and Dahlia—they grew up doing Shabbat dinners together—what my mother told my siblings and me after Reza died: 'Fortune and misfortune are intertwined.' We Delshads have had both. That's life."

Still, my overall takeaway was one of deft suppression. These were prudent offerings of understanding, replete with dollops of emotional honesty, in lieu of getting real. Whenever I'd try to probe the dynamics at play, digging deeper, let's say by introducing the lasting electrical current that is Julie ("How did the family's relationship with her evolve after Reza died?"), she'd reframe the discussion on preferred, impenetrable terms. Gina elided the core of my questions in the process, even while seeming to make a good-faith attempt at answering them. ("Taking care of two young girls in such circumstances, as a young widow, it's heroic, superhuman. We didn't know how she did it. We just offered our unconditional love and our support.")

I admired her dexterity even while I was frustrated by her approach. It was akin to that of the crisis communications advisers I dealt with as a journalist. The ones who'd mastered the shrewd craft of positioning a message at just the right invisible angle of sincerity and spin so it registered at a frequency at which, unless you really had your antenna up and optimally functioning, you couldn't even tell you were being played.

As she went on in this manner, I decided that her soft evasions weren't worth further inquisitive pressure. I have learned there are times when you engage and times when you knowingly act the fool, for a greater good, which in this case happened to be family détente. I'd soon be done with this book; Roya, Julie, and Dahlia would still be intimately linked to the Delshads.

Still, again, my time with Gina wasn't all highly polished bullshit. There were moments of what felt to me like unwary openness interspersed with the rhetorical gamesmanship that made this trip to Trousdale Estates more than worth it. One that especially stuck with me came at the midway point of our conversation, as she reflected on her own persistent astonishment at the sheer sweep of her niece's journey. "The poet Rumi has this line, 'Unfold your own myth,'" Gina said. "I've never known anyone who has embodied that more than Roya."

I next connected with Roya's favorite relative, a second cousin whose grandmother was the sister of her late grandfather. His name was Daniel. The same age as Roya, he worked for the family firm, serving as a lieutenant to Nouriel and David on commercial real estate deals. At his suggestion, we met in a popular Persian ice cream shop on Westwood Boulevard called Saffron & Rose, where he did the ordering in exuberant fashion. He insisted we share the namesake flavors, plus scoops of cucumber, pomegranate, orange blossom, persimmon, jasmine, and medjool date. Then, while we waited for this bounty to arrive at our tiny table, he advised me on the "chewy mouthfeel" of his ancestral country's uniquely thick ice cream, how it derived from employing ground orchid root.

Tall, mustachioed Daniel Gohari, wide of smile, was exuberant in general. He possessed a blithe humor, as well as a padding around his big-boned frame that avowed a devotion to Saffron & Rose more meaningfully than any series of punches in his customer-loyalty rewards card. I found him delightful and winning, understanding at once why Roya had long connected with him so well. "My mom always liked him too," she told me before our ice cream shop meeting. "I think he reminds her of my father: funny, easygoing, energetic, proud to be Persian, but uninterested in being hemmed in by it."

Daniel, his golden Star of David necklace barely visible in a partially unbuttoned dress shirt amid a dense profusion of chest hair, had a firstborn son's assurance in discussing dynastic affairs. Whether due to his generation or gender or otherwise, he was far less concerned with betraying the Delshad name than Gina, freely musing on the internal clannish undercurrents and outward status snobberies accrued in the decades since fleeing hard-line Islamic theocracy for their safe harbor of America. One digression: "Our pastime was sitting on the terrace of Porta Via on Canon Drive," he said, "talking mad shit in Farsi about all those flashy fucking Saudi tourist-kid royals driving by, revving their joke neon Maseratis and Lamborghinis and Ferraris like imbeciles during their Beverly Hills Ramadan Rumspringas. It's like the circus coming to town."

I later asked Roya if she'd participated. She said she did. "As wealthy as my cousins were, they were anchored to reality," Roya explained defensively. "They weren't diplomatic immunity loaded. These were *teenage sheikhs and their courtiers* who'd have *raped* Dahlia *if given half a chance*!"

Daniel said that he didn't remember Reza since he had died when Daniel was very young, but he attested to the aura of heartbreak that trailed him. He confided that as a boy he'd had alternating crushes on Julie ("I mean, come on") and Dahlia. "I don't know how many times I'd insist to my friends she's 'just my second cousin,' not my first, as though that made it substantially more OK," he said. Roya, meanwhile, he'd "clicked with—we were sort of best friends. She's just cool, you know? What's the word? *Droll.* And really smart, a thinker, a hustler, an original. I knew she'd go places from the time we were little. Actually, I always kind of thought she'd end up joining the business."

I asked for his take on Roya's self-confidence. He sighed. "It wasn't good, but I don't know if you're going to get anything particularly astute out of me," he said. "Look, we also bonded because I was a fat kid with, obviously, my own issues—my very fit parents were constantly on my case to, I think, be more, I don't know, *on-brand*. I've lost my baby weight now." Daniel laughed, self-aware. "I could stand to lose a little more, starting by not meeting people in an ice cream shop!" His tiny plastic spoon nevertheless continued to plow through the persimmon scoop. "Growing up is shitty. She made it out OK, all things considered. Psychic scars, definitely." He laughed again. "Physical scars, you know, by her own doing, clearly. But she made it out." A moment later, he said: "Did she tell you her first real boyfriend, this Southern dude she met in college, was a former fatty? I've always given her such a hard time about that. I tell her there must've been a, like, Freudian desire to be with me." (Her response, when I passed this along: "Yeah, tell Danny I'm down to fuck *former* fatties!")

Speaking of problematic longings, I reached out to Dr. Pankaj

Viswanathan, the Beverly Hills rhinoplasty specialist who performed Roya's paradigm-shifting teenage nose job, then embarked on a torrid sexual affair with her years later. He was semiretired now. Even though I positioned a potential conversation as all good things—that she credited him with forging her interest in the field, and I was innocently inquiring about his formational influence—he was a difficult fish to get on the hook. When I did, via email, all he offered, after extracting a promise not to share his take with Roya (I kept my word), was a three-sentence poisoned dart of a mash note.

"She's incredibly bright, skilled, and caring," Dr. Viswanathan wrote. "Her flaw is boundary crossing, which is to say a lack of professionalism. For Roya, ethics appear to be situational, revisable on her convenient terms."

My exchange with Dr. Sandra Collins, Roya's mentor and USC residency program head, was as long as Dr. Viswanathan's was short. I wanted to learn more about Renew, the international program Roya and Terrance had been involved in, which she'd founded and still ran. But in a discursive, unhurried, end-of-the-business-day conversation with Dr. Collins at her private practice office suite in a sleek Century City high-rise overlooking the old Fox studio lot, we hardly talked about Renew's work—or for that matter, really, Roya—at all. Rather, she was eager to share, at length, thoughts she'd "kept returning to" ever since Roya's situation came to a head. These thoughts concerned a longtime friend, Dr. Barrett Akerman, whom she first got to know when the pair were both residents at Columbia. He was now a Renew board member and occasional on-the-ground volunteer.

Dr. Akerman was, like Sandra, an authority in reconstruction procedures. (While Roya habitually referred to her as Dr. Collins, Sandra insisted, in a pronounced upper-class Boston accent I didn't hear much on the West Coast, that I call her by her first name. She was warm in a media-trained way: pleasant, indistinct, and faintly hollow. It made sense that she was a frequent TV guest, the upright denizen of the cable-news and daytime-talk-show greenroom.) Unlike Sandra, who'd branched out, making her money and a good deal of her name on a nonsurgical facelift she marketed as the Collins Lift, Dr. Akerman solely focused on restoration work at the Mayo Clinic.

Her friend, Sandra explained, was a groundbreaking surgeon with side gigs advising NASA and the Department of Defense. Advising in exactly what capacity wasn't specified, and I unsuccessfully followed up online. He'd gained acclaim within his field by focusing his impeccable skill set on developing innovative techniques to address the worst possible cases: the face eaten away by cancer, the hand reduced to meat in an industrial accident. More recently, however, the same colleagues who'd lionized him had blanched as he began giving presentations and publishing papers about the elective augmentations he was dreaming up that would alter form and function in provocative ways—artificial photoreceptor rods for eyes and cochlear implants for ears yielding superhuman vision and hearing.

"There's a saying in this discipline," Sandra said. "'Human flesh is infinitely malleable.' When you do what we do, when you're fully invested in the central belief—that the body connects to the soul; that its modification elementally changes the individual—perception can become mutable too." She went on to confide, off the record and rather darkly, that Dr. Akerman had a few years earlier told her of an idea he'd yet to circulate beyond several of his most-trusted peers. It was a blueprint design for theoretically flyable human wings (torso fat pulled across bone that'd been appropriated from the rib cage, then shaped into gliders when the arms outstretched), which he was convinced within a couple of decades would be accepted by the medical establishment and the general public.

Sandra was sharing this because she'd felt conflicted when he'd told her about it. She'd recoiled. But he'd pushed back. How different was this, after all, from "every other intervention," whether educational or pharmaceutical, technologic or genetic, religious or otherwise intellectual, and on and on, that might challenge our baseline conception of what it means to be a person?

"You're born and you discover, if you're paying attention, two things: life's untenable and life's full of wonder," Sandra said. For whatever reason—the framed diplomas on her wall, that accent, her steady gaze, the truth of it—this pierced me.

Sandra went on to observe that Roya, like Dr. Akerman, had triggered her recoil before a reassessment had kicked in. "At root," she said, "they're both chasing ideas of liberty that exist contrary to social convention, and that's compelling." This felt like both a trivial summation and a false equivalency, since the specifics of her old friend's and her protégé's respective circumstances were so different. But my efforts to gain further insight were brushed off. Sandra had said what she had to say.

On the drive home from speaking to Sandra about those wings, I had been unable to get the grotesque, fantastical image out of my head: translucent-thin webbing shot through with light from above, borne aloft along the currents, unshackled from the dictates of history and physiology. It was potent and haunting enough that I didn't even begin pondering until the following day the probable bacterial infections (athlete's wing?) and other prosaic realities of such a scenario.

When I told Roya about all of this at our next prison session, she was far more enchanted than I'd been, wishing she'd been there, in the room. Talk of Dr. Akerman's plan had her free-associating on the science of phantom limbs, how the mind is known to rewire itself after losing an arm or a leg ("so you'd likely acquire a winged brain"). Ever the Getty Villa habitué, the Greek hobbyist-scholar show-off, she also riffed on the Daedalus myth of flight—"What's going to happen to Icarus this time? A sunburn?"—and, in turn, diagnosing Dr. Akerman as an avatar of the Minotaur "operating at the intersection of beauty and monstrosity."

Meanwhile, Sandra's remark about discoveries after you're born prompted Roya to muse on the yet-to-be-understood-by-doctors magic of in utero reparation. "The fetus cannot scar," she said. Roya added that while she used to pride herself on her expert suturing craft ("To be straight-up sexist, female surgeons are just much more adept at it than men"), leaving the most insignificant, vanishing of marks, she liked to share with her apprehensive patients a maxim of her own devising: "Scars are memories of living."

This was conspicuously broad-minded, given her aversion to blemish. She would never abide such disfigurement in herself. Then again, the past wasn't of much use to Roya, except as a well of pain. She lived in the present, and the future.

BORN TO MAKE YOU HAPPY

I dreamed of being a doctor. I never dreamed of having my own practice, of being a small-business owner, despite the you-go-girl pride everyone around me took in my accomplishment. My fantasies didn't center on the minutiae of entrepreneurship.

Yet I found myself immersed in it when I hung my own shingle. There was an incredible amount to deal with, most of which I had given no substantive thought to before. This included rent, insurance of various sorts (malpractice, liability), equipment of different kinds (furniture, computers), adhering to regulations (HIPAA, OSHA), setting up a payroll system, and overhead in general. I had second, third, fourth, and fifth thoughts about the whole stressful endeavor, undergirded by my rookie's profit-loss anxiety about staying afloat.

At the Bedford group, while there were all sorts of administrative duties, they were quarantined, long and smoothly operating. I was spoiled, able to focus most of my energy on my patients. Not so now. But I was already in too deep. To this day I question how things would've been had I remained at Bedford, or started something with another equity physician partner who was more experienced in running things.

When I left Bedford, I thought Norm was being gracious in electing not to enforce the noncompete clause of my contract. I still do, yet now I can't help but believe there was at least some understandable trace of mischief, perhaps wanting to see this less-than-grateful upstart blundering out of the well-built nest before her time.

To be fair, one of the many generous things Norm did when I informed him of my plan was to provide a list of consultants to advise me on starting and building a successful private practice. I spoke to a number of these people, but their quotes seemed way too expensive for what they were offering.

It was shortsighted. I should've had an independent expert giving me advice tailored to my professional niche and its unique market context. Yet I kept thinking I had this stuff covered between my mom, a career office manager who was already weighing in on a lot of the same things (not least because she'd recently retired), and, to a lesser extent, my uncles, who had taken the suite build-out off my hands.

My practice never lost money. It just didn't make much, barely anything in fact, and I hustled a lot with a tiny team. Our all-female office consisted of someone at the front desk who handled the appointments, a medical assistant who helped me with patients, and a billing specialist who filed claims.

We built our initial bookings out of referral overflow from other practices, primarily Bedford's (again, Norm's generosity). I went on a charm offensive around the Golden Triangle to get a toehold on this front, as it's rare these days for a junior plastic surgeon with a local group to even attempt to start their own outfit in the same area. Rather, they head elsewhere, somewhere lower profile by a large margin, where they can far more easily leverage and cash in on the "Beverly Hills" cachet they've accrued.

I was able to fill my calendar because I accepted insurance at disadvantageous, some might say discourteous rates, at the bottom of the Beverly Hills market—hence the lack of meaningful yield. One could argue my acquiescence, due to a lack of clout, *set* the bottom of the local market. These were prices that more established doctors, those whose practices were teeming with the preferred sort of patients (which is to say, cash paying), would flatly turn down.

My chief gambit in establishing my practice in this ultracompetitive realm was a willingness to work on the weekends, at least for the first couple of years. I didn't perform procedures then; the surgicenter I used was closed. But my office was open on Saturdays and Sundays. We took Tuesdays off instead.

On the weekends, it was just a physician's assistant, a front desk girl, and me. My regular staff was with me on Saturdays. On Sundays I relied on a rotating array of part-timers from other practices to fill in.

While I didn't love working six days a week—I'd grown accustomed to living like a normal civilian at Bedford, and free weekends were a big part of it—I figured it wouldn't be forever. I had perspective. It wasn't as exhausting as medical school and residency, with those crazy around-the-clock hours. Not by a long shot. I could tough it out, particularly since this tactic served the dual purpose of strategically clawing my way into the Beverly Hills plastic surgery scene and alleviating my guilt and angst about making such a quasi-reckless decision in the first place.

The unrivaled weekend appointment availabilities, along with my, shall we say, *flexibility* with insurers, had the effect of producing a patient population notable for its diversity. By this I mean I saw far more middle-class and even working-class individuals (I really should just say "women," since my clients were more than 95 percent female) than my colleagues in Beverly Hills. I lured this demographic in preponderance, turning myself into a shameless bargain-basement option that nevertheless still featured comforting prestige plumage. I was a Loehmann's of the scalpel, simply because I was *available* to see them, in practical terms. Their insurance plans would allow the visits, and Saturday or Sunday appointments meant they wouldn't have to request time off and be subject to the mercy of their superiors, from the sorts of jobs—often compensated hourly instead of salaried—that didn't offer any inclusive annual paid time off. These folks came from long distances, as far as Simi Valley to the north, the Inland Empire to the east, and Orange County to the south, which meant that a visit to my office was at least a half-day commuting commitment.

Perhaps not every young plastic surgeon seeks to supersubspecialize, but everyone I knew did, and I was not immune. There was money to be made by becoming the go-to of a particular problem and recognition to be received from colleagues for being its agreed-upon authority. At Bedford, I'd begun to home in on areolas and nipples as my areas of expertise.

There were reasons for this. I liked how these were by their nature more intimate procedures, the work seen by far fewer people (mothers, sisters, close friends; mostly, of course, sexual partners). And while the importance of the visual outcome is obvious—achieving undetectable incisions via adept suturing—the aptitude of the practitioner's craft determines the effect the patient didn't think enough about in advance: loss, or not, of feeling. Sensation, a keen alertness to its fragility and its complexity, is of crucial importance. It adds another dimension to what's at play in the operating room. Outside of vaginoplasty, there's no procedure where cognizance of touch response is as integral to surgical success.

I've got plenty of regrets. Never having the chance to truly master this space is one of them. I know it may sound odd, but it was shaping up to be my forte. In my own shop, as I strived to get it going, I didn't have the luxury to focus on just one thing. I played all the hits: tummy tucks, breast lifts, butt implants, nose jobs. (Septorhinoplasty, covered by insurers who were skeptical about claims of deviated septums, was by far my most common procedure and biggest moneymaker, carrying my practice.) I also offered comprehensive "mommy makeover" packages that were great deals—for the patients, if not for my bottom line.

Still, the benefit of the way my practice was set up was that I found myself, for a plastic surgeon based in Beverly Hills, working on a wide ethnic array of body types. The nipple and areola work would, indeed, cycle through with all the rest. Those procedures are quick and simple, so I got to do a lot of them. And when it comes to procedures, there's an arc connecting experience and excellence.

The two most common surgeries in this genre are areolar reductions and inverted nipple corrections. Rarely do women want larger areolas—it's always "I hate these pepperonis." Sometimes it's about making one areola or nipple look like the other, reconfiguring the shape via skin excision. Although if the conclusion is reached that one needs work, typically the patient's attitude becomes, Why not optimize the other while we're at it, and make them both perfect, given all the trouble? (I can't fault that attitude.)

Inverted nipples are common and can be agonizing, especially when they further invert upon contraction. Those afflicted are enormously self-conscious. Then there's the reverse extreme: nipple reduction—long, protruding, often sagging nipples that are the consequence of breastfeeding. They can be painful if they're not flattened.

The ladies in the office (we called each other "lady"; it just became a thing) once gave me a cake from one of those erotic custom dessert shops kept busy by bachelorette parties. It featured a nicely shaped pair of breasts and two long lit candles jutting from their centers. "Happy Birthday, Dairy Queen!" the cursive icing read. I felt the love.

They were all funny and fun like that. We were funny and fun together, and I miss them. Among my anxieties about opening my own business was being a boss: the hiring and firing and managing, with all the attendant interpersonal hard-assedness it entails. I'd never done it before. I'd forever been the student, the junior, the protégé. Maybe I just lucked out, but the ladies I ended up with all had their shit together while, as a bonus, being a reliable joy.

I chalk the success up to taking Norm's advice, which was to assess prospective staff at the interview stage on vibe. He explained that to him a résumé, while an indication of base qualification, was nonetheless a "mere hypothesis" that could only ever be borne out once on the job. What mattered was in-person rapport. "You need to ask yourself," he told me, "'Do I want to subject myself to this individual in the break room, at the holiday party?' 'Do I want to subject *other staffers* to this individual?' It's quality of life. Atmospherics correlate to morale."

Sonya, my front desk henchwoman, took no prisoners in ensuring that patients were kept in line, and by this, I mean not flaking on appointments. Her bubbly personality and Valley girl upspeak combated excuses both legitimate and not with lethal cheer. During confirmation calls, she would remind them of our steep penalty fees for cancellations within twenty-four hours or showing up more than ten minutes late. Her entire immediate Filipino family—mother, father, three elder sisters, and one elder brother—were home health aides. The baby girl had gone rogue after at first doing the same.

"I need more action," she told me when we met, about wanting to work in an office. Sonya was twenty-three years old. I would later learn that when (not if) she got married, it would most definitely be in a Monique Lhuillier gown—Lhuillier being Filipina—and that "gorg" Vanessa Hudgens was her idol, for representing her community in such a shining light, even if she's "only half, from her mama." Sonya bore a faint resemblance to Hudgens. I told her this once, offhand, and she levitated near the ceiling. So I kept on doing it at intervals.

Where Sonya was a classic extrovert, happiest when gabbing, feeding on energy, my medical assistant, Narine, effervesced on a much quieter and more intimate register. (I'll note here that I've changed all the names of my employees and patients in this chapter for their privacy.) She had a shy graciousness to her, a way of speaking that made you lean in. This was her first gig out of school. Her job was to be my right hand, and she participated in all my examinations. Narine's soft presence affected the delicate alchemy in the room as secrets were shared, dreams and fears aired. Vulnerable patients felt a kindred spirit.

I got a kick out of the daily interplay between the demonstrative Sonya and the more subdued Narine, who grew up in Glendale and whose rather gloomy conception of her Armenian ethnicity appeared to be defined by her passionate advocacy for genocide recognition—she volunteered for an organization seeking to raise its awareness in the U.S.—and interest in the life and ideas of the pathologist and physician-assisted euthanasia activist Jack Kevorkian. Sonya was a huge fan of the Kardashian women. They reminded her, in the best possible ways, of her female-dominated family, in their loudness and vulgarity and ecstatic intergenerational bonding over glamour and sheer, clear, bickering love for each other. She presumed that Narine, a fellow Armenian, would be another disciple.

Yet Narine, a lovely, petite toothpick with a Wednesday Addams thing going on in her posture and pale-dermis-to-dark-hair contrast, saw the curvaceous Kardashians as a burden, despite acknowledging they'd used their platform for good in spotlighting the genocide. She wasn't a hater, per se, but she wasn't enamored either, and she didn't like to see her "people" reduced to some "clucking swirl of extensions" in pop culture.

The big lecture I received from my mom before I opened the practice was on "cultivating a positive office culture." She deservedly felt she was an expert on this. Her main insight, beyond banalities involving setting boundaries and remaining attentive to the texture and nuance of morale, was "to be proactive without creating expectations." This meant bringing in a masseuse or a mani/pedicurist or Sugarfish for sushi or Sprinkles for cupcakes, but always unannounced and never on the regular.

When I think about those times at the practice, that sweet spot after I worked through the initial anxious hustle of getting it all running and before everything imploded, I return to the end of many days, after the last patient had been sent away, when we were each handling our respective paperwork. It was a narrow stretch, maybe fifteen minutes before Sonya had to catch her bus home. She had this radio by her desk, always tuned low to the Top 40 on KIIS. One day early on we were debating the Taylor Swift and Katy Perry songs that were most likely to age into eternal radio classics, the new oldies. "From KIIS to KOST," I said, referencing the local adult contemporary programming option. She looked lost. I turned the dial to KOST and cranked the volume. At that very moment, Seal was crooning "Kiss from a Rose." I intoned, "This is where you can find your favorite pop when it's no longer popular."

Her response: "I thought that was YouTube."

Unashamed, unapologetic Chicago fan Norm had turned me into an unashamed, unapologetic disciple of KOST. (Pronounced *Coast.*) It'd been Bedford's de facto office station—meaning, inclusive of hold music—for years. The dorky, rapturous easy listening was undeterred by either the latest fashion or in-house snickers. I once asked him why he was such a KOST loyalist, and by way of explanation, he told me that on the way home the previous night, he'd heard a Phil Collins triptych: "In the Air Tonight," "Another Day in Paradise," and "Against All Odds." I could see him drumming his fingers on the steering wheel of his Porsche convertible as he drove Sunset Boulevard. back to the Palisades, the top down.

In my office, the close of countless afternoons turned into goofy if heartfelt ad hoc KOST sing-alongs, part ironic girlie hormone indulgence ("Time After Time," "The Sweetest Taboo"), part sober karaoke ("Don't Know Much," "Africa"). My staff knew their Whitney and Stevie and Madonna. It was glorious, genuine cheese like the Peter Cetera and Squeeze hits that were the acquired tastes. Yet once the ladies opened themselves to adult contemporary, which is to say recent cultural history, they were all in.

I swear this was not forced frivolity. After the first few times, I wasn't the only one turning on and turning up KOST. It became a shared habit. Now if this all reads like a cliché teen sleepover of adult women backdating themselves several decades—or a movie montage of that sleepover—I wouldn't argue. We also discussed myriad boy problems in depth and at length, along with the latest twists on *The Bachelor*, *The Bachelorette*, and *Bachelor in Paradise*. Narine would pantomime Vanessa Carlton's piano playing in the video for "A Thousand Miles." Sonya would mimic the emphatic hand-and-arm gesturing of Boyz II Men performing "I'll Make Love to You." They would join me in a full-throated rendition, once they familiarized themselves with the lyrics, of Wilson Phillips's "Hold On."

So yeah, we were cutesy-annoying—hardcore. The sporadically game, often reluctant fourth-wheel participant in all of this was Jenny, my billing specialist. She was good for the Aaron Neville half of a "Don't Know Much" duet. Jenny arrived at my practice direct from Seattle, where she'd earlier done the same work for, in succession, a gastroenterologist, neurologist, and urologist. Originally from a small town a couple of hours east of that city, she'd chosen to move after breaking up with her University of Washington sweetheart and making the quarter-life crisis decision to move to LA to pursue her songwriting dream. "It was one of those now-or-never things," she'd told me a few months into our time together.

Unlike the three of us, she wasn't pursuing a career in health care. I almost passed on hiring her for this reason, except her references had such effusive words of praise about her work ethic and her meticulousness. And unlike the three of us, she wasn't a local. A lifetime of having to endure assorted flavors of dumb commentary about LA from nonresidents—which reached its ill-informed, condescending apex during my sojourn along the East Coast—has predisposed me, unfairly or not, against transplants.

To her credit, Jenny was very good in, and very serious about, her self-styled "day job." She was a true professional. Still, I was forever on guard around her, antennae attuned to interpret perceived disdain, whether from the subtle reproach inherent in the severity of her high-cut blunt bangs or the austerity of her dark attire or the mystery of her alien-crop-circle-ish abstract arm tattoo. "Sorry," she once said, batting away an inquiry into the inking, "it's a private thing."

So I was a little extra pierced when Jenny, our very own resident musician, boasting next-level taste (or so I gathered from errant spying on her desktop computer's open Spotify account), would decide to viciously warble a drenched-in-sarcasm "Kiss Me"—after all, I remain a dyed-in-the-wool *She's All That* fan. By the same measure, I'd be relieved on days when sincerity, that better angel of our nature, won out and she'd lean into an emphatic "You're Still the One" or, for that matter, a tender "You Were Meant for Me."

Jenny, through no fault of her own, brought out my insecurities. She was one of those smart, well-meaning women of a certain progressive-minded bent who'd built and sought to inhabit a complete moral landscape of authenticity—and, it was presumed, justice—through correct political, social, and aesthetic choices. Some were overt, others less so. The consensus edicts were clear when it came to cultural consumption. Among others: Wear minimal or, better yet, no makeup; embrace challenging art and entertainment, ideally created by diverse voices; eat organic and sustainable; shop local; support small businesses; seek out the homemade and the handcrafted wherever possible.

Her lifestyle amounted to a rebuke of my own laziness. I recycled and was prone to pangs of half-Jewish guilt. That was about it. Perhaps this was Jenny's point: Be the change you wish to see in the world, la-di-da. But I registered it all as an irritating affront.

So, because I'm a bad person, I have to admit enjoying how oblivious the other ladies were, time and again, to Jenny's with-it white-girl values. Exhibit A: that Jenny's decision to live at the less-gentrified southern edge of hipster Echo Park was met by a baffled and bemused Sonya with, "*Why* would you *choose* to live in super-dangerous Filipinotown when you could afford to live in a perfectly *nice* part of the *Valley*?" Exhibit B: that Jenny's elated discovery of delicious local Armenian chicken chain Zankou—prompting rare outright effusion: "I can't stop thinking about that garlic sauce!"—was punctured in the most *wah-wah* of terms by Narine with, "My family hasn't gone there since I was a kid, when the owner killed his mother and sister and then himself. My parents' friends knew the guy. To this day they insist his advanced brain cancer was somehow to blame. Mom and Dad never bought it."

Depending on how you look at it, I was either blessed or cursed to have Jenny's point of view, her progressivism (millennial socialist, forged by student loan debt and the Great Recession), at my disposal for what came next. I couldn't have gotten myself into the same trouble I did if things hadn't been what they were. Now, I'm not trying to spread blame, far from it. I take full responsibility; it's all on me. I'm merely providing context for my actions, in the interest of clarity.

There was one more way Jenny was unlike the three of us. It was plain when she first began working at the office that she thought my patients were somehow fundamentally suspect for undergoing plastic surgery. We never discussed it. She never said anything. I just *knew*.

But by that same measure, it was plain that within months, even weeks, her outlook had changed. Jenny saw and overheard the results. And by "results" I don't only mean physical. I'm talking psychological: the tears of happiness, the smiles. Again, we never discussed it. She never said anything. I just knew. She became a believer.

Another believer, a longtime member of the converted, set my downfall in motion. She didn't realize, probably still doesn't realize, that her act of good faith had such ramifications. To repeat, this isn't about blame. It's context.

Irena was a married Beverly Hills mother in her late forties with three children. She's a Russian immigrant, a stunning trophy wife unmarred by age, married to an American businessman: the full cliché. She'd started visiting Norm when she was still single two decades earlier and invested in the works. Over the years her husband had financed tune-ups, including mommy makeovers. How she paid for the early procedures was vague. She'd said, in passing, she'd been a model. I suspected, based on experience and intuition, she'd been an escort, meeting her Mr. Right in a *Pretty Woman*–esque scenario. At the most respectable, it was a millionaire-matchmaker situation.

Irena brought in her early-twenties Mexican housekeeper, Gabriela, for a consultation. Gifted procedures weren't out of the ordinary among relatives. Occasionally financing even occurred among friends. However, this was the first I'd experienced stemming from an ongoing business relationship. The ethics made me queasy. Yet I was set at ease by the palpable benevolence involved. (Of course, let's be real about the bounds of the bigheartedness: It's not like she and her husband sprang for Gabriela to see Norm; this discount doctor would do.)

Gabriela was a strong candidate for chin and jaw augmentations to correct a substantially recessive profile. "I had the same thing but in reverse; mine was overly jutting," Irena said, her Russian accent reduced to a trace by time, her thumb and forefinger charting her own features while holding her housekeeper's hand in sisterhood. The combined procedure involved a chin implant as well as a titanium plate for the repositioned jawline.

I was struck by the tender rapport between the housewife and the housekeeper. Gabriela's English was basic and Irena's Spanish was nonexistent. However, their affinity was visible in the shorthand of gesture and giggle that'd been established, I imagined, over years insulated in Irena's home.

There was something bittersweet about their dynamic. I was happy these Russian and Mexican immigrants born a generation apart had established a friendship across class and race divides. I was also saddened their bond was, to my mind, doomed by their original sin: transgressing their vast employer-employee duality. Then again, who was I to stand in judgment of people seeking mutual solace from the isolation of adulthood, however hopeless and money poisoned? Wasn't I doing the same thing by socializing with my staff—presuming to be on their level?

When later I had Gabriela away from Irena, I asked her if she really wanted this. She was, in my professional estimation, an otherwise cute girl with one unfortunate malposition. Gabriela said, in Spanish, "*Want* this? I've dreamed of this my whole life! I just didn't know it was a possibility." Waterworks commenced. Narine had a box of tissues at the ready, a soothing hand massaging her back. It wasn't yet noon. We were already on the third patient cry of that day.

The surgery was a success. On the day of the procedures, I met Gabriela's kind and tentative mother, who accompanied her to the surgicenter along with Irena. The recessive chin and jawline must have been paternal traits.

Irena granted her several weeks off to recover. Gabriela's new facial profile was in ideal balance. She was thrilled with the outcome. "It's better than I could have hoped," she told me, wiping away tears at a checkup several months later, once the swelling had almost completely subsided, "even when I allowed myself to believe in the pictures you printed out for me." She was speaking of the side-by-side image renderings I'd presented to her on my desktop computer at our initial meeting.

All was well—another triumph. Then, five months after the surgery, Gabriela was back in my office, this time with her identical twin sister, Alejandra. You can guess where this is going.

My heart sank: a definite fuckup on the most elementary patient history leading to what would've been a foreseen turn of events. I later learned, in a fit of after-action recrimination, we'd marked that she had two sisters and both were older. Due to a language impasse or unrelated breakdown or gross negligence, we hadn't bored down to the nuance that one of them was a mere *three minutes older.*

If I'd been aware, I would've warned Gabriela. She was cleaving from the story she'd shared with her twin, one of communal pain. Alejandra, who worked as a stock girl in one of the wholesale shops in downtown LA's Flower Market, would now bear it alone. Maybe Gabriela would've gone through with the operation anyway, taking advantage of the opportunity her benefactor had offered her and her alone—despite what would've been my pointed caution. Who knows? It was a fable worthy of Aesop.

No matter. Here the twins were, seated across from me, by my hand no longer identical. They didn't need to tell me of the new emotional distance between them, but they did. They didn't need to tell me of the new raw tension between them, but they did. They didn't need to tell me of the guilt and jealousy and betrayal, but they did. Narine, as always, had the tissue box at the ready. They made use of it.

Here were the facts. Alejandra, like Gabriela, had a green card, and insurance under Medi-Cal. Like Gabriela, she was a strong candidate for chin and jaw augmentations. The orthognathic element (jaw work) could be covered by her plan, since I would be citing medical necessity on account of TMJ, headache, dry mouth, and lip incompetence—several of these issues she did have. The challenge would be arguing that the genioplasty procedure (for the chin) was anything but cosmetic.

"I just want to look like my sister," Alejandra told me, in Spanish, tears streaming. She and Gabriela didn't need me to condescend to them by expressing the truth: that I truly, deeply, *crushingly* understood this exact impulse. So I didn't. Instead sentiment overwhelmed me and I told them—this is where it all went wrong, the point of no return—"We'll find a way to make it work."

Alejandra's surgery, too, was a success. She somehow was able to take the necessary time off from work to recover and still hold on to her job. And I ended up coding her genioplasty as medically necessary due to the worsening aftereffect of an inconsequential accident she'd experienced years earlier when tripping on a buckled segment of sidewalk on the way to her bus stop after work.

This worsening was a lie, the first of many, but not the biggest whopper, not by a long shot. At least in this case there was an underlying truth. The sidewalk spill itself wasn't total fiction.

I felt a pinprick of sin for conjuring the bogus aftereffect: the specific fact itself (having to do with an airway defect), the ease with which I'd done it. How much worse did I feel than I did when alleging a disputable headache or case of dry mouth? Not much. By comparison, the pleasure I found myself taking in doing what, all things considered, was a minuscule bad thing in service of doing what, all things considered, was a sizable good thing? It was immense.

SEVEN

My unsanctioned background check on Roya yielded her litigation history, or what was legible of it outside the cloaked domain of arbitration. There were several intriguing initial malpractice filings available in the Beverly Hills court system. However, each case's narrative soon disappeared behind the veil of a mediator.

I asked a few attorneys and surgeons about the number of lawsuits. They thought it was maybe a little high given the limited timespan she'd been in practice, but by no means definitively so.

I reached out to each plaintiff's litigator, inquiring if I might speak off record to the client. In most instances I received polite dismissals. A couple of times they'd offer, by way of explanation, that confidentiality is standard in settlement agreements.

Without a smoking gun, I simply brought up malpractice with Roya, framing it as a sociological matter, a reflection on consumer behavior. It was the correct approach.

She revealed herself. Not through some telltale detail of her past as a civil defendant or even any notable commentary on what, for many physicians, is an unnerving subject. "This is why you have insurance," she said, shrugging.

It was Roya's serene disposition as I probed her that struck me—

and stuck with me. Her equanimity on this topic just *felt* phony, although I couldn't place how. There was more here, I was certain of it.

Soon after that conversation, someone sent me documentation about one of the settlements. It was clear that this client turned litigant had been one of the beneficiaries of Roya's insurance scheme. The woman claimed her chin surgery resulted in a waking nightmare: first a gruesome infection, then a loose screw requiring a second procedure to tighten, and in time, persistent nerve damage that'd left her with lasting numbness across her lips. "Dr. Delshad thinks she's a saint," the sender wrote from an anonymized email address. "Don't buy it."

My first instinct was to confront Roya about it. But I checked myself. It served neither of us at this point for me to play inquisitor on this subject. Besides, I felt I knew what the result would be. She'd be ultradefensive and upset about my out-of-bounds prying. The breach would also undermine the rest of our ongoing work.

Still, my temperance had limits. The digital case file was expansive. A rabbit hole I couldn't help but drop down. Its nauseating image exhibits stayed with me, as did the woman's jolting impact statement. There was such specificity to her testimony: the psychological, the tactile. How eating and licking and kissing were no longer the same. "These human things have been taken from me," she wrote in her filing.

Roya monitored my ongoing reporting from the penitentiary. She quizzed me about not just what people said and how they said it but how quickly they agreed to talk in the first place and under what conditions. In turn, wherever possible, she'd gather and share her own intel on the discussions, relaying nongermane insights, in at least some gossipy cases selling out their confidence. I couldn't tell, and didn't push to find out, whether her rationale was that this was all in service of the presumed higher mission of our mutual project, or that she merely didn't think it was a big deal.

"Tina was crushing so hard over what a *sweet, thoughtful, handsome* guy you are," she'd teased during one of my visits, speaking of the grade-school friend I'd chatted with at her home in Hancock Park. "I warned her I'd spotted you first!" Roya had paused, arching her back in her baggy jumpsuit, materializing a devilish grin and a breathy camp falsetto: "Such a tough masturbatory choice: the desperate-housewife daydream—or the woman-in-prison fantasy?" I never got over her talking like this, the flirty-dirty-ironic thing, although I found a zen place of polite professionalism in not taking the bait, which just made her try harder to get me to do so.

There was something similar afoot in the way she teed up my imminent meeting with Dr. Penelope Greene, a cosmetic dermatologist and her former colleague at the Beverly Hills physicians' group that Roya had been a part of before starting her own practice. Still close friends—likely her closest friend, from what I could tell—Roya called her Money Penny, with some amalgam of envy and admiration, for enterprising Dr. Greene's then-in-the-works partnership with a major beauty brand to sell an affordable mass-market kit version of her expensive in-office skin treatments. As Roya framed it to me, in pleased wonder, "She's already successful, but she's on the verge of being super, *absurdly* successful before even beginning to lose her maximal fuckability. It's like the human version of a total solar eclipse."

I met Dr. Greene—or as she asked me to refer to her, Penny—for lunch on the courtyard at Spago. As it happens, we sat at the same table, two in from the street on the side closer to the bar, adjoining one of the potted olive trees, where I once dined with Buzz Aldrin and his since-divorced third wife, Lois. For a short *GQ* profile about Aldrin's surreal LA socialite retirement life that was pegged to his debut on *Dancing with the Stars*, we'd discussed the magnificent desolation of outer space, the depression and alcoholism that followed his NASA career, and his then-recent decision to undergo a facelift. He'd earlier told *Time* that a career enduring g-forces "caused a sagging jowl that needed some attention."

I could see Penny and Roya's friendship straight out, how they sparked. Penny, in her late thirties and single, with no kids, was sharp, savvy, amused. She also presented with the identical edgeless, straightened-and-swept look of cryptoconservative professional femininity that Roya had perfected before being sent to prison. She recalled a Jewish American Princess ready to conquer her prep school's twenty-year reunion. The similarity made me question what this brunette would look like with a radicalized, incarcerated Jewfro.

Not that it mattered, since I wouldn't be quoting her anyway, but Penny was keen to stipulate that this would be a purely off-the-record chat. This was in part because she didn't want the taint of the scandal to somehow affect the public relations rollout of her forthcoming product. Yet, she assured me, it was just as much a selfless consideration as a selfish one: Once the business was in motion and she'd solidified a position of relative tactical control, she intended to bring Roya in on it, in some to-be-determined capacity.

"I know she's got vague but very important plans for her social activism after she gets out," Penny said. "I also know she's grown accustomed to her *upper*-middle-class life, and she's got legal debts, so she'll need a day job between all of that do-gooding."

I told her Roya hadn't told me about this. "Oh, should she have?" Penny responded, slicing me with a hint of feigned alarm. I realized I'd revealed an unwarranted competing claim on intimacy. "It's gestating. We're figuring it out."

The other reason she wanted to talk off the record was that it turned out Penny had been aware of what was going on with the insurance claims. "Look, I told her to be careful, and I told her she'd be wise to knock it off," she said, her voice quieting, lest someone else hear. "I certainly didn't understand that the situation was ever anywhere *near* as extensive as it turned out to be, just in terms of the volume of patients who were being granted procedures beyond the scope of their policies."

Incidental life of crime aside, Penny still thought highly of Roya, seeing her as a potent force, "generous to the point of courageousness," a levelheaded person who made an atypical if seismic mistake. The fraudulent billing scheme was, in short, a pardonable transgression, one that Penny was satisfied to forget. "What happened was awful—for her," she said. "People will move on. Now, this book you guys are cooking up will arrest that process, bringing everything up again, and I've *told her that.* But whatever."

I took this opportunity to bridge Penny's skepticism with my own from-the-jump doubt about how the memoir might ultimately benefit Roya. I also floated my belief that Roya bore a propensity to make unwise decisions at odds with her strategic interests. (Of which, of course, the one that had gotten her locked up would be the most prominent.) As I'd wagered, Penny digested this not as an illegitimate psychological fishing expedition but a rare opportunity for bonding over the challenges of an exasperating, beloved friend.

"Some people," Penny explained, loosened after a glass of rosé, "are led by their hearts." Her tone said *led astray.* I offered silence. She went on, "It's like how she hooked up with Norm: It made sense even if it didn't make sense."

Penny's eyes flared as it registered that I might not know that Roya had been in a relationship with Dr. Norman Landler, the head of one of the most prominent plastic surgery groups in LA, where the two women had worked in neighboring suites. Until that moment I hadn't known, only having been informed of some forgettable investment adviser she'd casually dated during this period after meeting him at the gym. In an instant—mostly for her sake, a little for mine—I pretended that I had, skipping past the lapse, nonchalantly rejoining, with a shrug and a nod, as though I too were already bored of the subject, "I don't know if the Norm thing makes sense to any of us." Later, before she could even try to get upset about the revelation, I dressed Roya down for not prepping either Penny or me about *l'affaire* Landler in advance, to better avoid near calamity.

Penny, relieved by my improvisation, told me that, as close as they were, it wasn't something that the two had talked about until the relationship was over and Roya had gone to jail—even though it'd been whispered about at the time in their Beverly Hills office a few blocks west of Spago on Bedford Avenue. "Look, I'm not going to go on about her love life," she said. "I wouldn't want her talking about mine." So why then were we talking about it? What was the relevance? "You're going to speak to Norm, right?" I told her that as it so happened I'd been in the process of trying to set it up. Penny leaned in: "Along with her faculty adviser at USC—some reconstruction surgeon I've never met—Roya looked up to him most."

OK, so Penny was operating under the assumption that if she knew about the improper billing while it was happening, then Dr. Landler, who'd been Roya's mentor in business even before becoming her lover, did too. But when I broached this with Roya, who already was guarded on the details of her relationship with the then-married Dr. Landler ("He was nice; it was nice; it's over") in a way she wasn't with anyone else she'd been with, she was adamant she'd confessed none of her illegal behavior to him. "I was ashamed," she said. "It was different with Penny. I could tell her things that made me look stupid."

My face during this exchange at the prison must have betrayed my disbelief that their pillow talk avoided what I knew to be a salient issue in her life at that time. "I compartmentalized," she insisted. I observed that she'd just said she'd been embarrassed—so which was it? Roya didn't appreciate this pincer interrogation. "Drop it," she said, ice cold. We moved on.

Still, as touchy as she was about Dr. Landler once I was aware of their liaison, she made no bid to kibosh my already-in-motion attempt to talk to him. I thought this was strange until, after a few weeks of silence from his office, I received a warm, direct email inviting me to come by and figured that she'd already back-channeled the facts that a) I knew what was up, and b) I knew it was off-limits.

An alpha dog of gracious ease roaming his doghouse, so confidently groomed in his silver goatee as to make me question my own acute aversion to sporting such facial hair, Dr. Landler volunteered information, synthesized ideas, and thoughtfully asked me if I needed him to slow down or repeat a point. He spoke in eloquent paragraphs. It didn't surprise me that he had an occasional side gig as an expert witness in medical malpractice cases. He was smooth, engaging, and ferociously smart and made me feel sated as he walked me out of his office door with a fatherly hand on my back two minutes shy of the buzzer on our allotted half hour. It wasn't until later, when I reviewed my notes, that I grasped he'd somehow said nothing of use at all.

One worthwhile exception was that, like Penny, he thought what'd happened was a true tragedy. Dr. Landler (who, as opposed to the rest of the physicians I chatted with, never suggested I forgo the honorific title in addressing him once we'd exchanged initial pleasantries) spoke of Roya's "innate talent, honed skill, obvious compassion, and clear work ethic." He also explained, without sentiment, "To do something that foolish, you're duping people all along the way. But the first fool is you." This sounded to me like a man who'd come to accepting terms with his own thorny role in an interlude of bamboozlement, perhaps to some unknown extent his own, that nested within what should've otherwise been a simpler story of infidelity. I'd never resolve exactly what happened between them, nor determine how much law enforcement might've known or even cared. As much as I would in time learn of Roya, this remained a mystery.

On another day I chatted with one of Dr. Landler's several receptionists, Cristeta Mendoza. She'd previously worked the front desk for Roya. He'd taken her onboard after she'd lost her job when the Delshad practice imploded. This is what I mean by "gracious."

We met at a smoothie shop around the corner from their office. "I'd love to get into raw juicing," she told me as she ordered, "but the trendy cold-pressed thing is too expensive of a habit for too little product, and honestly"—she went *sotto voce*, vamping a glance in either direction, as though she couldn't be caught sharing such a verboten view—"I can't deal with that sugar-free taste. It's like, cayenne and wheatgrass and oil of oregano? *Ugh.*" As a devoted Orange Julius fan, I told her I understood.

Cristeta, a Filipina in her mid-twenties, spoke highly of Roya. "It's crazy what happened to her," she said. "Dr. Delshad got a bum rap. All she did was color outside the lines the teensiest bit, trying to make life better for chicks with pretty shitty lives." Cristeta, who maintained she never knew anything of the fraudulent billing, continued to look up to her: "I thought she was a badass before everything went down. I just think she's a much bigger badass now."

Her only bitterness, she joked, is that she wishes she'd gotten a marked-down procedure for herself. "Dr. Delshad knew I was hard up—she cut my checks!" Cristeta laughed. "Now I'm *still stuck* on the itty-bitty-titty committee until I figure something else out."

She pretended to give serious thought to the dilemma, hammily stroking her chin: "Let's see, taking out a second mortgage on the home I don't own? Drawing down my just-hatched 401(k)? Coupon clipping would be the most responsible thing to do. Then again, I'd be eligible for the saggy-titty subcommittee by the time I'd saved enough." She'd made her point. Roya told me she missed Cristeta. I could see why.

Next up was Roya's former medical assistant Tamar Sarkissian, a mousy but in her own quiet way striking young woman. She'd since landed another job an hour's drive east in traffic at a family friend's orthopedic practice in the Armenian enclave of Glendale, where she's from. "I probably should've been working here in the first place," she said, legs crossed, salad in a clear plastic container balanced on her lap, granting me her office lunch break while seated at a bench in a park across the street. This rendezvous had followed much protracted pleading, as well as a jailhouse email nudge from Roya.

It was plain that Tamar, like Cristeta, idolized Roya. That Roya was a self-made woman—in all its definitions—and that she'd charted a life of comparative adventure, otherwise known as drama. Tamar also appreciated, from her close vantage, how Roya handled her patients, both empathetically ("They always felt seen for who they could be, not just who they were") and the surgical outcomes themselves, noting as point of reference that she herself had a "private interest" in carpet weaving ("I know, *so Armenian!*") and Roya's attention to detail, artistry, craft, and general focus were "an inspiration." Basically, she said, locking my eyes, "Dr. Delshad is a sorceress."

Tamar hadn't been certain that anything illegal was going on while she was there. But she'd had her suspicions. For one thing, there were the seeming tensions between Roya and her billing specialist, Jackie. For another, there appeared to be a substantive uptick in "rabbits being pulled out of hats to make things happen for people." Enough to the point where Tamar was privately Googling for answers to quell her curiosity, which only confirmed her belief that there was something amiss about the escalated insurance approval rate.

So did she ever say anything? Tamar looked baffled. "Of course not." She explained it would've been rude and unprofessional. The fact was, she liked Roya and her job. "Let's face it," Tamar said, having already faced it, "I didn't really want to know."

Roya was eager to put me in touch with the first beneficiary of her criminality. Adriana Vasquez was a stock girl in downtown LA's wholesale flower district who'd received a chin implant and jaw correction to bring her profile in accord with her twin sister Josefina's, a Beverly Hills housekeeper whose employers had paid Roya months earlier for the same complement of surgeries. The sisters together met me in the living room of their parents' small, brightly painted house in East LA on a Sunday after attending church.

They'd each recently married and moved away to apartment units, like their older sister before them, within blocks of the family seat. They now lived with their husbands, both gardeners who worked on crews servicing the San Fernando Valley, just as their own father did. The twins, whose post-Roya defining features were bright eyes and beaming smiles, settled into opposite ends of a sofa, jean legs affectionately tangled together in the center. Their mother drifted in and out of the room, offering intermittent rapid-fire commentary in Spanish that by its pitch and her daughters' occasional subsequent course corrections I understood to be on-the-fly media training.

My limited, broken Spanish and their limited, broken English made communication difficult. The barrier restricted nuance and intimacy. This failure was my blunder. I should've brought an interpreter.

That said, I understood enough to know that the twins were straining to put on a show, understandably keen to repay Roya for her kindness. They didn't mean for this to be a rigorous discussion. Still, I found it frustrating that for the most part I couldn't elicit material beyond the banal. (Surprise: They were gratified with the work they received; they'd been miserable beforehand; it'd dramatically improved their lives.)

A memorable exception was a provocative musing at the confluence of race, class, and sex—which, whether purposeful or not, occurred when their mother was in the backyard. I'd congratulated them on what I learned had been near-simultaneous nuptials and now pregnancies. This triggered laughs and the joking-but-not-really observation that, postprocedure, they'd each expected that at least one and perhaps multiple wealthy, sexy suitors would've swooped in to court their newly lovely selves, elevating them to easier American lives. "Remember *Maid in Manhattan*?" Adriana explained, referencing the 2002 movie in which the titular Jennifer Lopez ends up with Ralph Fiennes.

As for why this white-knight fantasy hadn't transpired, there was a rationalization. According to Josefina, the Latina lure for men like me is a J.Lo-style bottom—but in their family that kind of extra-large posterior is only "fated" after giving birth. This wasn't like dealing with Roya. I could tell they weren't looking to goose a reaction out of me. They were just stating objective reality as they saw it. I considered parrying their preconception and thought better of it.

The bulk of our conversation had to do with how their surgeries begat, by their estimate, nearly two dozen Roya referrals. People were curious how these sisters had remedied their pronounced physical deficits. It was a miraculous event.

So, when asked, the entire Vasquez family discussed not only the generosity of Josefina's patrons but the magic of the venerated Dr. Delshad, who'd by the grace of God found some way to get Medi-Cal to pay for Adriana's procedures when the sisters didn't think it could be possible. (Concerned her luck would sour, the sisters didn't tell their parents until Adriana's surgery drew near.)

Partly it was the family's honesty. How could they keep such desired, conceivably valuable knowledge from their relatives, their neighbors, their coworkers, their fellow parishioners at Saint. Alphonsus? Partly it was the family preventing whispers against its good name. How else to explain such fortune? The Vasquezes were hardworking and honorable. They made it clear they had no access to, and would never draw a benefit from, the community's sources of easy money. It went unsaid, but I presumed various forms of trafficking-related income.

Roya hadn't told me how much of the patient demographic whose procedures got her in trouble was clustered in a single, tightly woven, low-income Mexican barrio of the city. It turned out she hadn't realized until after she was caught the quantity of individuals who'd gained access to her care that were all related by no more than two degrees of separation.

When I brought it up the next time we saw each other, kidding that perhaps she might be considered for sainthood, Roya nodded, running with the gag. "Beatified for beautifying," she said, pretending to turn it over in her head. "I don't know the first thing about canonization requirements, but"—Roya's upturned gaze acknowledged the room and the prison beyond it—"I certainly *have* felt persecuted."

She then told me what Adriana and Josefina never did. She'd already been blessed, so to speak, in a way that mattered. The twins and other surgical beneficiaries had seen to it that, from the moment she arrived in prison, certain other convicts from the same neighborhood knew who she was and what she'd done for them, in all its munificence. "It was made clear on my first day that I'd have zero problems," Roya said. "This gangster girl with a teardrop tattooed below the corner of one eye made an announcement in the middle of the cafeteria. She stood behind me with an arm around my shoulders."

The last person I talked to on my listening tour was Jackie Mayer, the woman who handled billing in Roya's office, which meant she dealt with insurers. Unlike her boss, who made far more trouble for herself with the hard-ass prosecutor by at first lying about her legal sins when confronted, she sang straight away and ended up with nothing more than 150 hours of community service and a calamitous internet search history.

Jackie was the last person I spoke with for two reasons. First, Roya was reluctant to let me contact her. ("She hates me—like, *totally* hates me; why do I have to be a good sport about this?") Then, when I finally prevailed on her about it, Jackie herself was for some time indifferent to participating in my process. ("So you want to hear me out and not even actually quote what I have to say about her? What's the point of that?") In a feat of persistence, charm, and talking out of both sides of my mouth, I landed my meeting. It took place in the dark in the middle of the day amid glowing red strung lights at her favored dive bar in Highland Park, the gentrifying Eastside neighborhood where she lived.

During a warm-up tango that mirrored my initial conversation with Roya—severe skepticism about my intentions blended with general get-to-know-you boilerplate—Jackie revealed that her anger manifested itself in a range of octaves. There was unalloyed wrath, droll shade, fatigued resentment, unnerving detachment. I got the impression that her fury, faceted and held dear, wasn't performative. This was where she remained in her post-Roya existence.

Jackie's humor was laced with more than an undercurrent of malice. She allowed that, "ruining my life aside," Roya was a virtuous boss, treating her and her colleagues well—"although she had this sort of Michael Scott way about her," referring to Steve Carell's character on *The Office*, forever awkwardly attempting to connect with his employees. She also acknowledged Roya's skill as a surgeon. But Jackie couldn't resist framing it as snark. "Yeah," she said, "bitch definitely knows how to cut you."

Jackie, only at best mildly attractive by nature yet not appearing to be much burdened by this situation, did not worship at Roya's house of physical prayer. She ascribed to an alternate feminine ideal, less conventional if not obscure. I'd been informed she was straight, but without knowing, I'd have taken her for a lesbian academic. Roya, sounding like a disapproving mother, clucked before I met Jackie that her former employee's aesthetic decisions "didn't do her any favors." Afterward, in what I thought was one of Roya's least appealing moments, among her first orders of debriefing business was seeking vindication on this point: "See what I mean?"

Much of my time with Jackie, who'd taken to an Eeyore-style fatalism that was by turns purposefully and accidentally funny, was spent excavating how "fucked" she'd been. That she'd had to declare bankruptcy to deal with her attorney fees, which tanked her credit score. That she'd since blown a bunch of money on a reputation-management firm in an unsuccessful attempt to fix her Google results as she focused her attention on the songwriting career that was her ostensible reason for being in LA in the first place. (The devastating search results were only slightly buried.) That she didn't have any money to blow on the psychotherapy she felt she needed to "move beyond all of this shit." (She wished she could sue Roya for emotional distress.) That she'd spent months appealing her rejection to be a ride-share service driver after she failed a standard background check due to her record. (A friend of a friend had pulled some strings, "so now I'm lucky enough to drive drunk dipshits around all night and hope they don't hurl in my Kia.")

Jackie told me she'd at last elected to speak with me, after consulting friends, because she saw through Roya's "image renovation" of a memoir project and felt duty bound to refute it, figuring me at least somewhat ethical for seeking out her counsel even if complicit in my contractual obligation to abet the author. Her antagonism left little room for empathy. She claimed to have grokked Roya's phoniness from the get-go.

"Come on, Wes, it was literally painted on her face," Jackie said. "The 'Dr. Barbie' vibe she went in for with that makeup and hair?" She felt vindicated by my revelation to her that her former boss was now peddling her actions as a social-justice narrative: "Help her write whatever, but just remember that there were no overarching politics to it at the time. It's weaselly to suggest otherwise."

Seeking a conversation rather than a rage spiral, I wondered whether this mattered all that much. Hadn't the disadvantaged gained rare access to life-bettering procedures they otherwise wouldn't? Perhaps how it all went down was unintentional, but hadn't it served as a useful case study in broadening the hitherto-negligible discussion about the constrained economic and emotional realities of a cash-based, elective field?

Jackie's expression was curdled. "Don't try me with the

Roya's-an-imperfect-vessel-for-an-important-debate argument," she said. "Save it for the suckers who haven't already been conned."

This prompted a step-by-step explication of how Jackie had been "ensnared" by Roya. The billing specialist caught on to the misconduct only several patients into the trouble. She'd asked her boss about it, and Roya had provided unsatisfying answers.

At first, Jackie had let it go. Then she realized she could be liable and circled back more forcefully. At that point Roya gave her "the full song and dance"—pointedly away from fellow staffers, over a special lunch at a nearby Italian place, instead of in the small office where Cristeta and Tamar could've overheard their discussion (even in Roya's suite with the door shut). As Jackie put it, Roya "preyed" on her bleeding-heart politics and her lack of knowledge about medicine.

"I was back to being a subordinate," Jackie said. "There was the briefest window where I had any agency. Once she had my buy-in, she just kept going on with it. It seemed like a mischievous but maybe righteous thing we were discussing, but ultimately a policy decision made by my boss that was beyond my comprehension. I didn't understand I'd agreed to be a coconspirator and accessory." It was all made easier when she saw the patients who'd benefited from their chicanery during follow-up appointments, taking silent satisfaction in their obvious joy. "There was a sort of quiet basking," Jackie admitted, her ire ebbing in thought. "You never experience anything like that working in a gastroenterologist's office."

I asked if Jackie supposed Roya worried about getting caught. "Whether it was arrogance or stupidity or some combination of the two, I don't believe she thought it was a real possibility," she said. "The recklessness is astounding, right? After our lunch we pretty much stopped talking about it. But I think she figured it wasn't *that* many patients, even though it *was*. Worst-case scenario, an isolated procedure here or there would end up disputed by an insurer who wouldn't budge, and the practice might just decide to eat the cost itself, sort of an altruistic act. She never suspected the whole pattern would be uncovered—that she'd lose her license and business and end up in prison." Having spoken with Roya about her thinking, I thought Jackie's analysis was astute.

Later, when I shared with Roya what Jackie had said, she was upset at the contention that she'd manipulated her subordinate into wrongdoing. "Jackie knew what was up early on, and Jackie was *game*," she said. Roya likewise could summon little empathy amid her own antagonism. "She's a big girl who doesn't want to take responsibility. I've owned up to mine, which is *nearly all of it*."

Since I wasn't interested in setting off nuclear-grade agita, I never told her that Jackie had called Roya's ex post facto social-justice repositioning of the fraudulent activity "weaselly." Nevertheless, there still would be much subsequent massaging of the limited Jackie material in the memoir before we got it to an agreed-upon place. One where it conveyed the pair's severely strained relationship in honest while tempered and circumspect terms. (Roya unfiltered: "I shouldn't have hired that ugly, miserable cunt in the first place.") The goal was for the pertinent text to be unobjectionable enough that Jackie wouldn't be compelled to issue some sort of rebuttal on social media or to the press afterward, thereby subsuming the rest of Roya's honed message rollout in a juicy catfight.

Back at the bar, Jackie was nursing another Negra Modelo, winding down her invective toward a key of, at my urging, volunteered pity. I'd told her I understood her view, that her experience was valid, that it would inform my own thinking. Yet I urged her, even if only as a theoretical challenge, to consider the most bighearted possible interpretation of Roya's faults, whatever it might be.

She'd been quiet for a while. Then she said: "It takes one to know one. Roya was a weird, sad, broken girl." Jackie peeled the label from the bottle. "Then she dealt with it in the most unimaginative way she could—by becoming this paradigm and exponent of conformist adult beauty. Well, she's 'pretty' now. She's still sad and broken."

CHAOTIC

In retrospect it would be easy to recriminate, to pretend there was some overarching plan, to lash myself over its fatal flaws. In the moment, though, my decisions—the bad choices piling up one after the other, with increasing frequency and arrogant abandon—were impulsive and disconnected. Not only did I not know I was heading down the wrong path, but I also didn't understand I was on a path at all. I was reactive, buffeted by the short-term pleasure of doing what felt right and the long-term delusion that there would be no unwanted repercussions.

For fourteen months, from the time I signed away Alejandra's fraudulent paperwork to the morning the California Bureau of Investigation raided my office, this all held out. In the interim, I floated along, otherwise focused on running my business and living my life. Which is to say, I gave little thought—at least far less thought than I should have—to the accumulating impact of these periodic illicit highs that I was experiencing while making insurance miracles happen for a tiny fraction of my total patient case load.

The one exception to this was when, early on, my billing specialist, Jenny, figured out what was up and confronted me. "This is wrong," she said one day, clutching a sheaf of printouts while seated across my desk. "And regardless, it's only a matter of time before the providers figure out what's going on."

I should've listened. Instead, I did even worse than ignore her. I rationalized my behavior, pulling her into my undertow: that it was no big deal, that the offense was no worse than physicians using medications off-label, that it fell into the realm of professional creative license.

Jenny—my subordinate, my responsibility—bought my bullshit. A conspiracy of mutual silence about the fraud would last until she immediately and understandably cooperated with the prosecutors at the California Department of Justice. Still, she would pay a public price along with me. For this I'm ashamed and I'm sorry. I have yet to forgive myself. I doubt I ever will.

Selfish ego played a colossal role in my supposedly selfless behavior. I'd talk to prospective patients during consultations and think, *I'm going to change your life in a way nobody else can.* I radiated the quasi-political demigoddess energy of a modern-day back-alley abortion doctor. On top of that, I felt like a renegade judge, able to withhold my support for any reason. Most often it was because people were too aggressive in asking for help ("I heard you can make things happen . . ."), which would sully the purity of my own altruistic impulse.

I *liked* breaking the news that I could make things happen. I *enjoyed* seeing the look in my patients' eyes. I *got off* on their tears of joyful relief the way a stand-up does on audience laughter in a comedy club. Go ahead and castigate me for my twisted savior complex, which was transparent in plenty of cases. Narine, my assistant, has told me she suspects plenty of the beneficiaries knew what was up and played me for a fool.

If that's true, good for them, because so what? Reprimand my motives. The results are still what they are. These were sins with net-positive outcomes since the real crimes transcend the acts. They're the inequities of genetics and the impossible economics of such procedures for most people. We all want to grasp a better life. If—somehow, some way—we do grab ahold of it, we sure as hell hold on.

I treated 116 patients under fraudulent pretenses before I was caught.

This was across three private insurance providers, as well as Medi-Cal and Covered California, the state's public health programs. Let's keep in mind the realities of the fallout. Jenny was tarred by virtue of listening to her boss. My other two employees had to scramble to find new jobs. I ended up in prison, my practice kaput, my medical license revoked, my reputation shattered. These behemoth corporate insurers, unbeknownst to them, temporarily felt the most inconsequential statistical pinprick against their profit margins that they later partly recouped anyway as creditors of my bankruptcy. And sure, a government entitlement was scammed, fine. What else is new? At least the money went downstream.

Meanwhile, the patients—all working-class and low-income women, nearly all minorities—who rarely catch a break on anything in this rigged world, much less a significant one, got to go right on living their better lives. Nobody could take away what I gave them, and none of those publicity-anxious insurers dared make them pay for their improvements after the fact. I'll take that victory.

So in a tale that's otherwise all about me, me, me, I'd like to take a moment to salute them. Between these chapters of my own narrative, many of my patients have bravely shared their before-and-after photos, as well as snippets of their own emotional journeys, revealing just a bit of the thoughtful, elusive inner selves shaped by their outer ones. Those who aren't dead inside are no doubt finding these stories heart wrenching. That's because there's no kind of plastic surgery story other than a heart-wrenching one.

Despite the popular misconception, you don't willy-nilly undergo a major medical procedure if the stakes for you and your future aren't huge. The only difference between these women and others—the ones who've gotten procedures, the many more who haven't and wish they could—is that they had no other option but the miracle that resulted in my career suicide. Their voices are my story; my actions are their story.

I stand in wonder at the varied human experience I encountered during my downfall. There was the stripper who really was trying to pay her way through school, in need of a superior chest. There was the retired adult film actress with what I came to think of as the Groucho Marx request: Now with a husband and planning to conceive, she desired facial alterations ("I don't care which") so she wouldn't be recognized by leering strangers anymore. "You don't need to make me look better—just different," she'd told me.

There was the smart young woman, who'd landed her first job as a local bank branch teller, with the most perfectly round, jealousy-inducing natural rear end who wanted it flattened, so she could breathe in a society that exalted her butt while precluding the rest of her existence. ("Let's disappear some booty and maybe I won't be so invisible, you know?") Similarly, there was the celebrity doppelgänger, a nightclub waitress, who sought a cheek reduction, known in our trade as a buccal fat extraction, so she'd no longer be thought of as "a poor woman's Selena Gomez, who I *don't even like*."

Not all patients were so idiosyncratic. But each was a strange and surreal request, illuminating some dark perch of perceived pain and desire. I respected their longing, remembered in it my own, the same formational urge that'd propelled me to a brighter future. I was happy to be their bridge across an otherwise wide and indifferent gulf.

I have many regrets. Yet my only true disappointment is that I'll no longer be able to help more women this way. Directly, in the operating room, my hands across their willing bodies, the scalpel opening universes of possibility.

EIGHT

Roya and I had developed a rapport in the months since I'd met her in the visitors' room at the California Institution for Women in Chino. Erotic tension lay at its center. An established pattern continued unabated: She'd tweak my pinched, stuffy professionalism with straight-faced, out-of-the-blue, comically aggressive flirtation that often came across like pure solicitation. I'd have called her out for sexual harassment rather than sticking to my MO of ignoring her if I weren't in the position of privilege (the free man, or just the man in the situation), if I weren't enjoying it on multiple levels (including as farce, which she intended) and if calling it sexual harassment wouldn't have played into her amused narrative of pinched, stuffy professionalism.

Our dynamic was that of office workplace spouses enmeshed in a complex deadline project, bickering, often at each other's throats over a creative idea, but largely energized. Except instead of happy-hour drinks, we toasted our efforts at high points with commissary-purchased Taster's Choice.

Roya loosened after our initial formal interview, turning at times too verbose. Our time restricted, my interest limited, my patience tested, I'd have to steer her back onto the trail. "But this might be useful!" she'd protest as I'd rein her in, the rushing geyser of anecdotes of meager value untapped once again, this time about some reverie on the quad at Penn or in a surgical tent in South America. I don't know what psychologists would say, but I've come to believe that allowing people to talk about themselves at length to a willing audience, in a free-form if to some degree guided ramble, might be a damaging thing in terms of the malignant swelling of the ego. "I think," I'd say, using my kindest voice, "we're good."

Now, this isn't quite fair. Roya proved to be curious about me beyond her hard-edged original interrogation. She later confessed she'd lifted many of her own questions, peppered as I was packing up at the end of our sessions and lingering in my mind on my drive home, from a social science study on building intimacy that had been making the rounds online for a few years. "I've memorized them," she told me. "They're like my tarot cards."

I remember she asked me, "Do you have a secret hunch about how you'll die?" (Cancer or a car accident.) And, "When did you last sing to yourself?" (That morning, in the shower, along with "Love Me Do.") And, "If you could learn a truth about yourself in a crystal ball, what would you want to know?" (The last time I'd have sex.)

Roya probed me best, though, when she wasn't around. Through her, I saw others as I hadn't before, and myself through a looking glass. It turned out she'd unmasked me—pantsed me, really—as pretty-boy privileged to the point of blindness.

Perhaps it was my upbringing, this aversion to open acknowledgment of advantage. But I'd never thought all that much about my own attractiveness, except how I might deflect it. My gaslighting tool set included diffident humor, knee-jerk denial, and quick-draw reverse compliments.

I didn't dwell on how my looks affect others. Roya's relentless goosing, however, had its intended result. I found myself alighting on past conversations, incidents, moments—ones I thought I'd forgotten, ones I'd dismissed, ones that'd meant nothing to me at the time. And I'd think: *How dense you've been.*

To this day I'm no doubt still thick with obtuseness. I've only obtained a dim glimmer of perception. Yet it's a comparative breakthrough.

I don't know if there's a way to directly speak to this stuff without skin-crawling vanity. So screw it. I'll risk the grossness.

Roya burrowed into me. By her example I contemplated the burden I imparted to others and the attendant stress I evoked through what she called my "unexamined beauty power," how "the sheer heat of your hotness can be a torment." When she said this, I responded that such a line could be someone else's corny come-on, rather than an indictment. She was unmoved.

As a result, I took myself under evaluation, or at least the public performance of myself—the radius of my effect. I reviewed a lifetime in knowing receipt of crushes, whether flash infatuation or long-carried torch: from the girls and the boys, then the women and the men. Most, by dint of the numbers, were unrequited. Had I been cavalier? Did I exhibit grace?

More broadly, I reflected on the ache of wishing to be desired and the doom of feeling—for whatever reason, valid or not, logical or not—you aren't somehow deserving of it. Roya was insistent that it was nothing less than a "primal grief." She asked me to empathize with the people I knew and, if I could "manage it," the people I didn't, who'd been "warped" by this. My thoughts came to center on one.

I'll call him Dave. He was one of my closest friends across grade school: smarter than me, quicker; funnier too. He possessed, it's factual to say, a more winning personality. Dave set you at ease. He was just a *good dude*. It's also factual to say, as our wiseass buddy Alex once put it behind Dave's back after lacrosse practice in our junior year, that he looked like "a knockoff version of Wes, produced in some third-world country," hampered by mistranslation "and cheap parts."

Dave crushed on several of the girls who crushed on me. We didn't talk about this much. What was I to offer? I did what I could as a wingman. The girls would say they didn't "think of him that way," or whatever. This was high school.

What came back to me, with Roya as catalyst, was what Dave said once, in a rare-for-him occasion of open self-loathing. Or at least open self-loathing he shared with me. It was at the end of yet another lake-house party, prompted by yet another soft rejection—someone, if memory serves, named Alison. I was dusting him off, joking it was only now early on a Sunday morning of a three-day weekend, and more tenderly, she didn't deserve him anyway. Dave was uninterested in the ministrations and told me so.

"You're the last person I want a pep talk from," he said, before apologizing. I didn't know how to respond, so I let silence dilate between us as we sat on a pair of Adirondack chairs under a full moon, the mist drifting. Dave exhaled, long and slow, then chuckled. "To be Wes the Blessed. What a life."

Let's not be mistaken. I've known longings. How they enrage, plague, decimate. I've hungered for what's been, in the end, out of my reach—a successful screenwriting career, a viable marriage. And despite my evident allure, I too am familiar with the experience of amorous interest rebuffed. What Roya showed me was the raw essence of my inheritance, its layers and its crevices. It was the rare gift of clarity.

I visited her at Chino once a week, bearing updates about the progress of my listening tour. In turn, she would at times have received word from interviewees about how things had gone, and we'd compare notes. She also demanded news of the world, and I attempted without success to trade it for gossip about daily prison life, which she was never willing to share beyond the most occasional, florid scraps of dubious validity, 95 percent of the time involving, say, full tampons wielded in spiteful fashion, meant to disabuse me of further inquiry. "Go watch some *Orange Is the New Black*, dork," Roya once said, rolling her eyes.

The sessions had fallen into a productive rhythm and structure. I'd start off by circling back to clarify points I'd better digested since previous visits, often after pouring through the transcriptions and cross-referencing notes. (I have a beyond-anal color-coded system that I won't go into here.) Then we'd push on toward new frontiers.

By the time I was wrapping up the listening tour, I had more than enough material to begin composing passages of the initial chapters of the book, which would concern her early years. What was key was capturing some sense of her voice and perspective and then transmuting it into something else—something more palatable. She was the first to express that an unfiltered window into her soul wasn't for the best. "This isn't an exercise in unadorned realness," she said. "Besides, that's not my brand, right?" Roya chuckled. "My brand is, uh, *adjusted* realness."

So the previous week, as I readied to leave, I pulled a manila envelope out of my satchel with the printouts. "For your review," I said. It'd been a surprise. I hadn't previously told her a delivery would be imminent.

The reason was that I didn't want the weight of its production and reception hanging over us. I knew she'd have insisted upon reading it right away if I were to have handed it over any earlier during our session, and responded in an unnecessarily agitated state, with embryonic takes—whether she liked the passages or not. We also wouldn't have gotten any other work done that day. Instead, I'd chucked the grenade as she headed back to her bunk. I rode off out of town while she absorbed the impact.

A few days later, during a short call, she told me that while she didn't appreciate "being Pearl Harbored on this," she'd come to grasp my intent, which had forced her to simmer. Roya went on, informing me, "I like where we're going." Still, "I've got notes."

So, when we convened the next time out, the passages loomed. She'd marked them in red ink, grasping them in hand as she trod into the meeting room, making sure I caught an eyeful of the bloodied pages before placing them on the table upside down, a later course.

First there was a related matter to address. Roya had an idea. She'd decided, after I'd spoken to Adriana and Josefina Vasquez, that she wanted me to interview a sizable number of the patients who'd received her fraudulently billed services to render in short vignettes their lives before and after the procedures. "I don't want cheesy 'Dr. Delshad changed my world' testimonials," she said, adding, "It's like, you know, 'show, don't tell.' We'd need to get them talking about *how* their existence is different now, the little things."

Roya explained she was a fan of the popular online series *Humans of New York*—known for its affecting reportage of everyday people's inner lives via lengthy quotes coupled with empathetic portraits—and believed her former patients should serve as interstitial stories to better buttress and illuminate her own. As she envisioned it, similar vignettes would run between her chapters in the planned memoir, alongside before/after pictures she still had access to as well as appropriately understated glamour shots.

"We'll have the publisher foot the bill," she explained with confidence of the new portraiture, as though she had this already locked down—that her former patients would be willing to participate in this endeavor and her future publisher willing to fund it. "I'm sure I can get enough of them to show up on one or two weekend days in some rented studio in downtown LA. We can do it once I'm released."

She claimed she'd handle all the producing duties, including talent wrangling. I didn't want to get started on her qualifications, or lack thereof, as a booker—a tough job, I knew, from my years in the groves of glossy media.

Instead, I expressed misgivings about how this could backfire. How trotting out a cadre of largely Hispanic lower-income women each allotted a comparative instant to speak about their lives—as a sob-sister chorus and ad hoc defense force to their far wealthier sole savior who'd be hogging the main stage to restore her reputation—wasn't Roya's best look. But she insisted she'd already "thought a lot about it," had discussed it with several friends and exes "of color" whom she trusted, and that it was "all about the execution, like anything." Case closed.

While I thought it was problematic, I didn't mind playing Studs Terkel for a couple of days, especially since I was assured my fee would be adjusted, and it was. She also persuaded me by her other argument: The archipelago of mini photo essays between her chapters would allow the memoir itself to be shorter, which, after reading my yet-to-be-discussed initial passages, she was insistent on. When I remarked, while sighing on the inside, that the book might need to be published in a format more befitting a coffee-table book, given the newly dominant weight of imagery relative to text, she responded, "Great!"

"This needs to be a quick read—a *beach* read, an *airport kiosk* read," she said, her furrowed brows all-business. "I *know* my demo, Wes. It's people who watch a lot of TV and buy self-help and chatty, self-effacing personal-essay collections. They'll have a glass of wine in their hands while they're reading this. They really want a good cry even if they don't know it. And the pictures and the vignettes will provide a nice, needed break from me." She added with a laugh, "I mean, if I wasn't me, I'm pretty certain I'd only be able to tolerate me in small doses."

I considered this. "The sugar to help the medical insurance fraud go down?"

I'd meant to goose her, but she blew past it. "This memoir needs to be an instrument and catalyst of inspiration. It's got a utilitarian purpose—to make the world a better place. That's the service angle. The people who'll be reading this thing, the ones who've been following my situation and mostly casting judgment: Let's be frank, it's women like me, not women like the ones who got the surgeries. They need to see themselves not just in my shoes but my patients' shoes."

After a break for commissary-derived granola bars and Jolly Ranchers, we reconvened to discuss the passages. As she either unselfconsciously or entirely consciously propelled a watermelon Jolly Rancher around in her mouth—bulging from cheek to cheek, clattering against her teeth, lassoed by her tongue—Roya registered, point by point, her precise thoughts on the sampling of material I'd left with her. She was considerate enough to start by praising things she liked. There was the rather folksy-charming voice I'd begun to conjure. ("I'd actually want to hang out with me.") There was the briskness of pace. ("No lie, I'm the kind of reader who bores easily—even if it's the passionately told story of my own life."). There was the seeming ease with her feminine perspective. ("I didn't know you were a cross-dresser, Wes.") And there was a sense of humor that resembled her own. But not too closely, for everyone's sake. ("It's like if you tweaked my DNA to be eighty-five percent less of a cunt.")

Generally, Roya explained in approval, "my inner life has been given the glam-squad treatment: It's more presentable." I asked if she was sure she didn't want to be *less* presentable and truer to her genuine self in all its unruliness. The now-diminished Jolly Rancher came to a halt between her molars. Then it shattered. "I know who I am, the real me: marginally likable at best. Even in your optimal possible light, I'm . . . a lot. Do me all the favors I can get."

She displayed zero angst, only serenity. This was the last time I would question her certitude. She wanted me to be the nonconflicted plastic surgeon of her personality.

So anyway, that was the praise. Roya's line-by-line critique consisted of bracketing text she wasn't enthused about alongside the letter *D*, for *dull*; circling words she thought were "poncey"; and crossing out sections she believed "didn't get us anywhere." I was impressed by the dyspeptic rigor. She'd missed another calling as a grizzled newspaper editor out of central casting, replete with green eyeshade.

Then there were her "larger concerns": issues of fact, interpretation, inclusion, or omission. I'd submitted three passages, each less than a thousand words. They all were returned to me with one or more points of such disputation.

Some were minor, and not my fault. Exhibit A: I'd rendered a scene from a middle school dance at which Roya's crush, Raj, had asked her sweet, shy best friend, Tina, to dance instead. She'd relayed the anecdote with Toni Braxton singing her chart-topping "You're Makin' Me High." I was privately kind of scandalized that the DJ was allowed to play a song whose blunt lyrics begin with masturbation. But I figured I'd been a sheltered kid in straitlaced Pennsylvania, and hey, it was Beverly Hills.

Turns out, on further reflection, Roya realized she'd mixed up her 1996 R&B hits. It'd been Braxton's far more G-rated—and conveniently, far more lovesick-appropriate—ballad "Un-Break My Heart" that had scored her adolescent despair.

Other issues were weightier. In one instance, I'd portrayed an awful moment at the Beverly Hills surgical practice she'd worked at prior to establishing her own shop. A woman had jumped to her death from the rooftop of a neighboring building. They later learned she'd been recovering following a facelift performed by a prominent physician.

Roya and her colleagues watched it all happen from their office suite. She'd told me of an evocative, detailed recurring dream—perhaps better classified as a nightmare—in which, through mutual tears, she'd successfully talked the woman from the ledge. I thought this spoke to her deep empathy for patients writ large, as well as served as a revealing window into her subconscious, and elected to portray it.

She didn't think it was a good idea and enumerated a few valid points for excising it. Foremost, her fantasy was oblivious to the reality of the event, which would've obviated any reasoned conversation on that rooftop. To her mind, rendering such a dialogue, even framed as blamelessly imagined, "isn't fair to her loved ones."

Roya also rightly felt that anyone who tells the story of their own dream, no matter its legitimacy, in a context under which the audience isn't their parent, sibling, or significant other, is prima facie annoying. Ergo, relaying an anecdote in which she's positioned "as some sort of redeemer, especially when I didn't actually do anything," is bound to backfire. "If you're already worried, I suppose understandably, that I'm going to come across as having an unappealing savior complex—which, by the way, all doctors do; it's a known occupational hazard, OK?—this isn't going to help," she said.

In another case, she vetoed an aside to an anecdote of pubescence. It pertained to how her mother, Julie, once caught her as an insecure preteen posing nude in the mirror. Specifically, in the formal pose of the statue of Venus at the Getty Villa in Malibu. While after the run-in, Julie had said all the right mollifying things to defuse the embarrassment and lift her daughter's fragile self-worth, Roya had overheard her days later, on the phone with a friend, making a lightly jesting comment about the situation. The punch line of which was referring to Roya as "the goddess of awkwardness."

Roya, at that very moment the most delicate of blossoming flowers, was privately "flattened" for months. She never told her mother why. In hindsight, Roya explained to me, she understands that Julie hadn't been cruel; merely enjoying, as a parent is wont to do, a moment of the absurd. Yet at the time the idea that her mother—her everlasting bulwark, who always said and did the right thing—would joke about "something like that," and do it after so tenderly ministering to her, felt like a fathomless betrayal. It in fact sent her spiraling to her single, brief flirtation with self-harm. She grazed a wrist with a steak knife: "It was never more than a scratch."

I authored that story. Roya, seeing it in writing, nixed it. "The idea that I was so shattered by something so trivial she'd said in confidence decades ago to someone else, and that I came so close to seriously hurting myself over it, and that I never told her about any of it then or—even worse—since . . . for her to read that, it would devastate her," she reasoned, her voice soft. "It might be illuminating, somehow, I guess. It's just not worth it. She worked her ass off to be a good mom. I'm not going to gift her with a regret she didn't even know she was supposed to have."

Roya had a few other general clarifications, which she ticked off from her notebook. For one, she felt the need to inform me she was aware that "below-average and average-looking" women can and do get hit on all the time. For another, she wanted to underline, if she "hadn't already," that all sorts of nonsexual benefits accrue to beautiful people, from employment to friendship to common courtesy. "The world is just a nicer place to be when you're a pretty person," she said. I didn't challenge her with her own sister's testimony to me.

I took this occasion to float a pair of questions I'd been curious about. The first was theoretical: If Roya's plastic surgery utopia were achieved, wouldn't there be nobody left to envy, and therefore no satisfaction? "It's the inverse," she scoffed. "This isn't about jealousy or spite. It's about wanting and craving and fulfillment and pride."

I'd also been pondering why she'd exhibited so little seeming interest in the attractiveness concerns of boys and men. Didn't her empathy extend to them? They have their own challenges: distinct, nuanced, incalculable, full of pain and promise.

Roya took this in. "They do," she said. "You're right. They're vast and underconsidered; not taken seriously enough." She allowed a moment for our agreement to take root. "It's just not my mission, which is already expansive to its detriment."

Even so, I wondered whether venturing more of a big-tent approach, within the rhetorical frame of her book, could win even further converts to her cause. After all, she'd told me, her goal was to build "a movement of understanding." Why not attempt to speak to the hearts and minds of the other half of the population while she was at it?

She weighed this, too, explaining with no small amount of fury that the male medical establishment had a history of "gender-based prioritization" in various scientific advancements, "especially those at the nexus of sexuality and desire." Take the advent of impotency pills, which she noted arrived on the market decades ago. "Meanwhile, just as one example, all we have for IUD insertions, which can be *insanely painful*, is some fucking numbing gel and, if we're lucky, an over-the-counter-strength painkiller after the fact," Roya nearly spat. She continued, "You'll excuse me if, just this once in the annals of comparative sociomedical progress, it might be ladies first."

We wrapped business early for the day and filled out the rest of our time together shooting the shit. I told Roya about a brief visit home to Pennsylvania several days earlier to see my family. I'd found myself on my eldest brother's suburban living room sofa, on the receiving end of an enthusiastic and knowledgeable lecture from my fourteen-year-old niece, Sarah, about the supreme coolness of the latest phone app that she and her friends were all obsessed with. This one rendered a custom-augmented version of your face in high-definition clarity as you spoke on video chat. Zap that zit. Makeup automatically applied. Add extensions. It wasn't meant to be cartoonish. It was "totally realistic."

Tap to reduce baby fat. Smooth out wrinkles. Straighten teeth. Switch the color of your eyes. Add a tan. Become paler. Decrease or enhance your forehead or chin or cheekbones or nose with a swipe—or, better yet, allow the algorithm to calculate the ideal shapes and distances. Select photos of celebrities (or, really, anyone) whose features you find aspirational, and the computer modeling will do the work of morphing your own appearance toward them. Users create one or more facial "presets" and click them, as if donning a veil, when they enter a conversation.

Later, I asked my brother and sister-in-law what they thought of the technology—and why they allowed their daughter to use it. They gave me weary looks, offering little except resignation. "We'd fight it," my sister-in-law said, "but what is there to fight, really? You can't hide from a future that's already here."

I was less accepting. Perhaps it was my childless naivete showing, but this registered to me as a significant acceleration toward dystopia. I felt queasy while my niece, who to my understanding was no victim of body dysmorphia, explained exactly how she'd airbrushed herself. A consolation to her old-fashioned uncle: Sarah confessed that, as in real life, her parents wouldn't let her wear certain "provocative" lipstick and eye shadow, and she'd also been denied the ability to plump her lips to create the bee-stung quality she desired.

Soon she'd turned her attention to me, downloading the app to my phone and showing me how to create a preset of my own. With little ado, first my teeth were whitened and then my crow's-feet were removed as her finger hovered, zoomed, swiped, pinched, clicked. A bit more fussing relieved me of the bags under my eyes. In less than a minute I looked a decade younger. I was startled, but Sarah was blasé about the magic, expressionless as she reviewed her handiwork, only pausing to wordlessly amp up my "glow," some admixture of hard-to-pin-down generalized coloring and flush that made it appear as though I'd had a good workout that morning instead of being in the midst of recovering from a red-eye cross-country flight.

In that moment, right after she'd walked out of the room to fetch a snack, I was at once mortalized and immortalized, humbled and turned near-invincible. There was a test mode where you could examine your altered nature, blinking in the funhouse mirror. I leaned in close and held my gaze.

In the days that followed I found myself stealing away, returning to the view in private wonder. You also were able to manipulate your hands and fingers, as well as your neck. I discovered that the app wasn't only a digital fountain of youth and beauty. You could, in theory, go gray and add wrinkles and sunspots and weight. It was just that, according to articles I read about the app, so far, the proportion of people who did so, except for those venturing into costume-party irony or avant-gardism or both, was small. "Our data is telling us that ugly and old are niche, marginal interests," one of the cofounders explained.

Another offering allowed you to transition your features along the gender spectrum, masculine to feminine and back again. The whole thing was a giant trip: summoning the identical twin of the opposite sex you never had. I couldn't conceive of encountering such wizardry before I'd established a firm sense of who I was.

The app's developers also said they were working on similarly credible, nuanced transformations for the whole body, which would be part of a premium-priced product. When I got to this part, Roya picked up on the unspoken business model: desire and its discontents. "Pixelated penis pumping," she mused, impressed by the nascent bonanza. "It'll be pervasive, inescapable fraud."

She thought more about it. "It'll just end up either killing off actual sex, since chicks are bound to be disappointed by the real thing, and guys will know it, or else it'll explode the phalloplasty market. Which would be amazing since phalloplasty recovery is *painful*, or so I've heard."

Not having taken the bait, Roya brought up, before I could—because I'd been thinking about it—her own online false-representation swindle. The one in which as a teenager more than two decades earlier she'd taken suggestive pictures of Dahlia and sent them to men she was flirting with. She observed that if she'd had this app then, she wouldn't have taken Dahlia's intimate imagery. Roya also said, longingly, "I lived in my imagination. I knew exactly who I'd be. It took so long to get there, and it was very hard. To think that others—people that I loved and people that loved me and that I wanted to love me—could see me as I'd wanted to be seen back then? And that I'd be able to *see them seeing me*? And maybe even *understand that me*?" She grew teary and then quiet before she spoke again. "It would've been easier."

When I experimented with the app on my own in Pennsylvania, I toggled toward decay, flinching as I shriveled and warped, age's brutal assault time-lapsed to seconds. I stared death in my face. Then I scrolled along another axis less traveled by: the journey that leads to ugly and begins with a nearly immediate stop at average looking—and therefore invisible. My musculature and bone structure had begun to contort, the slightest asymmetries blossoming. What Roya had called my "stunning" hotness melted away. I stared this death in my face too.

Amid a fight and occasionally to start one, my ex-wife liked to contend that my looks had limited my capacity for maturation. She meant this as an insult but also an assessment of tragedy. That being handsome in the extreme had at times been a crutch and a shield against misfortune, as well as an undue propellant on the long path to contentment. She once compared the situation to how celebrities lose touch with the normal arc of personal development the very moment that fame hits. Maybe she had a point.

Since my return from Pennsylvania, I'd become obsessed with the app, its portals to other dimensions. I kept peeking, unstoppably curious. Yet I hadn't taken it out of test mode to see what friends, family, colleagues, ex-lovers, and strangers might think of these other versions of me. I wasn't brave enough. I'd never had to be. Not like Roya.

"It would've been easier," I agreed, taking her hand in mine, taking in the dream girl's face, the one she'd dreamed. "I'm sorry it wasn't."

She smiled. We'd never touched beyond the brief initial handshake when we first met. There was a security camera watching us and the guard positioned outside the door. Roya didn't let go, even though sustained contact was an automatic penitentiary infraction that would tack more time on to her dwindling sentence and end our sessions.

I pulled away. "Let's be careful," I said. "You only have five weeks left."

She leaned forward. "About that. So, I know where I'm headed, at least for the first month after I'm out." Roya explained that her USC mentor, Dr. Collins, had been by during regular visitors' hours three days prior and offered to lend her the key to the vacation cabin that she and her wife owned along the scenic coast of Mendocino County, a few hours north of San Francisco. "She said it's a good place for thinking and planning. I told her I had plenty of time in here to do both. She said, 'Then just enjoy the view.'"

I offered that it sounded wonderful. "It does, doesn't it?" Roya said, making a show of the dramatic pause, turning it over in her head, already there, on a vertiginous foggy hillside above the thrashing sea. "I'm glad you agree, because you're going to be there with me."

I shuffled through all the reasons why this was, as I termed it, inappropriate. The two most important being that Roya deserved true alone time and that she really ought to maintain a professional distance from me, at least until we completed our endeavor.

After allowing me the litany, she responded in an even tone, serene: "Wes, I'm going to fuck your face, repeatedly. You should know that by now. Among other activities, of course, sexual and otherwise—and between bouts of you churning out pages of this memoir for my review at a steady pace." She let her studied poise ease in the direction of a smirk. It was very Roya to frame an amorous invitation as a sadistic power play. "You should also know I'm a screamer. A cabin in the middle of several wooded acres is a good idea. Highly appropriate."

What was there to say to this? Roya went on, "You want to tell the story of my life and work, which is the story of my body? Then *know it.*"

TROUBLE

The California Bureau of Investigation raid on my office was low-key. I never saw a gun. There were no raised voices or burly agents leading the charge. A pair of polite if no-nonsense women in vests, who looked like moms that ran track, met with me in the waiting room while the rest of their team initially hung back by the elevator bank.

For the first of many occasions, time slowed. Sonya, wide-eyed and perplexed, peeked her head into my office suite just after I'd arrived in the morning, a few minutes before we were expecting our first patient of the day, and said, "There are some people out front who say they need to speak with you. They say they're with the, uh, government?"

The lead detective, pale and ponytailed in an unmarked dark baseball cap, spoke first. She had an everywoman's corn-fed Anglo features that I imagined were ideal for undercover work, either dulled toward erasure or dolled up to entice. "May we talk?" she said, holding a trifolded sheaf of papers I would soon learn was a search warrant.

I'm now an ex-con. But at that moment I was, or believed myself to be, foremost a good girl, a teacher's pet emeritus, an anxious lifelong follower of rules who operated safely inside them. Someone whose worst documented infraction against the law had been a lane-change violation and some parking tickets. So my instinct, when I realized what was happening—that I was in trouble, big-time—was to obey. I said that I was happy to cooperate, and that my staff could assist. They explained that we all needed to stand aside while they executed their warrant.

I stood shaking against the reception counter. Sonya, Narine, and Jenny were silent beside me. The CBI team filed into the office with their briefcases. The second lead detective approached. She laid a steadying hand on my arm and explained that it might be wise to consider sending my employees home for the day. Although they'd need to "retain your bookkeeper, who we are hoping can assist us." Then she added, locking eyes, as much in empathy as in practicality, "Now's the time to call an attorney."

I'd subsequently learn that I'd been scrutinized for many months. First, one insurance company's investigations unit noticed that something was rather flagrantly up. Then that one cross-checked information with the others and made sure, in collaborative fashion, to catch me even more red-handed in what would come to be known as my "discrepancies."

They did this by, in certain instances, sending several claims back to me to verify and further elaborate on information concerning patients' histories. I would then again directly sign off on them. In other instances, during recorded phone calls, I answered what turned out to be incriminating questions meant to clear up minor inconsistencies of submitted case narratives. I remember nothing special of any of these inquiries into my "special cases," as Jenny and I referred to them. Which goes to show how blind I'd become to the seriousness of what was going on, the danger I'd put myself in.

Finally, the private insurers complained to—excuse me, *tipped off*—a state-level fraud inspection unit. The government discovered my mistakes involving the public health plans. At that point the full weight of The Man mobilized to take down this particular woman.

This will sound stupid, and that's because it's a shining example of human stupidity, but it was only when the evidence the insurers had amassed was shown to me days later that it all truly clicked. The amount that I'd done wrong, how far afield I'd strayed, what deep shit I was in. I don't know whether my ego had been sleepwalking me through a ton of denial for more than a year or I just hadn't thought enough about what I'd gotten myself into (maybe both). However, seeing this inarguable paperwork brought to bear by unknown forces arrayed against me, I was at last wide-awake.

I called Fred, who put my mom on speakerphone. They headed over from Manhattan Beach, arriving an hour later while the raid was still ongoing, right around when my first lawyer showed up. It was Fred's old friend Arthur Coefield, a name partner in a criminal defense group whose nearby Century City office was located a few floors beneath the civil litigation firm where my parents met.

Given the circumstances, I was fortunate. My mom was supportive, saying and doing all the right things. Among her first words upon embracing me at my temporary command station, Brighton Coffee Shop, as I finally succumbed to a full meltdown: "You've been through worse. You'll get through this."

It was remarkable, as though she'd read a book about what to do in the event your child finds herself in legal peril with the government. In the weeks that followed, I kept waiting for a deserved lecture about the reckless foolishness of my behavior, until it at last sank in that my behavior had been so out-of-bounds egregious it'd transcended her instinct or need to lecture me about it. Fred, meanwhile, was all action and pragmatism and composure during the subsequent legal process, start to finish. Of course, I was lucky to begin with to have a stepdad who was a retired attorney and therefore was tennis buddies with the likes of Arthur, able to summon him at a moment's notice.

I wasn't arrested on the day of the raid. Instead, I was informed by the California Department of Justice through Arthur that I was going to be the target of an indictment, which he then clarified meant that there would be sufficient evidence to charge. Arthur, back at his office with me late that afternoon, in turn noted that there was nobody for me to cooperate against and therefore explained, in the sweetest, kindliest way possible—the way you inform your tennis buddy's stepdaughter when your tennis buddy and his wife are also seated beside her in the room—that I was fucked. Or, as he put it, "cooked." Back at the coffee shop I'd already confessed to them all within minutes of their appearance that I was *guilty, guilty, guilty.*

Arthur, himself semiretired, advised me to get in front of the situation to the best of my ability by straightaway offering to plea. He soon handed off my case to a quite handsome and charming junior partner, in possession of a toothpaste smile, who in other circumstances—me not being his client, or him not already being taken, or this not being reality and instead being one of those romance-laden David E. Kelley legal dramas—might have ended up as my lover. Instead, this knight in designer-suit armor negotiated the terms of my surrender.

At this point, it should be noted that prosecutors mostly *don't even bother* with cases in the private sector where the loss is valued at under $1 million. Mine was, ahem, just shy of seven figures. It's considered small-fry bullshit. Not worth the departmental investment. The thinking is, *Leave it to the well-financed corporate insurers to sue the alleged reprobate in civil court until the defendant is ruined. That'll show 'em.*

However, I'd primarily defrauded government programs. It didn't matter that this was my first offense or that I profusely apologized or that I was offering to plea. I was fucked. End of story.

I had next to no interaction with the prosecutor—who, I will note in all professional objectivity, had the sagging jowls of a woman a decade older than she was. Go ahead, call it bitchery, but I'm convinced this salient fact played at least some crucial role in her outlook toward me. After all, the sheer size of the meant-to-be-distracting pearls strung around her neck told me she could, if she were so inclined, afford to tap my specialty to rid herself of them.

While I understand the prosecutor's job was to fight against me for "the people," I couldn't help but interpret her approach as lacking in any meaningful generosity of spirit. My attorney took pains to explain during a session at her office exactly where I was coming from, how I'd come to do what I did. Yes, wrong as it was. The prosecutor, in other words, was on the receiving end of what I'm sharing here now. An abbreviated version, but it was substantial enough to understand the complexities of the situation.

Her response was to mouth platitudes about taking responsibility for one's actions and to imply that my lawyer had perhaps been taken in by my womanly charm, with the implication that she was immune. I wound up agreeing to twenty-five months in prison, which meant with good behavior I'd be out under supervised release in twenty.

I posted my $200,000 bail and was soon staying, for the clock-ticking nine weeks until I would begin serving my term, in the guest room at my mom and Fred's place. The judge knew I wasn't a flight risk. I wasn't part of any suspected organized criminal activity. I didn't possess any foreign passports. And to my embarrassment, as I like to consider myself something of a cosmopolitan, I hadn't spent—even accounting for my Renew journeys with Dr. Collins—what he characterized as "any significant amount of time" living abroad.

I experienced every aspect, every *single* aspect, of the government's processing of my demise from an absurdist remove, in the same scary-but-surreal way, faintly comic. The CBI raiding my office, being cuffed and having my rights read to me, the taking of my mug shot and fingerprints during booking, the theatrics of going before the judge in the courtroom. These were activities you talked with friends about or idly thought about or watched movies or TV shows about. These were not things that would ever involve you. My overriding thought at each of these moments was always the same dumb, amazed thing. It was the thought I had when I finally had sex for the first time . . .

This is actually happening right now. This. Is. Happening. Right. Now. Holy. Fucking. Shit. This is my real life!

What played out far more quickly than the government's processing of my demise was the related one taking place out in the world. My attorneys never allowed me to speak with the media, as anything I said could affect my case. And aside from an initial short, perfunctory statement about how "Dr. Delshad looks forward to addressing this matter," they also gagged themselves, refusing to engage except to confirm or deny things off the record.

I don't know who tipped whom off, but what happened was all over the place, internationally, the next day. It was startling just how viral the whole thing became, and how quickly. My mess, anything but masterminded, was packaged as a perfect gem of shrewd scandal. Still, even amid fresh shock, I can't claim not to have understood the interest. After all, given my own lowbrow reading proclivities, *I* would have clicked on an online story headlined, in just one emblematic instance, "HOLLYWOOD ROBIN HOOD: Govt. Raids Office of Hot Doc Who Grifts Plastic Surgery Gifts to Poor Patients." Particularly since the publication was astute enough to juxtapose the alleged objectionable behavior with a flattering, and therefore extra-infuriating, headshot of its villainess-subject. (The photo had been taken from my business website.)

Based on the time stamps of the online stories, a couple of early reports served as press bulletins for other outlets to pick up. As the first day wore on, they multiplied throughout the media, replicated and expanded, abbreviated and distorted. You could also tell because a couple of identical minor factual errors, later updated in the initial dispatches, materialized again elsewhere in several of the follow-ups.

It blew up to the extent that multiple late-night show hosts made hacky monologue zingers about the situation, which was a bummer. If you're going to be lampooned on national TV, you at least want the joke at your expense to land, right?

It's strange. While I romanticized gorgeousness as a kid, I never much fantasized about fame. Now here I was, infamous in a flash, the star of my very own photo-driven post on a highly trafficked, celebrity-oriented, pseudonymously bylined gossip website, where pictures filched from my Facebook and Instagram accounts were interspersed with a gleefully mean-spirited write-up in which I was referred to as "the 9021-ho."

Honestly, though, I was so consumed in real time with the emotional, legal, and financial realities of the fiasco itself that I didn't think much about the public response until later. You know, when I had plenty of restless, jobless energy to expend in that Manhattan Beach condo on, say, Googling myself. I marveled at the sprawling catastrophe that had befallen a self-directed search query. It had previously yielded nothing more than anodyne references to educational and professional accomplishments.

Now the results were so marred it was hilarious. We're talking back to the *seventh* page. Who even clicks that far?

Yet when I did get to the public response, I went deep. I became a dedicated scholar, curiosity toxically mixed with obsession and boredom, reading and watching everything, dusting off every last comment, looking under the rock of every last person, anonymous or otherwise, who bothered to contribute.

There were levels to it. The news articles, dry and factual (or, in some cases, not entirely factual), were of limited interest. What I was into was the bloom of ego-stoking hot takes, the furious and reflective and wry essays on women's-content websites assessing and digesting my actions. This demographic had reacted to what I'd done, ill-considered as it may have been, as a purposeful cultural provocation. Which was kind of awesome.

Some of these were hostile, putting me on blast. This was fine but not instructive, since nobody could hate me better than I could hate myself at that point. The defenses of my behavior, though, were not just comforting but illuminating. I hadn't thought of myself as a modern-day folk hero. Yet that's how I was embraced in many circles, principally on social media by those younger and more politically alert than me. My transgression was contextualized, to my gratification, as a noble swindle in a society that's devolved into a far more egregious, near-total culture of scamming.

I should also admit I was then largely ignorant of the socioeconomic undercurrents at play. These women informed the foundation of my thinking about what transpired—along with why it matters. Apparently, I was a “clandestine Marxist radical operating deep inside the late-capitalist patriarchal slave state.” *Fuck, yes.* Tell me more, adjunct professor!

Most fascinating to me were the comments in response to the articles and the commenters themselves. At first the freewheeling, implacable carnival of judgment stung. Who were these people who didn’t know me to bully me about my mistake? To casually amuse each other at my expense? To bloodlessly assess my appearance (all right, mostly positively) even though they should’ve been aware I’d sooner or later come across what they wrote? Were *they* all so perfect? Please.

There were moments when I wanted to create aliases and fight back undercover on my own behalf, conjuring a shadow army of wittily incisive defenders. Those moments were followed by the recognition that nothing could be more abject an endeavor. At some point, after scrolling through enough of the sheer volume of accumulated opinion—a small fortune of strangers’ two cents, spanning from the damning to the praising—it all fizzed out to noise, and I was OK.

There wasn’t anything about it that was personal, even if my instinctive response was to construe it that way. I was mild entertainment in the form of a news story. I’d become nothing more than a useful distraction from humanity’s perpetual baseline boredom. Somehow this calmed me.

This distraction could be anyone or anything else, and right now it just so happened to be me. I imagined myself as the lioness on the other side of the glass in a zoo enclosure, gazing back with indifference at the crowd’s fleeting if forceful attention, in full knowledge that this horde would soon shuffle on, braying among themselves at the next exhibit.

These people, some hidden behind screen names and avatars, others anchored to their words through Facebook accounts, were interesting to me less for what they argued—there were only so many ways to catalog approval or disapproval—than for who they were. Occasionally they’d frame banal insight through anecdote, their own or loved ones’ experiences with (or desires for or regrets about) plastic surgery coloring their views. “Sometimes I think my mama might’ve finally had the conviction to leave my POS father if she’d only had the money to get that nose job—or better yet not settled for him in the first place," HerRoyalThighness reflected. "It would've solved multiple problems, come to think of it: I wouldn't be here, loathing my own body all of these years!!" More than anything, I sensed familiarity. These could've been outtakes from my own consultations.

I'd click through the pictures in their social media accounts, homing in on their faces, studying their features, in most cases fate's bestowment and in the remainder the adjusted work of their free will. What tugged at me was a pattern I registered across this demographic matrix. Again and again and again, on a trip to Lisbon or in a backyard outside Denver or at a prom in Georgia, I'd see them—the doubtful smiles.

Whether they'd spoken well or ill of me, no matter the objective attractiveness of their features, these women had something in common. It had to do with reciprocal sexual desire. They didn't trust that their faces merited a smile in return. I knew this, *truly* knew it, could read it in the confession of their eyes, because those doubtful smiles were once my own.

It was a crushing realization. My career was wrecked. My medical license was soon to be revoked. I'd no longer be able to utilize my skills to do my part to combat that aching uncertainty inside so many.

Just as crushing to realize was that for all the talk about me by strangers online in the days and weeks that followed the raid, I was surprised by how few friends and colleagues reached out to me. I mean, in a substantive way. Yes, there was some limited if sincere hope-you're-doing-OK stuff, but overall, it came across as arm's-length. Even if they were all waiting to find out if indeed I was a crook, it wasn't like I stood accused of a *violent crime*. I'd, uh, misguidedly "robbed" insurance companies to help poor people! I was *the Robin Hood of Hollywood*! Sheesh.

It was all super isolating. This wasn't helped by the fact that I didn't have much to do except find ways to divert myself from the dread of the countdown until the day I was set to self-surrender, which I'd moved up as close as possible, wanting to get started with my sentence so I could, well, get it finished. Say what one will about the existential despair of prison life—and don't worry, I'm almost there—the clear-eyed, expectant wait for it is its own unique wretchedness, a permanent curdling in the stomach.

I was restricted from assisting in any way with the dissolution of my practice. This included placing my patients with other surgeons, as well as random stuff like off-loading furniture, filing bankruptcy paperwork, and shredding client files the government acknowledged had no bearing on its case. Which were, I will note, nearly all of them.

My mom, the retired office manager, couldn't have been more suited to this task. She undertook it with a grim grace that was capped when she presented me with a big cardboard box of mementos. I threw most of them away. But I did keep, among other key artifacts, my framed diplomas (can't take those away from me, bitches!), as well as my monogrammed white coats and a cute snapshot with Sonya and Narine, in which the three of us strike the *Charlie's Angels* pose.

With a ton of free time, I binged TV shows, saw a psychiatrist, worked out at the suggestion of my prison consultant, and hooked up with a series of surfer bros and volleyball bros and other assorted local Manhattan Beach bros sourced through several dating apps pretty much indiscriminately and with an apocalyptic despondency. This was what I talked about twice a week with the shrink, to her mild weariness, since I wasn't much interested in plumbing the more substantive depths that may have led to my lawbreaking. Always, I'd like to add, the hookups occurred at the dudes' places: Mom, Fred—if you're reading this chapter, even though I *specifically warned you not to*—I swear I never took even one of them back to my room at the condo.

My attorney recommended the prison consultant, herself a grandmotherly former white-collar inmate at Chino. Her alumni status was why the consultancy paired me with her. She'd done five years for tax evasion. Nominally her insider's scoop was to acclimate me to the idea of going there, since my fear was colossal. I think she helped alleviate it a bit, although it's hard to say given the dosage of Ativan I was on. Aside from a lecture on the subtleties of body language miscommunication (which boils down to "don't do anything that could be interpreted as disrespecting anyone"), her key practical suggestion was that I should complete a more advanced self-defense class than the short seminar I attended in high school to combat sexual assault. I did. The main takeaway, though, was that she thought I was "blessed, all things considered." Unlike many other women in custody there, I didn't have children that I'd be "constantly and dizzyingly" feeling guilty about.

The other thing I did is I hung out alone at the empty beach on weekday afternoons. It was already deep into autumn and never warm or blue skies enough to be dressed as I insisted, which was in an exuberant bikini, a floppy hat, and oversize sunglasses. It was full goose bumps and shivers amid the wind gusts and squawking gulls even before my arrival on the sand, where I'd roll out my multicolored towel and plant my likewise-multicolored umbrella. It was silly to the point of preposterousness, and yet I kept doing it. I was so hardheaded and embarrassed about it all that I didn't even bring it up to the expensive therapist I was seeing.

And it gets worse. Knowing I was going to be cold, instead of bringing a sweatshirt or responding in some other reasonable manner, I decided to keep warm by busying myself with the most bizarre activity for an adult woman. I started, with frenzied energy, *digging holes.*

Yeah, holes, in the sand, like a child. They were deep and wide enough to stand in without crouching and still be unable to see over the top. For real: probably like twenty of these in total. I dug them with a plastic shovel-and-bucket set my mom and Fred kept at their place for when his grandkids visited.

On several occasions, lifeguards would drive by on the beach in their LA County pickup trucks. They'd inquire, not in flirtation but rather with a measured I-might-be-dealing-with-a-psycho cadence, just what I was doing, noting a hole that deep and wide was a safety hazard that needed to be filled in right away. To reassure them they were dealing with someone who had their marbles, I replied, "It's probably a metaphor."

Maybe it was. Or maybe, as I'd cheerfully tell the little kids who'd innocently ask me about it as I shoveled away on the beach (the excavation took upward of an hour with those dumb plastic tools), it was "just for fun." Or maybe, as I'd not-so-cheerfully tell the older kids who'd not-so-innocently ask me about it, it was "to curl up and die."

When I finished digging, I'd drape the towel across the top, shading the cavity beneath. The air would be cool, the sand damp, the sound of the waves and the wind hushed. Seated in the lotus position inside, for a moment I'd take off my bandeau top, shoving part of it into my mouth, like a hostage. And then, tears overflowing, I'd scream.

NINE

Those final weeks until Roya's release ticked away, gathering force with the urgency of a held breath. After all my relentless hand-wringing and speechifying about professionalism, she'd undone me anyway.

I busied myself. There were my other, extant freelance journalism projects to focus on, since I figured I'd be zeroed in on the memoir while holed up in the coastal boonies. I also surveyed a few close friends about what I was getting myself into. The responses ranged from *Niiiice* to *I didn't know you also work as a gigolo, Wes; what's your rate?* to *She sounds like a psycho—keep an eye out for the hatchet.*

Julie gave me a knowing look when I stopped by her Manhattan Beach condo again about a week before Roya's release date. I was there to pick up three suitcases of clothes, toiletries, and other items she'd packed at her daughter's request. "Have *fun*," she said, while I loaded my car, stammering about the work to be done. Later that day, Dahlia sent me a text consisting of eggplant and peach emojis, without further elaboration. I didn't respond.

The you-guys-are-totally-gonna-do-it awkwardness coming from them aside, I thought it was strange that the Delshads didn't seem at all bothered that Roya wasn't itching to see her family right after she was sprung. But perhaps there was some mutual psychology to it: that they all needed some time to reacclimate to the idea of her out of lockup.

Roya heading out on an extended getaway with a seemingly nice-enough dude was, maybe, a gradual point of reentry.

After I accepted her cabin summons, Roya herself had been uncharacteristically low-key in our last two meetings at the prison. She didn't speak again about what our time together in Mendocino might hold. Instead, during those final sessions she turned her attention to a topic she had so far avoided: life in prison, her own as well as the lives of her fellow inmates.

It was bleak stuff—loneliness, despair, heartache, boredom, and rage. These were stories of mental health on the brink. Roya wiped away tears after relaying one characteristic anecdote. It was about a woman she knew who'd attempted suicide when she'd learned that her five-year-old son had been beaten nearly to death by her brother-in-law. This guy and his wife, the fellow prisoner's sister, had taken the boy in after she'd gotten caught writing bad checks on behalf of Nuestra Familia. Composing herself, Roya ran an arched foot up my pant leg under the table between us, ruefully snorting, "Boner killer?"

I'd grown used to the long drive east to Chino out there in the Southern California megasprawl, at the edge of San Bernardino County. In good traffic, the commute took more than an hour. In bad, which was most of the time, it was easily twice that. Stop-and-go the whole way. I listened to a lot of Tom Petty during these journeys.

The Wednesday when Roya got out of prison was the first commute I undertook in total darkness, from departure to destination. She was set to be released at six o'clock in the morning. I promised her I'd be there waiting.

Everything about my time with Roya was memorable. It's why I feel compelled to share the experience. Yet this part is a lot more intimate than the rest. So let me switch gears to tell it.

The heat runs high in his car. The defrosters hum. Bob Seger is cued to croon "You'll Accomp'ny Me." He idles before dawn by the curb in the prison parking lot. His eyeline fixes across the decorative gravel to its double doors.

Three minutes past six, an eternal delay, she bursts through them. Her hair, even in the darkness, is as unruly as he's ever known it. For the first time, she's wearing not a baggy jumpsuit but her civilian clothes: the hoodie, T-shirt, sweatpants, and sneakers she arrived in.

He emerges into the chill to greet her, still a distance away. He's imagined the embrace, the kiss, the conversation. "Save it," she shouts, choking up, breaking into a trot, jabbing the air to points beyond. "Let's just get out of here."

They do, but not far. She told him earlier that she wanted to head straight to the cabin ten hours north, "without passing Go." Now that she's in possession of her freedom, there are pressing concerns. She's hungry. And before that she wants "a real shower."

The short drive to Chino's Holiday Inn Express is wordless. Her eyes are closed. Her breathing is metrical, as though to forestall shock. They've yet to touch.

The room is corporate, clean, modern, anonymous. It's blue gray beige. She takes her things out of a suitcase and, without comment, disappears. The water pressure makes its exertions clear through the wall.

A sliver of pale morning breaks through the blackout curtains. He watches the news from the bed and registers none of it. She's steps away. They've spent a good deal of time together, intimate in its way, but none like this. They're still, at root, each other's holograms. Now they are to be, it would seem, each other's humans.

The shower is off, the sink and blow-dryer on. Then there she is, all of her, striding forward. An idealized form made real, nonspecific in its perfected faultlessness. There's a banality in the beautiful.

Before he can speak, she's atop him. Her tongue wishes entry. She expresses appetite and technique, if not passion.

He's still absorbing this—the suddenness of everything, the lack of discussion—when she pulls away. "Scoot down," she says firmly, repositioning his head upward on the pillow. "I have a promise to fulfill."

She envelops him. Her swirling tufts of pubic hair nuzzle his cheeks, reach his chin, graze his eyelids. Warm, sticky wetness flushes his lips. It's overwhelming: the immediacy of the salty-sweetness, the pungency of the scent, the vividness of the sensation, the totality of the act.

She lifts and drops, slightly then heavily. In control of her progression, linear and circular, she works her way over and across and into him. He brings his hands around her bottom, as a reply and as an instinct, even if only to anchor himself. She pulls them away.

Then, with as little segue as the kiss, she's done. She tells him that he can "fuck me now," commanding he hurry up and undress as she turns off the news. While he complies, struck witless by the onslaught, she issues an admonition: "I will be so pissed if you blow your load before I finish."

Already throbbing and covered in her glaze, he blanches. She rolls her eyes, looking back at him as she assumes a doggy-style position and he unwraps a condom. "I've waited twenty months for this," she adds, her tone softening. "Don't be an asshole."

He guides himself into her and sets a rhythm. She's far less verbal than he imagined, aside from the weakest of moans. Just out of prison, he thinks, she's not yet herself. He focuses on her pleasure, a surveyor mapping unexplored territory, hyperalert to infinitesimal fluctuations.

Muscles tense. Skin sweats. Breath exhales. They are in sync as one. In time she finishes, again devoid of audible flourish. Soon after, so does he.

There is no pillow talk, no postcoital embrace. She returns to the bathroom to rinse again. When she's done, she suggests he do the same, and when they pass each other at the sink, she announces: "I want pancakes. And sausage."

At a nearby IHOP, she orders what she desires. Although she'd left the prison in her plain attire, her makeup was fully done, the purposeful glamazon chafing at drab constraints he'd first met. Now, in this banal place, she exists apart from the waitresses and the trucker patrons.

Her designer camisole is tucked into formfitting high-waisted jeans.

Her oversize white sunglasses nestle in the exuberance of her curly mane, shinier and bouncier than he's seen it before. The effect is meant to be lustrous, luscious.

They didn't talk on the ride over to the restaurant. He was still processing and she was letting him. But as he pokes at his scrambled eggs and extra-crispy bacon, he grows annoyed with the silence.

"So, uh, what happened back there?" There's a clear edge to his voice, more than he wanted there to be.

Her eyes dart, po-faced. "We . . . fucked?"

"I'm not your slam bag."

She laughs. "Evidence to the contrary."

He persists, hurt. "Did you even enjoy that? It was hard to tell."

She makes a show of slicing a sausage down its length, then across, to ready a bite. "I'd give it a C, maybe even a C-plus. It wasn't as awkward as I was expecting. Decent starter sex, given the circumstances: my dry-spell nerves and the weird pent-up energy between us and that unexpected retro-macho thing you curveballed me with when you showed up this morning, which *definitely* threw me off." Assessment rendered, she forks and devours the meat with a smirk.

This negging is classic her. Nevertheless, he's been baited. He asks about the retro-macho thing.

She cocks her head. "Seriously?" Her fork is still in the air. Its tines are directed toward him in appraisal, motioning up then down in repetition. "Newly cultivated stubble since the last time I saw you two weeks ago. Bomber jacket out of, I don't know, a Ryan Gosling film. Playing dad-rock ballads in your car. Your car, it turns out, being a—what, a vintage Mustang?" (It's a mint-green 1973 Dodge Challenger with a black vinyl top.) She cracks herself up. "What happened to my favorite clean-cut postprep who'd visit his moll crush in the cooler? Is this like a heritage-aesthetic personal-brand shift or a hand-me-down early midlife crisis?"

She reaches for the syrup dispenser, drizzling her pancakes from on high in loop-de-loops. Her tone rises to comic effect. "You know I love pretense, so I'm not judging. It's just going to take a few more minutes today of getting used to."

He's more naked now than he was in the hotel room. Her delight in calling him out, the accuracy of her unsparing frankness: It leaves him fumbling yet electrified. He gets it, that everything that's transpired since she'd walked out of prison has been an assertion of dominance.

He smiles, fine with it. She can fuck with him; she can fuck him. He knows who he is. Or at least he thinks he does. "Next time," he promises evenly, "will be soon, and I'm going to be calling the shots."

GPS sends them on a route through the desert. The interstate is big rigs. It's bugs on the windshield. Scrub brush runs infinite past the distant hills.

By the time they pass Edwards Air Force Base along the 58 heading west, she's zonked out in the passenger bucket seat, mouth lolled open. He expected this. She told him she hadn't slept at all the previous night and little the week prior, anxious with anticipation of her departure.

He scrubbed the Challenger ahead of the journey. Armor All had wafted from the gleaming vinyl interior. But her fragrance, which she hadn't worn in prison, is stronger. It engulfs the car, citrus and cream and musk. He can see the perfume maker marketing it: *indolence and insolence*. His window cranks open a crack.

She probably thinks someone did the scrubbing for him. Yes, he bought the car because it was cool. He also purchased it in a state of junkyard-worthy disrepair. The seller had been a retired longshoreman in San Pedro.

His inspiration was having read a passed-along copy of *Shop Class as Soulcraft*. He spent three years working on the car. He'll never tell her about this, the tremendous amount of meaning derived from the experience, unless she asks.

As they close in on Bakersfield, she's still totally out. Drool collects in the crook of her shoulder, dampening her camisole. It's endearing. It's hilarious. It's suggestive. He doesn't wake her up.

She'll use him. He's her rebound after a bad breakup with life. Would he even care for something more? She's not, historically, his type. He's never been one for outward messes. The damage he's discovered in the women he's been with is buried far deeper beneath the surface.

Yet since they met, she's exerted an inexorable pull. His occupational interest, her sheer visual splendor, and the singular magnetism of her often-trying temperament don't altogether explain it. She's lassoed some strange part of him. He knows so much about her now; he knows nothing at all.

She stirs—groggy, squinting, petulant—in Central California. At her request, they exit the 58 just past Los Banos in search of a Del Taco franchise advertised along the road as it ribbons through the vast agricultural dullness. "I've had a craving," she says, "for coming on two years."

At an adjoining gas station, he refills the Challenger's tank and scrubs the insect carcasses off the windshield. She departs to order the fast food with cash he palms her. He watches her stroll away to Del Taco, just as he watched her walk to the restroom at IHOP while he paid the check. Then, as now, he takes in her magnificence: its erotics self-engineered, its powers self-made.

At the same time, he takes in others taking her in, the fellow tank pumpers and vehicle passengers of both genders. Some try not to be obvious, but most don't bother. Their gazes are lustful, envious, censorious—even all at once.

She evinces an evident appreciation of this. It's in her bearing and her gait. Her confidence radiates an aura. She's a treat and knows it.

The nap has revived her. But the revelation that he's never eaten at Del Taco animates her. She preps their lunch as he drives on, a giant Cherry Coke perspiring in a console holder between them with a single straw to share. "Back in my day they only had Del Scorcho sauce," she informs him. "Del Inferno is pretty new."

The grilled-chicken soft tacos are laid open in her lap over wrapping paper. The sauce from packets is drizzled over a mayo-ish cream. She studiously rearranges the shredded iceberg lettuce and the semimelted grated cheese.

Her head is craned in concentration. All the while she intones, with a stoner's sincerity, "You need an *even distribution* of ingredients. Same with the chili-cheese fries." She's already doused a small pop box of the crinkle cuts with Del Scorcho. "You don't want any bites that aren't sauced. It *ruins* the *mouthfeel*."

She commandeers his digitally enabled stereo, pulling up Britney Spears's "I'm Not a Girl, Not Yet a Woman" on her phone. "The vintage car, the road trip: I'm feeling very *Crossroads* right now," she says as she turns the volume knob to an overbearing level and vamps, her fist a microphone.

She's tapped into what turns out to be a favored Britney playlist. Two songs later he's pleading for a reprieve. What comes next is a run of Peter Cetera's "Restless Heart," Toto's "I'll Be Over You," and Richard Marx's "Now and Forever."

For a while he lets her do her thing, amused. Then he becomes convinced it's all an elaborate put-on. "What's your deal," he half asks, stifling a laugh.

She turns toward him, removing her sunglasses in theatrical slow motion. A line of skepticism has formed between her brows. "My deal is adult contemporary. Clearly."

"I get that. You're into guilty pleasures."

"I don't believe in guilty pleasures." Her inflection is serious, more than he'd expected. "People have pleasures, and they sometimes, sadly, have guilt about them."

She questions his taste at some length—the established hierarchy, what compels its resonance, how sociology and psychology may come into play. His artistic preferences are those of a would-be sophisticate of his demographic. They're those of his time and of his place. They're predictable.

It emerges that he's snobbish. Indeed, she determines that he's insufficiently in touch with the commonweal. It's decided that he's in need of a cultural revolution.

This is fun for her, a game for a long car ride. She declares he'll be "properly rehabilitated" when "even *you* can derive true, nonironic joy" from Michael Bolton. He laughs. The mere mention of the name is shorthand for absurdity. The line of skepticism between her brows returns as she sips the last of the Cherry Coke and places the empty plastic cup by her feet. Then she adds, "You're proving my point."

Without further segue, she pulls up Bolton's "How Am I Supposed to Live Without You," hits play, unclicks her seat belt, and launches her lips hot against his ear. "*Keep your eyes on the highway*," she says, her voice an unfamiliar velveteen purr.

Belt unbuckled, fly unzipped: She operates with the swiftness of a safecracker. There's no commentary. She grabs ahold of him, pumps a few times for hardness, and swallows.

The joke is on her. He hears nothing. All he registers is her consuming touch.

Her curls pool and bounce across his lap. He has one hand on the wheel. Now the other runs through her hair. It catalogs sensations, cupping her head, encouraging. It's an illusion of command.

He's never sought out road head, never requested it. Pleasure would always be laced with fear. To surrender to the ecstasy, to tumble into it, would be to lose his bearings, to heighten the risk of a crash. There's something masochistic about it. How fitting, he thinks, while she rather showily sucks him off, that she seeks to indulge him in this way. She knows, as ever, what she's doing.

He's rubbery. She licks his shaft, kisses it, retreats upright into her seat. "What's up?" she says, a sweetness remaining, holding on to him, gently stroking. He explains, couching his concern as a riff on performance anxiety. The sweetness dissolves; the grip is removed. "Are you really bitching about a blow job? Is that even possible?"

It's a Michael Bolton playlist. In the silence that follows, he can hear the soundtrack again. The display on her phone is activated: "How Can We Be Lovers." His reflex is to make note of the obvious farce, turning the moment into grist.

But his mood is undercut by his exposed, wilted dick. It's clammy from her saliva and the circulating air. He routes it back through the opening in his boxers, zips his pants, buckles his belt.

It's several more hours until their destination. They'll ride the rest in awkward near silence, the playlist passing through "Soul Provider" and "That's What Love Is All About" before she switches to something else, then entirely gives up on music. By dusk she's dozing off again in the Bay Area traffic snarl.

It's dark. He's alone along the 101, just as he was when he was barreling through Southern California before dawn. He passes Petaluma, Healdsburg, Cloverdale. Then he transitions west to the coast on the 128.

He's kind of hungry. He kind of needs to piss. He's kind of frazzled from more than ten hours of driving, along with the emotional whirlwind. But he keeps going. The heavy mulch fragrance of oak and pine races through the slot of his open window.

Then the continent suddenly gives way. They're in Mendocino. The Challenger's V-8 preens across bluffs in the moonlit night and salted air.

In his head the cabin was rustic, homey. In reality it's modern, minimalist. What matches his imagination is its small size—one open-floor-planned room—and its secluded location. It's along a rugged, wooded ridge with an unobstructed view of the Pacific far below.

She pries off her shoes with opposite feet and swan dives backward onto the bed. There's no change of clothes, no removal of makeup, no brushing of teeth. As she drifts away, inaugurating a mild snore, her expression is serene.

He unpacks the Challenger, eats a few granola bars discovered in a cupboard, lies on an adjacent sofa in the cabin. They've been intimate. Sleeping together is another level.

Lights are off. The endless day is done. A lunar glimmer remains.

Drowsiness clouds in. He watches her with palpable awe. The snoring has amplified, a tinny rattle. She twitches in her slumber.

Weeks unfurl. Out of next to nothing, instant hothouse domesticity. Even stranger, maybe: legitimate workplace productivity.

There's plenty more awkwardness. But the cooped-up setup is

kindling. A mutual cognizance of their end date—the one-month stay—makes the whole thing feel crazy-romantic and whacked-out adventurous rather than claustrophobic and foolish.

He writes. She edits. He revises. She provides more notes. They bicker about it all, amiably and industriously. This project, their purpose, moves along.

A secretary desk is situated against the floor-to-ceiling window cantilevered over the plunging hill. A density of foliage sways in the foreground: manzanita, chaparral, willow, fir, dogwood. There's not another structure in view. Red-tailed hawks slice through the sky. It's enthralling at first but proves distracting. Soon enough he's opted for the kitchen table, facing a wall.

The desk and its stylish, uncushioned wooden chair—another reason for his departure—become her throne. She's set herself the task of wrangling the patients who benefited from her crimes into sitting for portraits and interviews for the book. The goal is to humanize and contextualize what, as she puts it to him, "they gained in real terms out of the insurance companies' rounding-error abstract financial loss."

Her tone on these calls is alien to what he's known of her. She alternates between maternal and sisterly, professional and just-us-girls. The tenor is conspiratorial. She enlists them in her cause.

She asks them about their lives, relationships. How they've changed since their surgeries. They explain. "Well, that's just it," she tells one woman, triumphant. "The way I see it, this 'you' was always there. I just helped make her more visible." Her eyes moistening, to another: "No, no! I didn't give you the confidence to leave him. That confidence is your own."

Some calls last a minute or two. With others, she's on the line for an hour or longer. She's in no rush: These constitute her final follow-up appointments. There will be no more patients.

He registers the melancholic twinge in her voice. She can attempt to tilt public opinion. Regardless, the state medical board will not reinstate her license.

During these exchanges, he often thinks of that leaked client settlement. The one he's kept silent about. Those awful images of the woman's face. Her pained avowal.

What of the inconvenient others? The ones he knows of and couldn't reach. The ones he doesn't know about. She won't dial them. Their stories won't be shared.

Most calls end in success. She updates the spreadsheet on her laptop. Often, he's unaware she's notched a victory since he wears noise-canceling headphones to focus on his work while she's chatting at full volume steps away.

On occasion, she'll sidle up, removing the headphones. "Another sale!" she says, beaming, playful. "My cunt needs a kiss." The dynamic has changed since their meetings at the prison. Always charged, what'd been teasing has turned tangible and unremarkable. He no longer resists.

So much time together incubates the range of intimacies. They exchange deepest professed secrets, often inconsequential, and seeming trivialities, often consequential. They gossip about the Mendo townspeople they scarcely interact with and the tourists they entirely steer clear of when visiting Patterson's Pub and Moody's Organic Coffee Bar and the aisles of Harvest Market.

They cultivate a private, byzantine language. It's minor in-jokes and sayings, forged in inflections and imitations. It's all conveyed less for its negligible entertainment value than as a self-referential affirmation and ongoing commentary on the hermetic, temporary life they've stumbled into together.

Through sheer dumb repetition, these sacraments of familiarity accrue worth. He'll find any way possible, for instance, to wax on at meals about how the dish in front of them must be consumed in a particular way. Otherwise—his voice plaintive, his eyes looking afar—"it *ruins* the *mouthfeel*."

Since they first met, he fantasized about her as his lover, not as his roommate. She does her full makeup and hair routine even if she has no plan to leave home. The thermostat must be set untenably low. Groceries are organized in the refrigerator under a baffling, complex, and opaque decision-making regime. Tomorrow's outfit is picked and laid out before going to bed. Flossing occurs up to four times per day.

He convinces himself that she'll end up alone. Her mother was right to worry. He hadn't thought about it until he'd begun circling her in this cabin. Now he can't stop. He isn't sure if she realizes this yet, although he suspects she's long accepted it. The prospect pains him.

There's a gravitational pull to her. There's also an impenetrable center. He knows this from his inquiry, in all its professionalism. He knows this from his liaison, in all its unprofessionalism. His ego precludes the possibility that she hasn't fully opened herself to him because he's just not the one.

She chased and captured her own physical perfection. It's receding, betraying her grasp. When she's sleeping beside him, he can see it in her mild encroaching wrinkles. She's already launched the antiaging counteroffensive. He's seen the serums and the pills, a battalion arrayed in the medicine cabinet.

With her innate grit and nerve, he wonders how much better off she'd have had it if she'd been born a man. That essential freedom: to devour beauty without the expectation to manifest it. He lances the thought. Her life, its trajectory, is inextricably codified by her womanhood.

When not working, they engage in the most conventional if gratifying activities that could be expected of a couple of their demographic, time, and place. They take day trips: wine tasting in nearby Anderson Valley, weed tasting in the adjacent Emerald Triangle, strolling along Glass Beach in Fort Bragg, driving through the Chandelier redwood, hiking in Russian Gulch State Park. They take pictures of themselves doing these things, posting them to their social media accounts. They scrutinize how they look.

They endeavor to impose their respective sensibilities on each other, acts of affection and attrition. Books are read and skimmed. TV shows are binged and abandoned. Films are watched in one-for-you, one-for-me fashion.

Her heartfelt enthusiasm for adult contemporary wins him over. She isn't into it because she's a nostalgist. She hardly even cogitates the lyrics. It's clear that she's just a sensualist, the melodies and hooks tactile.

Dated pop will never be his thing. But its emotional apparatus, powered on neon currents, is true. When she goads him into full-throated sing-alongs—Hall & Oates, Belinda Carlisle, Sting—he relents. It helps that they're in an isolated cabin in the woods and the hound is a fox.

Speaking of which: One evening she cues up Heart's "All I Wanna Do Is Make Love to You." He momentarily questions whether it's ironic and winking or cheesy and awesome if such a display is, in fact, a prelude to making love to him. Then he just as quickly lances that thought too, since it's a killjoy.

He's an anxious cook with a limited albeit reliable repertoire. She eats a lot of his whitefish po'boys, mushroom risotto, Vietnamese chicken-cabbage salad. Meanwhile, she's unsurprisingly expert with a knife.

In the kitchen there's a hint of her past as both a student and a surgeon. It's a space of practical creativity. She absorbs new recipes without frustration, deviating from their imperatives at will. She calls for utensils and cookware, maneuvering about the operating room aloft reserves of assurance. Her fingers are nimble along the slabs of meat, cutting against their grain. Her blade pulls the skin away from fish, separating fillets with skilled downward pressure.

Their sex life is intended as a conduit of intimacy. But it's only later, when she includes him in her hair care, that it becomes clear tenderness and understanding are channeled through other somatic means.

After she showers, she works shea into her curls to moisturize them, deploys a diffuser to dry them, and uses coconut oil to shine them. Then, seated upright and nude on the bed, she hands him a hair pick and lays her hands on his legs, now wrapped around her own. She bows her head and reminds him to be careful. If not deft, breakage and frizz can result—or at least painful snags she'll record by digging her nails into his thighs.

At her instruction, he picks from the roots in gentle, fluid motions. Mistakes are enumerated in whimpers. Success materializes as disorderly volume. She shakes her mane, fingers running through it across the crown. The bulk is a halo. Once satisfied, she turns, the scent whipping like a coconut pie thrown in his face. "Good," she says. "Now my bush."

Her bossiness ranges to her orgasms. The episode in that Holiday Inn Express in Chino wasn't a ploy. It was overture. She's unrelenting, even ruthless, in her quest for pleasure.

He promised to call the shots when they fucked again. In fact, he's steamrolled. Timing, frequency, locations, positions: She decrees.

He finds that he doesn't mind. Decision-free sex is emancipating. Besides, if anything, she's *too* interested, imaginative . . . exhausting. The sum variety of her yearning bears a ceaseless yet wretched quality. It reminds him of the weeks he and a college girlfriend spent working through a paperback Kama Sutra before she left for a year abroad. As if pressing against each other from every angle would make it impossible to cleave. They broke up anyway two months after she arrived in Florence.

On rainy days, which are many, her favorite thing is to run outside naked except for her ankle monitor bracelet, then lie in the muddy grass. Her rear is held to the sky. Legs dangle straight up and past her nose. Arms splay out. Hands grip the ground to support the upended pose. He lightly thrusts from above as he squats so as not to stress her neck.

Water obscures her vision. Dirt soils her hair. Blood rushes to her head, an operatic swoon. It doesn't take long before she shudders and seizes, beguiled.

The trickiness of this position and the concentration it requires disqualify chatter. So does its short duration. Otherwise, as with all things, she's a talker.

The set of headphones he wears while writing is often switched off yet kept affixed as a decoy so she won't blab. Silence is fool's gold to her. At least once a day he begs off for a solo hike to catch a break.

A week and a half into their time together, he loans her his Challenger. It's a three-day round trip to LA to stay with her mother and check in for the first time with her parole officer. The restorative quiet feels like a meditation retreat.

Their conversational mode is argumentative; their style freewheeling. Dialogue was their original communion when touch was verboten. Now the rapport has shape-shifted, unbound by prison strictures.

No longer is the interview form itself their vehicle of understanding, reliant on information extraction and imperfect performance. They're liberated from the countdown of the visitors' clock, as well as the tension inherent between free man and held woman. And now, of course, their physical frisson isn't hung in the air but consummated.

They learn that neither were high school debaters, a mutual surprise since both are joyous natural contrarians. Quarrel is primordial, as dogs wrestle, birds sing. They take frequent exception to one another, for sport as much as for belief, clasping opinions and fiercely defending them, a recreational pursuit.

Brutalism is dreamy, not depressing. Humor is innate, not learned. Sunrises trump sunsets. Mother Theresa was no saint. The turpitude that is Monopoly did more to brainwash unknowing young souls into rapacious capitalism than anything else in America. And so on.

This banter forges and fuels them. She's interested in keeping things light, given the telescoped circumstances. "It's emotional labor," she jests one night over dinner, purposefully appropriating the language of feminist struggle as she acknowledges their collective burden of marshaling the book.

At another point, over a round of beer and Scrabble at the pub, he once again frets that perhaps she should've chosen a woman to tell her story. She responds, in amused malice, no interest in placating him: "This tale, as far as I can tell, is about consciousness under the male gaze. Why not be channeled by it, for the final insult?" He has no riposte. So she continues, to seriocomic effect, "Hey, at least you're *well-intentioned* . . . and *cute*." He rolls his eyes, unhappy. "Whatever," she concludes, softening. "I get the last word. I'm editing you."

They develop a custom of walking along the coastal headlands late many afternoons. The two are strolling along a section not far from the main drag of town. It's the Tuesday before the end of their stay. One of their insubstantial disagreements turns into a real one.

He's been thinking about things her sister told him when they spoke months earlier. She shared stories of sexual harassment and abuse. The affronts inflicted and disrespect extracted as the price of her objective splendor.

She also observed that her sibling, the one who'd chosen this life, was silent about the experience. "It causes her whole post-wave-feminist-beauty-power-ecstasy-whatever thing to short-circuit," her sister said.

He's nearly done with the manuscript. She's never volunteered anything. He's realized in recent days that it's been a dereliction of his duty not to follow up.

So he does, beginning to scheme for an opening at the end of a thought-provoking if draining and gone-on-too-long debate. It's over the circumstances in which they've each forsaken or reassessed—or not—beloved works of art and entertainment on account of alleged predacious behavior by their creators or financiers. They've prodded at the topic enough to feel guilty, righteous, confused. Time to move on.

She muses, in an eddy, on "the real mind-fuckery" of harassment and abuse. That it insidiously taints, undermines, and leverages "all the good shit at your core." You take pride in being sweet, smart, single-minded, savvy, strong. It preys on what you thought were your inborn or practiced sources of power—accommodation, rationalization, ambition, perception, suppression.

Spoken like someone who knows. He asks her about her own history. She demurs: "Nothing notable."

He elides this, deploying his findings. Except now what was explained to him verbatim by her sister has been reworked. It's a moment of inquisition. Has she taken a perverse pride in at last being worthy of mistreatment?

She snickers. The eyes roll. The head tilts at an angle of *you*'ve got to be kidding *me*. Dismissiveness as spectacle. Yet there's no reply.

He tells her that her sister was far more forthcoming. Now a tempest flashes across her face. She makes it known that she's surprised.

It's a doubled revelation: that her younger sibling laid herself so bare during such a brief meeting and that he's only sharing information of such gravity now. To him the lack of prior disclosure wasn't purposeful. To her it's clear evidence of some deceit.

"Dahlia can be a drama queen," she says, her voice low. The slander is further muffled by both the wind and the fact that her mouth is recessed—along with the nimbus of her tresses—within the hoodie of her parka.

He believes otherwise and explains so. Again, he pushes, noting that her sister wondered whether she may be loath to acknowledge the downside of the physicality she'd achieved.

The tempest returns. His pulse quickens. His stomach churns.

Their conversation has stopped them along a thin dirt path on a high, jagged promontory. The riotous sea below is an aquamarine-and-indigo whorl of whitecap waves among the outcroppings. .He wishes he could laugh with her at their scenic providence. To argue here, amid the epic sweep of these elemental forces, is to underscore the pettiness of this clash.

She steps toward him, her nose wet, unbowed by the milieu. "..It's wild to me," she rages, "that after all our time together, you'd think I might not understand myself. I know *exactly* who I am!"

For the record, *that* was the boner killer. The trance was over. Our weird, fragile little thing had fractured.

Roya spent the next half hour just out of earshot in the middle of the headlands on an animated phone call with Dahlia. I know this because her sister was texting me throughout the duration of the call, beginning with "WTF????!!?!!!?" and ending with "I bet you're rethinking the cost-benefit ratio of all those BJs right now . . ."

Nominal apologies in each direction would be exchanged that night. I was back on the sofa for the first time since the night we arrived in Mendocino. But the rift would prove irreversible.

Two days later, in bed together again, legs entwined, Roya offered without notice an anecdote as a seeming peace offering. She described an episode during her residency at USC when a handsome superior, who up until then had been a "totally legit and cool" mentor, began hitting on her. She rebuffed him, he kept at it, and one day, when they were alone together, he "squeezed my ass so hard it left a bruise."

Weeks later, he cornered her again. Having just broken up with her boyfriend—he'd been "bugging" her about filing a formal complaint pertaining to the butt squeezing, and she'd refused—she "decided to hook up with the guy, to change the power dynamic." The session resulted in unexpectedly rough sex and physical pain.

I delicately asked Roya questions to explore her relationship with the mentor, the boyfriend, herself. She seemed . . . at a remove: about details, motivations, recriminations. At first, I chalked it up to a trauma victim's ambivalence and distance from a disturbing event. Then I felt a tingling chill—that spidey sense you develop in my line of work over time.

Something was wrong. Stranger still, it wasn't wrong in the usual way. The story didn't feel fabricated. It felt adapted.

Once the notion struck, I shut down. Exhaustion set in. I went to bed and, early the next morning, left for an early hike in the woods, dialing Dahlia as soon as I came upon a stretch of trail with reliable cell reception.

I shouldn't have shared what had been explained to me in confidence. People have reasons—conscious or not, valid or not—to lie. Yet my discretion and reason were breached by the thought that after all the trust I felt I'd engendered, Roya still may have felt so free to mislead me.

Dahlia listened. She was unsurprised by the call, unsurprised by the story, unsurprised by, yes, the usurpation of her life. "That's basically a carbon-copy version of what happened to me with my dirtbag manager at this bottle-service nightclub on La Cienega five years ago," she confirmed.

I asked if Roya had any real stories of harassment or abuse. There was a pause. Dahlia knew I'd been deceived and, to some degree, was dismayed about the fabrication. "If there are stories," she said, a knowingness in her tone, "they're not my stories to share." She went on, speaking in generalities about self-censorship and misdirection when it was transparent she was riffing on specifics.

"Many or even most" women, according to Dahlia, "perfectly understandably" don't want to be defined or define themselves by "the shittiest things that happened in their lives, that happened *to them*." They want to be defined in their personal narratives and their public lives by "positives and positivity," their own agency. Some compartmentalize the luckless parts of their histories and move on. It was easy to extrapolate what was unspoken. Roya, already defined in her public life by a shitty thing, had no interest in adding to a tally of unfortunate facts or suppositions that might further limit her ability to function in the world as she wished.

I acknowledged the rightness of this but stressed that Roya had agreed to an arrangement of candor with me. "Really, Wes," Dahlia said in sympathy, at the same time adopting a judiciousness I hadn't previously known of her. (Then again, she'd been placed in a tricky spot, between her dishonest sister and that sister's disloyal associate.) "Roya doesn't owe you anything about whatever it is she tells herself or others about her pain, whatever that pain might or might not be. Her compass is hers to keep."

I thanked Dahlia for her candor. She was correct, of course. Still, it didn't mean I couldn't feel irritated. I'd convinced myself that Roya and I were true collaborators, operating in symbiosis. As it turned out, at best I was high-end hired help. I should never have been so foolish as to believe otherwise.

I suppose I could've plumbed or prodded Roya about all of this. I didn't. Disenchantment overrode inquisitiveness. Long past antagonizing her, I was depleted of energy. I was ready to be done with this project.

The final days at the cabin would've appeared magazine-spread cozy from afar. The appealing couple together (she immersed in a book on the sofa, he with his laptop open at the kitchen table) shone in the butter-glow warmth of tasteful lighting as fog and rain swept past outside. At that table, as I got closer to the finish line on the manuscript for the agent we'd secured, I attempted not to sulk. As those days burned away, her falsehood contaminated the relationship we'd built, the entirety of the enterprise. If she'd lied to me about this, I was sure there were other fictions.

It wasn't the lying that bothered me. Memoir is fallible. Unreliable narrators are endemic to the form. I could roll with mendaciousness. What bothered me was that I hadn't been allowed in on it.

Beyond the paperwork, our deal was this: I would be granted meaningful, *dependable* access to her inner life, the places where deceptions and self-deceptions don't just go to hide but originate. In return, I would be a faithful steward of her consciousness, a conspiring messenger of her meaning.

Roya was aware that I was aware what was up. It was an unspoken standoff in which she either didn't want to be called out on her bullshit or own up to it, or didn't care enough, or wasn't ready to apologize. Or maybe she *did* want to discuss it and was just waiting for me to broach the issue myself. Too bad: This inquiring mind was closed.

This was her life. I'd just written a draft of it. Others could take their swings at her. I was clocking out.

Our Mendocino standoff manifested itself in a concluding stretch that improved from stony to, I suppose, cordial. Roya made one half-hearted effort at physical reconciliation, which I brushed off with murmurs that perhaps we should try again once we were back in LA. (Whereupon she sulked.) In truth, everything was starting to annoy me about her, including things that just days earlier I'd found endearing. Or at least, amid the good times, I'd overlooked them.

What comes most to mind is her cram-reading of a slew of life-in-prison writings that she'd rush-ordered online. They were all by politically radical, historically consequential figures: Nelson Mandela, Eldridge Cleaver, Aleksandr Solzhenitsyn, etc. It was a dubious attempt at excavation and cooptation. I found myself acting as a colander for her newfound, inchoately Marxist views and analyses, which shaded too much toward self-congratulation and martyrdom.

Despite it all, even as our affair waned, the beauty was still there, ever aflame. The morning we left, I went on one last solo hike at first light. As I returned up the path to the cabin, I caught sight of Roya through one of the floor-to-ceiling windows, dancing in the nude beside the sofa to the muffled sounds of Madonna's "Open Your Heart." Before I could turn away, she spun around, smiling in recognition. Roya approximated the striking moves from the music video with sweet, defiant confidence. I'd become another one of those leering, pitiable men in its peep show.

Open your heart with the key, she mouthed across the glass, her body a glory. *Open your heart, I'll make you love me. It's not that hard, if you just turn the key.*

CRIMINAL

"Prison is a prism." The experience changes you. I kept hearing that aphorism from the women I met who'd been in and out of the penal system on short sentences and were now back in again. The ones I spoke to who were serving longer stretches were often far less amenable to this idea of incarceration as transfiguration. Their view was that of waste. They had their own rejoining riff on the maxim: "Prison is nihilism."

I won't be chronicling the ghastly and unjust nature of the modern American prison industrial complex. Take it as a given: It's ghastly and unjust. Instead, please consult the shelf of extant literature. And if you *really* want to read a compelling indictment within the narrow genre of one privileged woman's induction into contemporary US confinement, I recommend Piper Kerman's *Orange Is the New Black*. I just feel leery about being a safari guide of the exotic realm of captivity, since I have this nagging sense that the colorful details may serve to distract and distance rather than focus and engage. Does knowing that women have taught themselves how to turn toilet paper into everything from extra menstrual pads (some inmates can't afford to purchase enough real ones with their commissary funds) to chess pieces (made extra firm with stale toothpaste) end up doing much except allow you to better gawp at them? I doubt it.

By the same token, I've also chosen not to record here the stories of the other prisoners I met at the California Institution for Women in Chino. Although those compelled should look up the much-reported-on allegations of widespread sexual abuse of inmates by staff members during my time there. The Feds are now investigating. I will note that I was spared. Being high-profile may have kept me safe.

The tales that brought each of us to prison often overlapped: inadvertent or at least not fully cognizant wrongdoing that resulted in unplanned, agonizing journeys. The vivid specifics, though, are largely their own—and due to their less-privileged circumstances, their struggles have been far more difficult. These ladies need to be able to speak on their own. I won't coopt their lives as passing anecdotes in service of my own.

This may be a mistaken strategy. Having heard my account of correctional woe, will you feel you've heard them all, never to bother with another? Still, I think it's the right one.

My humane swindle—yes, that's what I'm calling it; indulge me, this is the friggin' *slammer chapter*—benefited lower-income women, a wealth-redistribution scheme wherein the commodity value was laundered into looks. Now, for the first time, this Beverly Hills girl turned Ivy League graduate turned bougie cliché found herself living among that demographic. It was justice.

Prior to my surrender, I was worried about violence in prison. The reality was that I was not only protected but embraced by a group of gang-affiliated Hispanic drug offenders. Most had acted as traffickers for boyfriends or husbands. One of them had learned in advance from a family member on the outside about my imminent arrival. A patient of mine, one who'd gained from services rendered through fraudulent billing, had tipped off this cousin, whom she knew from her neighborhood. Inside, these women told others of what they framed as my noble act, and referred to me, in all seriousness, as Santa Roya. This was a significant validation of my already glistening inner martyrdom.

I was humbled and thankful. Still, socially, I gravitated toward the other white-collar criminals: the executives, small-business entrepreneurs, accountants, and real estate brokers who predominated among the money felons. They were primarily first-time offenders who admitted to making mistakes but never hurt anyone. At least they never physically hurt anyone. It was with them that I'd play cards, walk the track, veg out in the TV room, eat the gruel in the cafeteria, and wax floors for sixteen cents an hour.

One of the hardest things to adjust to at first was practical: sleeping in an overcrowded, warehouse-like environment of 170 frequently snoring women on bunk beds, where you're awoken multiple times throughout the night for inmate counts. The other was the deadening of the senses. There's the constant racket, which caused me to shut down, although over time you do get used to it. There's the sterility of the atmosphere, and then there's the muted, suppressed nature of everything about prison, particularly any gratification in femininity. I thought about it every day in the awful green uniform I wore and saw others' womanhood lost in: T-shirts, shorts, pants, jackets, sports bras, and these comical cotton granny panties.

This aesthetic desolation reminded me why glamour is so important to so many people. It's true that it's more likely to be classified as a sin rather than a virtue. This is odd since it's an aspired instead of innate gorgeousness, the consequence of beauty exalted beyond mere nature's gift. I'd argue that glamour is a calling toward transcendence, a secular analog of grace. When it's present, it amplifies the senses and allows for illusions. It can be a refuge from cruelty. Perhaps even a weapon against it.

I witnessed glamour manifest as a perennial resistance fighter. It was there in the torn pages of lifestyle magazines taped to the walls. It was there in the impromptu dance parties that broke out before lights-out, soundtracked to Bey and RiRi and Mary J. It was there in the attempt to make something sparkly-crafty in decorative celebration out of just about every holiday. It was there in the group activity everyone called glam-squadding—the elaborate hair-and-makeup-ing of a fellow inmate so she could feel special on her birthday, otherwise a teary occasion to mark on the inside.

Above all, glamour meant sensorial pleasure, as opposed to some idea of refinement or sophistication. There was this intense, extensive crocheting scene at Chino, which crossed age and ethnic demographics. Women created beautiful handmade blankets, socks, hats, gloves, slippers, shawls, and even tiny I.D.-holding purses. Some were bartered. Most were gifted. They were in bright, anarchic patterns.

Inmates flaunted their crocheted apparel and accessories. The items were referred to, lovingly and only semi-ironically, as "couture." I received a pair of patterned magenta, orange, and yellow socks a few weeks into my stay from a neighboring bunkie. It was an offering of wacky optimism, the interwoven yarn dyed in radioactive hues, a visual and tactile rebellion against the drabness of both the uniform and the surroundings. I picked up the skill soon after, presenting others with gifts in turn: upon arrival on the premises, or for winning the big Yahtzee tournament on Friday night, or just because.

What I found most challenging about prison was its sheer boredom. Contemporary life operates at a frenzied churn. Some lament it. I thrive on it. I'm sure there are those who'd consider a forced detox equivalent to a silver lining. They're the same people who'd hear about the inedible food in custody and think, *The perfect way to lose weight!*

There's only so much meditation you can do. There are only so many laps around the track. There are only so many books you can read. There is only so much gossip to be exchanged. There are only so many letters to write. There are only so many random hobbies to pick up to fritter away the hours. At a certain point you enter or reenter a fugue state, one that regresses you to childhood, its frustrations and limitations, veiled by the darker existential abstractions of your adult self. It fucking sucks.

A byproduct of tedium is solipsism. I ended up stewing a lot on boredom itself, the full menagerie of repetition and routine, endlessness and ennui, apathy and inertia. How it all functions. What it all means.

I became an armchair philosopher of the subject, venturing boredom as a hidden and underconsidered animating force in the world, rivaling and perhaps even outperforming its opposite—passion. I'd regale bunkies with my crackpot (or not!) theory that it can be traced as the key undercurrent through our political, economic, cultural, and personal realms. I'd do this by citing cherry-picked examples I won't regurgitate here, in part because I'd only open myself up to substantive critique, and what fun is that? Furthermore, that boredom is now undergoing its biggest transformation in the history of humanity, with technology eliminating much of it, or rather converting it into another category: distraction.

I had riffs on boredom as luxury commodity pursued by the affluent and boredom as psychological perfectionism, the mindfulness movement seeming to me to view the empty head as the highest sign of mental health. To that point, one fifty-something neighbor told me that ennui could be freeing. The diffuse mood is an individuating force that leaves your brain unmolested. She'd spent two decades raising children at home and treasured the hours in the middle of the day when she was alone. "That's when I knew myself best," she said, wistful amid the clatter of the cafeteria.

Boredom was an affliction, a dead end, until it proved catalytic, idleness sparking self-knowledge. My half-baked ideas brought me into contact with a smallish, self-selecting circle of Chino thinkers—autodidacts mixing with possessors of advanced degrees. I'd listen to their free-flowing populist-anarchist-reformist discourse, laced as it was in conspiracy, suspicious of authority, against all established orders. There were sweeping opinions and grand policy prescriptions for the drug war, education, the environment, health care, surveillance, various kinds of debt relief. The unifying thread was a mistrust of the market system and the men who control it.

At my elite college I'd been enmeshed in what my fellow conversationalists termed a "neoliberal professional path." I wouldn't have even known where to find the Penn dorm rooms where the would-be system-smashing kids were just then questioning their fated tickets into America's ruling class and learning to "interrogate" (a favored word among the Chino group), denigrate, and otherwise sniff at our collective future of neoliberal professionalism. Now cast out, I was radicalized too.

These inmate intellectuals, in their fuck-you attitude and disinterest in conventional mores, conjured the conditions for me to begin envisioning and workshopping fervent utopic ideas of my own. Notions of politics and policies I might previously have thought far-fetched or absurd, notions you likely will now find far-fetched or absurd, didn't just make perfect sense but seemed a scorching necessity. The most fundamental of all is the clear need to establish, as soon as possible, a new gynocratic world order.

I was then unschooled in feminist thought, although my operating premise was simple. Men have been in charge for thousands of years. They've screwed things up for everyone, particularly women. Time to hand over the reins. I'm not speaking of bringing about mere equality. What I want is straight-up sisterhood domination of all institutions in all societies for—conservative estimate—*many* generations, commandeering authority for at least long enough that there's no living memory of the patriarchy. Chief anticipated pluses of female rule include a drastic global decrease in annual statistics pertaining to violence and whining.

I'm no tactician, and I understand how improbable this may appear. Given the ongoing assault on abortion rights, we've yet to even seize the means of reproduction, let alone the means of production. Still, as I looked around the prison camp, I kept thinking: *What an ideal place for an uprising to begin.*

I'd lie awake night after night and fantasize about my bunkies, this ragtag band of untapped revolutionaries, humiliated and misshapen by a society that'd so often failed them, brought together under the auspices of a regime that would soon learn to regret the strategic mistake of state-mandated separatism.

In my imagining, they—we—had finally *seen* each other. A dream had arisen of a better world. Then an oath had been made to claim it.

One day this movement overpowered the guards, appropriated their armaments, and hijacked their vehicles in the vast employee parking lot, then caravanned southward, up into the Santa Ana Mountains that lorded over Chino. I had no idea what we matriarchists would do when we got there. How we'd evade capture. How we'd battle and grow as a guerilla force. How we'd vanquish near and far before establishing peaceable governance in tandem with like-minded women we'd inspire across a global reach. I wasn't focused on any of that.

My fantasy preferred to dwell on how the revolutionaries had taken shelter among the high-altitude, steep-slope wilds. Dusk was upon us. Our prison uniforms were overlaid by a riotous display of multicolor crocheted capes, hats, scarves, stockings, belts, vests, and other accessories. There was frenzied talk in the dying day of plans for a spectacular blitz early the next morning, racing into civilization, no time to waste.

Before we set out, still in darkness, the glam squad would apply the warrior paint: bronzer and eye shadow, lipstick and concealer, mascara and nail polish. Everyone's hair would take care of itself, turning windblown on the rushed trip back down the mountain.

But first we'd need our beauty sleep. History would soon know our conquest by the trail of glitter and dead.

TEN

You go in. If you're lucky, you end up too deep. Then you must escape—intact, if not the same.

I've found that no matter the story, the arc holds true. Not just to report and write about others with the correct blend of empathy and distance known as fairness. It's to persist in doing a vampiric job whose fieldwork includes betrayal.

Disentanglement can be problematic, uncomfortable, debilitating. Saving the toughest questions for last—the ones likeliest to sever any normal relationship, or else quash it from the start—often assists in the extrication. Interviewees consider this sandbagging. Interviewers know it as good tradecraft, the best medicine for all involved.

You're their mirror, the repository of their vanity, a salutary presence composed of curiosity, stamina, and charm.

When it came to Roya, my professional remove had dissolved in the face of, well, her face, as well as her dyspeptic nature. I realized now that she pegged me from the jump. Roya had reeled me in, beating me at my own game.

It was OK. Some stories you tell. Some stories tell you.

Our relationship unfurled to its reasonable conclusion. We returned from Mendocino and didn't see each other for weeks. I decompressed.

Roya went to live for a spell with her mother and stepfather in Manhattan Beach while getting set up with a day job at her friend Dr. Penelope Greene's skin-treatment-kit start-up. She'd be some sort of product liaison, doing a lot of, as it was relayed to me, "interfacing" with lab researchers, dermatologists, store owners, and investors. It would be a low-profile position, ideal for reentry into the white-collar workforce given her troubles, and would take advantage of her medical background and clinical experience. "I'm really grateful for it," she told me. She had bills to pay, including legal debts.

As a practical matter, Roya also needed the cash flow to finance her longer-term, far more brazen second act, which she'd begun to contemplate in prison. It would be a wholesale personal rebrand, a pivot in the marketplace. She was intent on transforming into a type of self-help guru.

Not that Roya framed it that way. In her words, she wanted to become a "health-care-policy-reform activist," advocating for a future of "universal plastic surgery coverage." Yes, you're reading correctly. She knew that, given where "the medical insurance and political conversation generally has been" in recent decades, it likely wouldn't be a battle that she'd see won in her lifetime. Still, she hoped to "be the spark" that might catalyze such an over-the-horizon "civil rights" triumph.

I thought Roya was joking when she first floated this. She wasn't. No matter, at the least, the many pragmatic challenges in seeing through such a revolutionary proposition. She considered herself an ideologue, not a wonk, and her audacious stance became the call-to-action coda of her memoir.

She told me about the work done for her by an online-reputation-management company she'd hired. It first helped clean up Roya's embarrassing search engine results by burying the negative ones in a sea of interlinked favorable information. As a reporter who'd taken silent pride in besmirching quite a few Googleable reputations with investigative articles I'd published, it was a fascinating if still-opaque peek into the black-magic algorithmic machinations undertaken to suppress them. Afterward, the firm slowly upped her then-meager follower count on social media. She played coy when I asked about that. I can only assume it involved the shady deployment of bots.

During this period, she had a website designer create a new DrRoya-Delshad.com, based around her forthcoming book, and got into teaching herself public speaking, listening to audiotapes about its strategy and secrets. A parallel newfound obsession with TED Talks became corrosive to our partnership as she fell sway to the seduction of buzzwords and other linguistic cant. We had more friction over the wording in the final chapter than the rest of the memoir combined.

Our agent had to referee the dispute, which reached an apex with my middle-of-the-night proposal via a group email chain that maybe I should just take my name off the project. The hill I was at that very moment dying on was my demand to eliminate Roya's multiple insertions, in assorted objectionable usages, of the term *disruption*. The agent's wisdom, landing in only my inbox from Manhattan before I awoke the next morning: "You know the line 'Happy wife, happy life'? When it comes to ghostwriters, try 'Want another client? Be compliant.'"

The point was taken. I sucked it up and we completed the book without further incident. Although I did prevail on Roya to dial back on quite a bit, if not all, of the bullshit semantics I detested.

In the end, though, it was a good thing for me. The spell was broken. It was easier than I thought it'd be to part ways when we wrapped things up.

Now, it wasn't like we were abruptly finished when our deadline passed. There'd be more teasing, more in-jokes, more hookups of varying intensities. We lingered and reverberated in each other's lives. But the volume and amplitude of our association dwindled to near nothing.

I find much to admire in Roya—the consonance of her sense of self and the dissonance of her sense of the world. How she's articulated her aloneness through the project that is her life. A struggle in which the trauma of the body can be renovated into a radiant future of one's own invention. It's intoxicating.

Roya's also plenty irritating. She's more than a little disturbing. If

I'm being honest, perhaps there's a hint of repulsion on my end too. I'm uneasy yet exhilarated by her actions and her justifications, or maybe by my culpability in expressing them. I still haven't worked it all out.

I haven't, in fact, worked out much of it at all. This stems from a central misstep: Even at the height of our time in Mendocino, I didn't comprehend that I'd maybe fallen a bit in love with her.

To be sure, this was never a love story, or even much of a lust story. Rather, it's a fable of intimacy and its accruals. It was only later that I began to understand how invested I'd become. That what we'd both taken for a fling had left me, at least, changed.

Our dynamic, at its reduced core a paid helpmeet to a client, was unequal. She led. I interpreted.

Yet it was also profoundly close. My sustained immersion with Roya felt synaptic. To this day, at random, I find myself inhabiting her thoughts, her passions, even her inflections. Then I'll question: Is this an indicator of affection? Empathy? Longing? Obsession? Is it even healthy? Roya's thoughts, after all, were often self-deceptions. Her passions were at times illusions. Some may argue delusions.

I've gotten inside the minds of—and extricated consequential revelations from—advocates and ambivalents, billionaires and vagrants, charlatans and straight arrows, believers and doubters, windbags and near mutes, egotists and self-erasers, nutcases and cool heads. Rarely, though, has this transference left much of a lasting dent in my worldview. I go about my business at a distance.

Not so with Roya. I'll grant the obvious: The physical component of our relationship made it unique. However, she imbued me with something alchemical and potent, something that I believe speaks beyond the dregs of infatuation.

The sheer capaciousness of Roya's desire for a tomorrow on terms she'd defined, the dizzying intensity and ferocious sweep of it, is a comfort to a far lesser dreamer like me. She embodies a magnetic can-do romanticism. It's (I loathe the sentiment and platitude of the word, but what the hell, the cards are out now anyway) *inspirational.*

I'm not given to soaring fantasy. It demands a symbiotic vulnerability and enthusiasm I wish I wielded yet know I lack in sufficient measure. Roya, though, set a daring example, a vector toward boldness. The effects range from the colossal (an amplified appreciation of wonder, which I'd argue is always beneficial for a journalist) to the tangential (think too much about it and your prose may begin to turn, *ahem*, conspicuously purple) to the inconsequential.

Of the latter, Exhibit A: One rainy afternoon in Mendocino, over yet another round of Scrabble and beer at Patterson's, it was revealed that I'd long harbored a notion to somehow bring to market a venomous party game, my own make-it-rich Cards Against Humanity. I didn't have most of the details worked out. But I knew it'd hinge on the frustrating yet fun gaps in the English language where a social phenomenon, often involving an unvirtuous aspect of human nature, has no name. The stuff of existence where you'd think there's just got to be a German word for it, but no dice. I *did* have a suitably punning name picked out for the game, though: "Schadenworde."

Examples might include the guilty feeling of failing to summon interest in a topic of weighty concern that nevertheless bores you. Or the personal affront that is others' superior ethical behavior. Or the perverse belief that someone else will assume the worst of you in any given situation. Or the secret relief of learning that circumstance has absolved you of an undesired responsibility.

Roya was thrilled about this. She had her own contributions, often on-brand: the crestfallen experience of meeting someone you'd anticipated being more attractive; the utilitarian downer when you can't reciprocate another person's licentious craving. She also inverted schadenfreude itself, pointing to the ghoulish pleasure one derives in awareness of others' vexation over your good fortune. Roya believes this urge is a motivating factor in a considerable portion of social media lifestyle-flaunting.

Anyway, Roya embraced the concept, in all its smallness and squalor. Not just with her customary neg-ish needling. Although there was some of that, too: "Entertainment for assholes! It's always in demand."

For Roya, when she grokked the flicker of essential sincerity hanging around my dumb idea—maybe this was more than just a thing you joke about over a pint at a pub?—it became vital to her that I value it. "Wes," she said, leaning toward me, fingers splayed across the table in theatrical emphasis, a pure vessel of earnest gravity, "if you're lucky enough to grasp some notion of what you want, whatever it is, *don't let go.*"

Schadenworde has yet to move forward. Still, the pep talk was appreciated, and the point remains. Beyond Roya's barbed personality resides the instinct of a guru.

I never did learn whatever it was that Roya was holding out on me—the thing Dahlia knows. I had my theories. Regardless, this was moot. She had decided it wasn't in service of the message she wanted to share, and she's the author of her tale.

At one point, back in LA, Roya told me that her work with Penny had gotten her thinking for a minute about becoming a makeup artist. She reasoned, at first, that the field was an analog to the profession she'd been excommunicated from. They shared in alteration, differing in duration.

I asked why the flirtation was brief. Roya turned quiet, explaining she'd thought it through and the thing about makeup—which she was wearing at the time, stunningly applied as always—"is that in the end it's an elaborate mask to conceal flaws, and I didn't want to consign myself to masking. Not when I'd already known the power in dealing with what's underneath."

We talked about aging throughout our conversations together. She had a battle plan, a complex and ambitious set of rearguard actions she'd already begun enacting, worthy of the effort she'd put into enhancing her body in the first place. Roya knew she was at her apex, cresting it, peak desirability soon ebbing.

The tragedy was tender. I had no doubt Roya would expertly prolong her—as she put it—fuckability. "Then what?" I once asked.

"Death!" she joked, at least by the pitch of her voice. It was left unclear in Roya's mordancy whether her skill in combating corporeal deterioration meant she'd remain alluring until ill health won out, or she'd kill herself when she felt her appeal had been eclipsed. I didn't pry further. I was too bummed out to pursue that truth.

The book's photo shoot that Roya had arranged took place over the course of a weekend a few months after we got back from Mendocino. Her mother and sister were among those she recruited to assist at the production studio as several dozen of her former patients had their portraits taken on a soundproofed stage in front of a curved wall to suggest an infinity background. Each woman received the affordable skin-treatment kits from Penny's start-up as thank-you gifts.

I was there but didn't see much of Roya. She'd told me afterward she felt like a bride at a wedding: the focus of frenzied loving attention, time passing by too quickly, everything over before you know it, never finding an opportunity—after all that choosy consternation—to enjoy the catering. (Roya hired a taco truck specializing in Jalisco specialties on Saturday, then one focusing on Sinaloa offerings on Sunday.) The reason I didn't see her was because I'd been secreted in an adjacent greenroom to conduct the interviews that would later be condensed into revelatory fragments and then placed alongside the edited portraits. I got what we needed: meaningful admissions in a prismatic array of voices. Yet it was exhausting.

One woman told me, "I actually had a perfectly fine nose, but it reminded me too much of my *tío* who did, uh, inappropriate stuff with me. I adjusted it, an escape. My dad and his sisters gave me such a hard time about the change. I still haven't told some of them why."

With the subjects' permission, the sessions were captured on video. Afterward Roya reviewed the totality of the footage. She was familiar with client passions—the many thrilled with a surgical result, the few who were upset. For whatever reason, she hadn't spent much time considering the substantial breadth of ambivalence in between. Perhaps these individuals don't self-report to their surgeon.

The interviews yielded a cumulative recognition. The women considered their procedures a boon and even a "blessing." However, by and large the trajectory of their lives hadn't much improved.

Depending on the person, a quantum of confidence had been instilled—leading to an arguable if indefinable and immeasurable furtherance of happiness. Still, I was informed time after time, these patients' blessings hadn't alleviated the overarching challenges that governed their lives, the deep and extensive structural issues at play. As one put it to me, in a quote I loved that didn't make the book because it wasn't on message: "People now look at me. I'm *noticed*, yes. But I still don't feel *noted*."

This shouldn't be a surprise. Yet it somehow came as a shock to Roya, who'd so internalized the potential and promise of her craft, whether legitimate or specious, to liberate from burdens. She'd leaned ever harder on the notion amid her troubles.

So these findings from her own patients sent her into nothing short of an existential crisis. Weeks went by after she watched the interviews. Roya didn't respond to my calls, texts, or emails. I contacted her family. Julie, concerned, explained her daughter had been in a mysterious "funk," although she didn't believe it had anything to do with me. Dahlia, unconcerned, said that, as far as she could tell, her sister was "back to her normal moody self."

I resorted to roping in our agent to get Roya to resurface. She did at last, inviting me one evening to her newly rented apartment for a conversation. It was a sparsely furnished studio in Santa Monica, walking distance from the office of Penny's start-up and a five-minute drive from her favorite place since childhood, the Getty Villa, which she now visited most weekends.

Roya was resplendent in full regalia, from the fireworks mop of hair to the lip gloss and hugging jeans she knew entranced me. She'd ordered Thai. She apologized for "going AWOL." She'd needed to "digest some stuff, some delusions." Had she come out the other end? "Yeah," she said, unnervingly bereft of the acerbity to which I'd grown accustomed. It was then that she described how the interviews had thrown her through a loop. Somehow, though—Roya resisted repeated attempts to clarify—faith had been restored. "It's a perspective thing," she explained without elaboration. I thought yet again about the woman with the botched surgery and the confidential settlement, wondering if she was ever on Roya's mind. The right thing and the wrong thing to do at this stage, now that our collaboration was complete, would've been to ask her about it.

But I refrained. It seemed hostile. Besides, the book itself would bring about whatever fate awaited her. By publishing her self-serving account, she'd invite further questions and tempt detractors. I felt my role in her life now was just to be kind.

We talked for a while. She told me about the prepping she'd begun with a well-regarded public-speaking coach. Roya intended to spread her policy gospel through paid speeches. She blew past my literal and figurative squint, laying an unromantic hand on my thigh at her dinner table for emphasis: "This is how you build a constituency for a movement." I looked deep into those sea-green eyes. She wasn't kidding.

Not only that, Roya wanted my "honest take." How would her efforts be received? I demurred, telling her I wasn't in the predictions business.

She pushed. So I told her she'd attract a lot of curious folks and she'd win some of them over—or at least force them to think in ways that they hadn't before. This satisfied Roya, who glowed at the analysis, and saved me from further explanation.

It wasn't my honest take, though. I didn't share it because I knew she wouldn't have accepted it. What I would've said, if I thought there was any point in sharing before she found out what the world thought of her, was that, yes, there was a chance she could very well be embraced as some sort of radical progressive thinker and empathetic seer. However, she was just as—or more—likely to be seen as a nightmarish huckster peddling a vision of self-realization that'd been limited by a warped life experience and narrow imagination.

Dinner was cleared and tea served in her adjoining living room. We sat beside each other on her sofa. She took hold of a glossy book from her coffee table. It looked like a wedding album, a one-off custom job with heavy paper stock and a professional cover photo. Except the waist-up, soft-focus shot on the front was of Roya alone, exuding a decorous feminine glamour.

Embossed platinum text ran across her midsection. It read *Transformation: Journey with Me.* "My mom had this, from when she received the contents of my office in boxes from the government," Roya told me. "I thought it was gone. I just found it in the storage unit the other day." She ran her hand across it in familiarity. Then she placed the volume in my lap. "I used to tell the ladies"—her employees at her practice—"that this thing's my 'closer.'"

I paged through the book. It was a series of stark before/after surgery photos of Roya, a chronicle of her years-long chrysalis. She narrated the voyage I already knew beat by beat as my eyes traveled from image to image, her voice a blend of expressive depth and deft saleswomanship.

Roya had packaged herself for commodification. "Procedures address both what's on the outside and what's on the inside," she intoned with a mild singsong artificiality. "What's on the inside is often insecurity. The adjustment I'm here to make is toward confidence."

I didn't know what to say, attempting not to judge, half curious why she would show off what was, in fact, other doctors' craft, rather than Roya's own work. But then her point was larger: She's an evangelist for the possibility of change, and she's already walked this path.

I remarked that some version of the book could, perhaps, be turned into a PowerPoint slideshow for her planned talks. "Serena"—her speaking coach—"and I are already working on it," she responded. "She's graphed the applause lines." Suppressing a sigh, I proposed we incorporate the material into the visual mix of her memoir, somehow threading it along with the clients' photos. She agreed.

Toward the end of *Transformation* was a several-page, scrapbook-like assemblage of Roya's childhood photos, most of which I'd seen before at her mother's condo. I was reminded again of how I'd been struck by Roya's smile in those images—the smile that didn't believe it was worth a smile in return. I hadn't asked her about it afterward, even though I should've. I hadn't found the right moment, and besides, the further away from the visit with her mother, the more I questioned my understanding of the pictures. Maybe I'd overinterpreted them.

Yet here the images were again, and their sadness held. I told her what struck me about them. For once Roya said nothing. Playing mute, she took the book out of my lap and into her own, opening the inside back rear cover, which was affixed with a gimmick: a thin mirror with an etching at its bottom that spelled out, in flowery cursive, *Choose Your Own Journey.*

Roya flashed the mirror at me. I saw my face, quizzical and intrigued. Then she returned *Transformation* to my lap, the mirror still open and now reversed, calling herself to account.

She looked squarely at her reflection. Roya Delshad beamed—teary, ecstatic.

STRONGER

I miss the operating room. It still staggers me that a portal of opportunity—for both my patients and myself—that I worked so long to capture has slipped my grasp forever.

After I was busted, I spent a great deal of time wondering what would replace it. Then it hit me that my conception of the operating room had to grow larger. It should encompass not just some corner of a surgicenter but *society*, and not just whichever body was then under my care but the *body politic*.

OK, I know that this sounds megalomaniacal, but hear me out. When your life implodes and you're locked in a cage, you're going to think either small or very, very big. Intrusions and profusions of grandeur are preferred.

A book of popular science I read in prison spurred mine. Gifted to me by Dr. Collins, my mentor from USC, it was Yale ornithologist Richard O. Prum's *The Evolution of Beauty: How Darwin's Forgotten Theory of Mate Choice Shapes the Animal World—and Us*. I blazed through it in an evening while seated cross-legged on my bunk. Then the next day I highlighted line after line and took copious notes in the margins as I slowly circled the track.

Prum's treatise chronicled his parting from the strict orthodoxy of evolutionary biology to embrace Darwin's too-long-neglected theory of aesthetic evolution. A distinctly feminist concept, aesthetic evolution argues that female members of a species pick their mates with ornament in mind, as opposed to the utilitarian logic that governs counterpart male behavior. Meaning, lady chickens are into roosters' hot plumage, and we chicks have a more than functional interest in good-looking cocks. (What, am I playing too blue to leaven this capsule academic lecture? Well, my bunkies, the toughest of crowds, enjoyed it.)

The opposing adaptationist view is an unromantic and rational belief held by the patriarchal scientific establishment ever since Darwin's time. It contends that forces such as climate, predation, competition, and geography ensure that only the healthiest and hardiest sexual partners are selected. Meanwhile, all outward stimuli are expressed in service of decoding evident fitness.

Aesthetic evolution theory squares with several things that already made intuitive sense to me (and likely to you) before I'd even heard about it. Among them is that, *duh*, the female orgasm isn't required for anything—certainly not procreation—except pleasure. And, as Prum put it late in his book, "women are not only sexual objects but also sexual subjects with their own desires and the evolved agency to pursue them." That's right, sing it, bird man!

In prison you're asked—*tasked*—to consider how you'll positively contribute to humanity if and when your freedom is relinquished to you again. I realized then and there that my calling is health care reform, albeit of a perhaps quixotic sort. My experiences, however checkered and problematic, have forged me into an advocate.

I'm neither a policy wonk nor a political strategist, and I'm not going to pretend to be. I'm aware that right now the most basic medical rights of dignity and mercy are still the subjects of a pitched battle in America resulting in half-measure legislation and unceasing litigation. We can't even agree on a universal standard of foundational public care, much less how to administer it.

Still, I dream. Our crisis is manifold. It's layered. We haven't even begun to conceive of its breadth. Beyond the emergencies and the preventative maintenance that should, in a more just country, be our shared burden, I judge there's yet more responsibility to ameliorate inequity.

What I mean is that, as the wealth divide grows and designer genes become more commonplace in a totalizing visual culture—where superficial signifiers determine success in the personal and professional spheres, especially for women—I believe a moon shot is required. We need to address disparities in attractiveness through technocratic intervention. I'm open to any efficacious practical solution, including market-based initiatives. Although I suspect government at the federal level will in the end need to take a leading role in what I'm talking about, which is beauty reparations.

I'm sure to many this notion registers as unreasonable, silly, and even crazy. That's OK. Much of what's now the social safety net began with fringe ideas. I'm still young . . . ish. I intend to persist toward a victory that, if it ever does come, may arrive long after my ability to witness it.

Should such history one day be seized, and its pioneers sanctified, I hope future portraitists and sculptors of the movement won't fret over idolizing my good side. Thanks to cosmetic surgery, I'm *all good side.*

Confidence is currency. Let me conjure an admittedly utopic vision in the hope you'll join me. One in which everyone can chase their full happiness unimpeded by the external hereditary imbalances of birth and the cruel residue of doubt that follows. Nobody is left behind. All have access to their most desired and desirable selves.

It begins with the patient consult. You've fantasized for so long about your future, some glittering panorama, the exalted ache of it, that distant paradise. It's out there, the consolation of transformation. Beyond the wilderness of a lifetime of uncertainty, past the stark facts of your born flesh, its shapes and its lapses.

The doctor will see you now, truly *see you*, and determine how you see yourself, how you *wish* to see yourself. The plan is drawn up, discussed, open for questioning. If both parties agree, the cathartic pageant of technical magic is set in motion.

In our land of looks the prospect of equality reigns. Capital's crucial, undeniable relationship with attractiveness is accepted, which is to say its attendant desolate injustices acknowledged. Ergo, once-impenetrable financial barriers to procedures have long since been annihilated.

Surgery will, of course, still be surgery—a rumble with chance. Medicine will advance by the arrival of this end-of-the-rainbow epoch. But the endotracheal tube may yet leave your throat sore, at least for a little while. Bruising will take time to heal.

You'll perhaps, too, still say some embarrassing things as the general anesthesia wears off in the recovery room. Not that you'll remember or anyone else will care. After all—woozily, then clearly—you'll be on your way. That path before you is your own now. It's limitless.

But first, the cocoon: You quiver in this corporeal limbo, bloodied and bandaged, a swollen mess of dislocation. Postop reality wallops. An elegiac euphoria courses beneath the compression garment. No matter how long or hard you thought about going through with this, it's surreal that it transpired. Here you are, in your lucid pain. Your form has been altered.

There'll be zero new memories in the old carapace, whether it was modified in modest millimeters or at significant scope. That former self is *gone.* No doubt: It's a poignant devastation, a special grief, even as a better tomorrow nears.

You did all of this—went through all of this—for you, first and last. Nevertheless, you can't help but care what those you love or merely know think of the work that's been done. It's only natural among social animals.

Of course, their reactions are anchored in their own shit: their own biases, their own histories, their own bodies, their own longings. Some responses will validate. Those of others will undermine. All these people, fairly or not, judge you now against the version you've elected to vacate.

Not so strangers. How satisfying, to at last be regarded on terms you've set. Their obliviousness is powerful, a totality that functions as benevolence. It's the closest you'll come to reincarnation. The effect is pure, visceral, vivid pleasure.

But then: What of it? Who will you have become? Who's this new you? What unfair expectations might be placed on this being? What excessive burdens?

You're aware that this isn't wish fulfillment, right? That there will never be a perfected life, one devoid of sorrow? That a besotting exterior won't do a thing about the grotesquerie inside? Maddening, huh?

What will you do, considering your blessings? Will you become bighearted or uncaring now that you've gotten yours? May the world you perceive be barren or abundant? What happens when life bows to you, iridescent, seduced by your loveliness? Do you lap it up? Do you recoil?

If you recoil, what happens? Wallow in guilt? Surely you know that nobody cares about the feelings of extraordinarily pretty people? Since you used to not be one, and you didn't either?

So what now? Perchance you'll yearn to pay it forward? Like, say, seek to lessen unfairness in some fashion? Or is it just inane to believe there could be, after all, a causal link between the aspiration to look good and the aspiration to do good? Maybe don't answer that?

Maybe instead your instinct rushes inward? Thrilled by the response to your splendor? Stirred by the illusion made earthly? Hushed by a retrospective despair that it took you so long to live this way?

You can't stop looking at yourself, can you? Has pride replaced envy as your most cardinal of sins? Isn't this all understandable—a natural side effect, even—when a dream so vibrant and luscious and wild and heartbreaking comes true?

It's OK if answers aren't at hand. Delirium may have set in. A fantasy realized will do that.

Out of the shower, steam in the bathroom, towel a turban, all else nude—wipe the mirror; the endeavor is complete. Go ahead. Run a finger down the bridge of this new nose once again. Gaze in profile at that reshaped derriere. Luxuriate at the mere thought of others taking in the spectacle of those heaven-sent C cups.

Now witness the body, whole. Glimpse it as quicksilver, yet resolute. Life's mutable, a mesmerizing improvisation. Its evanescent sacrament is beauty. I know this to be true. So do you.

ACKNOWLEDGMENTS

August Brown, my Virgil in this endeavor, believed from the start in what became *In Pursuit of Beauty*. The wise Jade Chang provided crucial guidance every step of the way. Early readers Amelie Cherlin, Padraic Foran, and Patrick Wood helped me see my words anew. I also owe debts to innumerable writers, teachers, and mentors who've shaped me.

My visionary agent, Shane Salerno, has been an unrelenting champion of *In Pursuit of Beauty*. Michael Signorelli's perceptive editing elevated the book. The team at Blackstone Publishing has been thoughtful and generous.

Authors are the consequence of many things, their families perhaps most of all. I didn't become a doctor like my father, Ronald, who took me on his hospital rounds when I was a kid. However, this book is in part an exploration into the drama and weight of medical practice. My mother, Amy, a passionate reader and freethinker, instilled the reckless confidence that forges a novelist. Meanwhile, my sister, Janet—in the way of no-nonsense siblings—has long ensured that any resultant self-regard remained in check.

An ode to beauty wouldn't be possible without an extraordinary, multifaceted muse. My wife, Kieumai, is the ideal. Lastly, my indomitable children, Rose and Clark: They are young enough to have arrived after I completed the first draft of this book, yet also now old enough to grasp that their father conjures stories for strangers, too.